I WOULD
DIE
FOR YOU

I WOULD
DIE
FOR YOU

SANDIE JONES

MINOTAUR BOOKS
NEW YORK

First published in the United States by Minotaur Books, an imprint of St. Martin's Publishing Group

I WOULD DIE FOR YOU. Copyright © 2025 by Sandra Sargent. All rights reserved. Printed in the United States of America. For information, address St. Martin's Publishing Group, 120 Broadway, New York, NY 10271.

www.minotaurbooks.com

Library of Congress Cataloging-in-Publication Data

Names: Jones, Sandie, author.
Title: I would die for you / Sandie Jones.
Description: First U.S. edition. | New York : Minotaur Books, 2025.
Identifiers: LCCN 2024043477 | ISBN 9781250910035 (hardcover) |
    ISBN 9781250910042 (ebook)
Subjects: LCGFT: Thrillers (Fiction). | Novels.
Classification: LCC PR6110.O6387 I96 2025 | DDC 823/.92—
    dc23/eng/20240924
LC record available at https://lccn.loc.gov/2024043477

Our books may be purchased in bulk for promotional, educational, or business use. Please contact your local bookseller or the Macmillan Corporate and Premium Sales Department at 1-800-221-7945, extension 5442, or by email at MacmillanSpecialMarkets@macmillan.com.

Originally published in Great Britain by Pan Books, an imprint of Pan Macmillan

First U.S. Edition: 2025

1   3   5   7   9   10   8   6   4   2

*Dedicated to anyone who believed they would
one day marry a rock star.
Be careful what you wish for.*

1

CALIFORNIA, 2011

"Have you called the police?" I ask, opening up my notepad and writing today's date in bright-red pen.

"No, I didn't know what to do," says the caller at the other end of the line. "You hear of these things happening at night, but I had no idea I'd see it with my own two eyes in broad daylight."

"Unfortunately, it's going on all the time," I say, already alert to the forthcoming opportunity. "Perhaps you'd be interested in signing our petition to put a stop to it."

"I'd be happy to," says the woman.

I allow myself a small smile, knowing that *one* signature has the power to make a difference. At least, that's what I tell myself when I spend endless hours on street corners, only to come away with just a couple more names to add to the slow-growing list.

"Another imbecile?" asks Brad, coming into my office as I put the phone down.

I nod. "A couple of young girls have been harassing the seals up at La Jolla beach, frightening the pups and abusing the moms."

"Jeez," he says, scratching his head as if it's the first time he's heard the like. "The sooner we get this petition filed, the better."

While I love the fact that my husband says "we," it's not as if he's the one up to his neck in the bureaucracy and the task of taking the beach closure to a vote at the next city council meeting. Sure, he always volunteers to lend a hand when there's trouble or when there's something practical that needs doing; he's spent many a weekend taking our eight-year-old daughter, Hannah, down to the beach at dusk to tidy up after inconsiderate day-trippers and nosey tourists have left the life-threatening remnants of their picnics for the seals to navigate. But on a Monday morning, he gets up and goes to work at the naval base, where his responsibilities start at nine and end at five. He clocks in and out—*and he gets paid.*

Not that money has ever been a factor in my decision-making, especially where the seal colony is concerned—but it would be worth all the money in the world to at least see my efforts rewarded. San Diego has more than enough beautiful beaches for the public to enjoy, so why can't we allow the seals one tiny cove to rest, swim, and birth in safety?

"Do you want me to go up there?" Brad asks. "I've just about got time before work."

As always, he seems to know when I need that little bit of underpinning—that extra beam in my support structure to stop me from lagging.

"It's all good," I say. "I'll check in with Hank now—see if he can send someone."

"You're doing great," says Brad, leaning in to kiss me. His beard tickles my lips and I smile—it's a relatively new addition and despite my initial protestations, I must admit I rather like it. It frames his face, like the hair on his head used to.

"If you turn upside down, you'll look like you did when you met Mommy," Hannah likes to tease.

Brad always laughs, but I'm sure it's not lost on him how the passage of time has changed us. To me, he looks just the same now as he did when I first saw him walking into Danny's Bar twenty years ago—and I hope he has the same warped perspective when he remembers *me* from back then.

Dressed head-to-toe in army uniform, he'd come in alone and asked for a bourbon on the rocks.

Having lived and worked in a military town for three years, I'd quickly learned not to ask questions I didn't want to hear the answers to. But something in Brad's eyes was begging me to say something.

"That's a pretty heavy drink for a Tuesday night," I'd said, putting the tumbler down in front of him on the counter.

He'd knocked it back in one, the ice cubes clinking against the side of the empty glass.

"I've had a pretty heavy day," he said, holding it up for another.

"Do you want to talk about it?" I asked, setting the bottle down beside him.

"We lost a good one today," was all he said. His relief at actually being able to say it out loud was palpable.

"We're losing good ones *every* day," I said ruefully, turning to look at the wall of remembrance we'd set up when the Gulf War had started claiming casualties. "And until we all learn how to get along with each other, it's going to keep happening."

He'd smiled, his face metamorphosing into something I wouldn't have thought possible just a few seconds earlier. And despite vowing never to entertain anyone in fatigues, my stomach did an involuntary flip.

"You're not from around here, are you?" he asked as I busied myself with wiping down the counter.

It was a question I was used to, but still it caught me off guard.

"I'm from England," I said, hoping that it would be enough, while knowing that it rarely was.

He nodded. "It was either that or Australia—I couldn't quite make it out."

"Americans rarely can," I said, smiling.

"So, what brings you here?" he asked, looking around. "To the lil ol' town of Coronado?"

I'd taken a deep breath and begun to share my well-rehearsed backstory. But had I known then that I'd still be lying all these years later, perhaps I would have told him the truth.

2

The doorbell interrupts my thoughts, and as much as I can't wait to see my favorite person, I rue another day having slipped past me without my achieving what I set out to do. Though I'm relieved to see from the grandfather clock in the hall that at least one of the hours I thought I'd lost has been credited back—it's only two o'clock. So it can't be Hannah back home from school just yet.

"Hello?" I say with a big smile, ever mindful of Brad's observation soon after we met: "You Brits are a hard-to-read bunch," he'd said, laughing. "I'd never know whether you were greeting a lover or a convicted murderer. The look on your face is exactly the same."

I'd been mildly offended, not knowing what he meant, but took notice of the warm welcome I received in the coffee shop the next morning and how the person in the street would smile when I stepped in their lane, wishing me a good day, instead of scowling and tutting. I hadn't even realized I was so British, but from that day on, I vowed to be more American.

"Nicole Forbes?" asks the woman on the porch, with a look of exaggerated expectation.

"Yes, how can I help you?" I say, still beaming, blissfully unaware of how misplaced my expression is about to become.

"Hi," she says, thrusting her hand forward awkwardly. "My name's Zoe Mortimer and I wondered if you could spare me a few minutes."

It's then that I hear it: the clipped syllables of a British accent. My defenses are immediately on high alert, barricading me into the fortress I've worked so hard to fight my way out of. But I reason that this woman—girl, really—whose name means nothing to me, might be about to offer her support to the conservation effort.

"What can I do for you?" I ask, my smile no longer quite so genuine.

"Could I come in?" she asks, looking around furtively, and I wonder if she's from the city council, here on unofficial business. The thought that next week's hearing date for the petition might have been canceled immediately gets my hackles up.

"Of course," I say through gritted teeth as I beckon her into the hall.

Watching her step across the threshold is akin to watching Bambi step onto ice, and I suddenly realize that whatever news she's come here to deliver, it isn't good. I steel myself for being told that the hearing isn't going ahead, that a decision has already been made, that—

"I'm writing a book," she says. "And I wondered if I might be able to ask you a few questions."

A rush of relief runs through me. "Of course—I'm always happy to do anything that might help the seals' plight."

Her expression changes, her earlier trepidation replaced by a forced confidence, as if she's having to psych herself up. She flicks her dirty-blond hair out of her eyes and pulls her shoulders back.

"I wonder if you could tell me about your relationship with Ben Edwards," she says, abruptly.

The heat that I'd thought I'd learned to control at the mention of his name creeps up around my ears, sending warning signals to my brain. The woman's face becomes hazy, and although I can see her mouth moving, I can no longer hear what she's saying over the thunderous roar that's reverberating around my head.

I move toward the front door in a daze, desperately trying to claw back to one minute earlier, when I thought the worst thing this stranger could say was that the seals would remain unprotected.

"I . . . I . . ." I flounder.

"I understand you were there that day"—she looks away, as if the memory pains *her* more than *me*—"when it happened?"

The weight of her words makes it sound as if she's underwater—or maybe it's me, drowning in an ocean of secrets.

"I-I'm sorry, I don't know what you're talking about," I bluster, my tongue feeling like cotton wool as it attempts to wrap itself around the lie. "You need to leave."

"I just wondered what it must have been like to witness the demise of the biggest band of the eighties in such tragic circumstances. Conspiracy theories abound even today, twenty-five years later, but I just wanted to know, from someone who was there ringside, what *really* happened."

"You've got the wrong person," I say, more forthright now.

"But you *are* Nicole Forbes?" she asks again. "Formerly Alderton?" She puts her bag, which I imagine being weighed down with the secrets of my past, on the hall floor.

The passive-aggressive action leaves me in no doubt that this woman has no intention of going anywhere. But she can't stay here—I won't let her. I won't allow the home that I've spent the past twenty years transforming into a safe haven for my husband and my child be violated by the nightmare I've been running from for even longer.

"You need to leave," I seethe, with my hand on the open door.

"I understand your reticence," she says, cocking her head to one side in a hollow attempt to impart sympathy. "You and Ben were close, and I get that you don't want to relive it all over again, but . . ."

I lean in close, the tip of my nose just a few inches away from hers. "Whatever you think you know, you're wrong. There's no story here, no conspiracy theory; it was what it was, and justice was served." I stand tall and take a deep breath. "Now get out of my house."

She smirks, as if to let me know that conceding defeat now doesn't mean she won't try again. "Well, as long as you haven't spent the past twenty-five years picturing his face and wondering what might have been."

I don't wait for her to cross the threshold before forcing the door shut and sending the bolts across, as if it will somehow stop those very thoughts from infiltrating my beleaguered brain. I wait to hear her footsteps on the path, forgetting to breathe as I imagine every flowering rose on either side of it wilting as her dark shadow deprives them of sunlight.

I suck in a breath as I collapse onto the bottom stair in the hall, my eyes desperately scanning my surroundings, looking for something familiar—to prove that nothing has changed. Yet *everything* looks different. I don't recognize the coats on the stand, and I can't reconcile who they might belong to. Even the photo of me, Brad, and Hannah that sits proudly on the sideboard doesn't jolt my paralyzed nerve endings into action, our faces suddenly seeming alien to me.

I close my eyes, willing myself to still the pounding of my heart—to stop it from beating through the wall of my chest. But the darkness only makes the light shine even brighter around Ben, who's smiling down at me in my mind's eye. I try to ignore the image, if only to prove to that woman that she's wrong, that I *don't* spend every waking moment thinking about him, and every sleeping one dreaming about the two of us together in another lifetime.

"*Fuck!*" I cry out with frustration as I clench my fists and slam them into the unforgiving wooden banister.

I thought I'd left that world far behind, if not from an emotional standpoint then certainly from a geographical one. I've ensconced myself so completely in this place I call home, buried my old life within its foundations so deeply that I thought it could never be found. So how come a stranger has managed to uncover what I've spent years hiding?

As I pull myself away from the image of Ben and the pain and sorrow he always evokes, I'm suddenly blindsided by the thought of Brad. The guilt jolts me out of my reverie, the here and now perpetually in conflict with the past I've forced myself to forget. I ask myself for the millionth time what my honest and loyal husband would make of my betrayal if he were ever to find out who I *really* am. Would he be able to overlook my tumultuous former life in favor of the peaceful harmony we've since created together? Or would he be unable to see past the deceit, no longer able to trust the wife he thought he knew?

Sometimes, even *I* wonder whether she's a figment of his imagination, invented to stop the rot of grief and the bitter regret of lost opportunities that had befallen her. But on those days, when I question myself more than anyone else would dare to, I can't help but feel proud of how well that imposter feigns normality. Of how she's able to reconcile losing the love of her life in such horrific circumstances, and then subsequently losing everything else she ever cared about as a result.

But it seems you only need to scratch the surface to find that the old Nicole Alderton is still very much there. Zoe's appearance has unleashed her from the cage she's spent all these years thrashing around in. And I honestly don't know how I'll get her back in.

3

"Hey, Jared," I call out to the driver of the school bus as he opens its folding doors. If I were of sound mind, I would notice the questioning look on his face. But my brain is so frazzled that I can't see anything, the past hour of overthinking doing nothing but clouding my vision even further.

"Hey, ma'am, no Hannah today . . ."

I can't tell if it's a statement or a question, but either way I can't compute what he's saying. I force a deep breath in, willing myself to calm down so I can put his words in the right order, so that they make sense.

"Hey, Mrs. Forbes," says Olivia, our neighbor's daughter, as she bounds down the last two stairs of the bus.

"Hey, Olivia, Hannah last off as usual?"

"She's not on today," she says, as if it means nothing. "Her aunt picked her up."

Olivia's mom gives me a wave from the other side of the street, as a rancid heat infiltrates my bloodstream.

Absurdly, I laugh. "Jared?"

He shrugs his shoulders, but a flicker of alarm momentarily clouds his chubby features. "She's not on my list for this afternoon's drop-off."

"But of course she is," I say, losing the moisture in my mouth. "She always is."

Jared shakes his head as he consults the clipboard hanging from the dash. "Nope, she's not on it."

"But . . ." I start, as the turmoil of Zoe's presence returns to haunt me. The shock, the panic, the terror, has rendered me useless; unable to function at the most basic level. *Think, Nicole, think.*

Was Hannah going to track and field after school? Have I missed an email inviting her to an afternoon tea to reward her effort grades? Did I prearrange a playdate with one of her friends? I can't separate the myriad of possibilities that are crowding my brain. All I know is that she most definitely didn't go home with her aunt. *Because she doesn't have one.*

I almost fall over myself as I run back to the house, the adrenaline turning my legs to jelly.

"Brad! Brad!" I scream, even though I know he's not there.

The house is exactly as I left it, which seems odd when everything else has changed.

As my trembling fingers hover over the phone, I don't know who to call first. My instinct is Brad, but he's going to know even less than I do, so I opt for the school office, praying that they can offer a perfectly reasonable explanation as to why an eight-year-old in their care has failed to reach the safety of her mother's arms.

"Hawkswood Prep," comes the cheery voice of Miss Santos, the school secretary, who up until now I'd had down as a jobsworth. I so desperately hope she lives up to my expectations.

"Hi, it's Nicole Forbes here—Hannah's mom."

"Oh, hello, Mrs.—"

"Hannah's not on the bus. She's supposed to be. Olivia got off, but Hannah didn't. Jared, the driver, says she wasn't on the list, but I know she was, because why wouldn't she be?" It all comes out in a rush of staccato statements.

All she has to do is give a resounding sigh of relief; a reassurance that she's got this, that she knows exactly where Hannah is . . . yet there's nothing but a painful silence. It may only be a couple of seconds, but it tells me everything I need to know.

"Olivia said she'd been picked up by her aunt, but that's impossible . . . So, where is she?"

I look around the front room, willing Hannah to burst out of the costumes trunk, ready to recite her favorite lines from *Tangled*, but her Rapunzel dress lays painfully dormant.

"Mrs. Forbes, we spoke about this last week . . ." she starts, talking to me as if I'm a forgetful child. "You called to say that Hannah's aunt would be collecting her from school today."

What?

"I'm just checking my records," she says tightly, but there's an underlying panic that she can't disguise—as if she already knows she's screwed up. If time wasn't of the essence, I would take a warped satisfaction in waiting to be proved right.

"You need to tell me where my daughter is, *right now*."

"Ah, here it is," she says, with a smug tone. Or is it relief? "You called last Wednesday at 11:27 a.m. to give permission for Hannah's aunt to pick her up—I have it here in my logbook, and I am most particular about these things."

How does that even make sense?

"Check again," I snap.

"Mrs. Forbes . . ."

"Someone has fucked up, so you need to tell me where my daughter is, *immediately*."

"Mrs. Forbes, I can assure you . . ."

I hang up, not needing to hear her empty assurances, and immediately dial Brad's number.

"Hannah's gone," I sob into the phone. "She wasn't on the bus and the school don't know where she is. They're telling me she was collected by your sister . . ."

"But I don't have a sister."

"Exactly! So where is she?"

"I'm calling Hank," he says, before the line abruptly cuts off.

I pace the kitchen floor as I wait for one or other of them to show up, or at least to ring and tell me how they're going to find her. But in the meantime, I can't help but picture where she might be. My imagination takes me into the darkest corners of my mind, and I can hear her calling out for me from a cell-like room. A steel door is holding her against her will and a stained mattress lies ominously in the corner. She knows she's somewhere she shouldn't be, her inno-cence even tricking her into believing she'll be in trouble for being there, but still she calls out for me, her need to feel safe far greater than how mad I might be.

I torture myself by remembering our trip to the library a couple of weeks ago and her excitement at going off to find a book for us to read. When she didn't come back within a reasonable time, I'd thought little of it—I'd often find her sitting cross-legged wherever she'd found something of interest, her eagerness to read making her forget that she was supposed to bring it back to me. But as I tracked through the aisles of the children's section, with no sign of her, my heart grew heavy. I'd quickened my pace, wishing I had X-ray vision to see through the bookshelves to ease my rising anxi-ety. I knew she was there—where else would she be?—but I had an inherent need to be put out of my misery.

"Hannah?" I'd half whispered, half called out. "Come on out now. Where are you?"

When I reached the end of the bookcase, she'd jumped out. "Boo!" she shrieked excitedly.

"That isn't funny," I said.

"*He* told me to do it," she said, dissolving into fits of giggles as

Brad sheepishly peered around the shelves. Despite being pleased that he'd surprised us, I couldn't help but admonish his insensitivity.

"Why would you tell her to do something like that?" I snapped. "I was going out of my mind . . ."

"We're in a library," he said, laughing as he attempted to grab my waist. "What do you think's going to happen?"

"You never know," I said curtly.

"I think we've got a pretty good idea," he'd said, smiling at my fearful expression.

But he shouldn't be so complacent, because I know people can be taken from you when you least expect it. Like now.

Hank's blue lights puncture the rapidly darkening skies, illuminating a room I hadn't even realized needed lighting.

"You need to find her," I sob, as I fall into his fatherly embrace. He may be the police chief of Coronado, but he's a friend first and foremost, and Hannah's disappearance will be hurting him almost as much as it's hurting me. "Something's happened—I know it has."

"Let's not be jumping to any conclusions," he says, his soothing tone belying his grave expression, which suggests he already has. "I'm sure there's a perfectly reasonable explanation."

"She's eight years old, Hank, and someone has deliberately set out to take her."

"I spoke to Hannah's teacher on the way over here," he says, guiding me into the kitchen with a firm hand in the small of my back. "She's confirmed that a woman did indeed collect her and that she introduced herself as her aunt."

"Oh my god!" I wail, as I imagine somebody else playing mother to my little girl. "What does she want? Why Hannah?"

As soon as the words are out, I wonder why it's taken me twenty minutes to ask myself that question when the answer is so glaringly obvious. How had I not made the connection? How, in the maelstrom of emotions that have descended upon my brain since Hannah's been missing, could I have forgotten the woman at my door? The woman who had even got as far as the hallway under the guise of being someone she wasn't. The deafening roar in my head renders me speechless.

"Nicole!" calls out Brad as he runs through the open front door and rushes toward me.

I fall into him, my legs giving way as he bears my weight. "Where is she?" I sob.

His bottom lip wavers, but he pulls himself up short before it has a chance to manifest into anything more. Though I know if it wasn't for me, he'd have been on his knees before he'd even made it through the front door of the house that bears so many hallmarks of his little girl. Her red rain mac hangs redundantly on its hook, her wellies, still caked in mud, stand to attention on the mat. I'd hazard a guess that he can even smell her, and I can't help but feel strangely envious; her natural sweet scent having already lost itself on me.

"We'll find her," he says, looking to Hank for backup, both literally and metaphorically.

An unnerving silence resounds and a guttural sob catches in my chest as children on the other side of the street play on their tricycles in their front yard. It's a scene that's played out every day. Except today everything feels different. Instead of seeing the gleaming pink and blue metal frames reflecting the sunset, a dark cloud seems to be casting the longest of shadows, and instead of their little chuckles of delight, all I can hear is my past howling at me.

4

The heat is oppressive, as it always is on those five days a year that London registers over seventy degrees Fahrenheit. Sweat drips down Cassie's back as bodies press tightly together like sardines in a can, waiting for someone to set them free. If she'd known it was going to be this hot, she wouldn't have worn her denim jacket, but she'd not trusted the weather girl on the TV this morning, even though she'd warned the elderly to stay inside and reminded animal lovers to keep their pets hydrated. In fact, Cassie had laughed in the face of it even further by wearing lace gloves and weighing herself down with layer after layer of plastic jewelry that sits heavily on her chest and around her wrists, making her skin itch, but impossible to scratch.

If she stands on tiptoes, held up by the pressing crowd around her, Cassie's just tall enough to see that she's on the wrong side of Oxford Street. If she were closer to the HMV record store, she'd be able to shelter in its shadow, but the sun is high, beating down on top of her head, making her feel like she's cooking from the inside.

"Get back!" yells a power-hungry policeman. He raises his truncheon and needlessly jostles the edge of the ever-growing, excitable crowd.

Although the threat of authority looms menacingly, Cassie can't help but feel empowered at the thought of revolting against it. She imagines being embroiled in the riots of a few years earlier or standing on the picket line of the long-standing miners' strike, demanding to be heard, and although this isn't quite the same, she doesn't doubt that the police wouldn't hesitate to use the same brute force if they felt their superiority slipping from their grasp.

As if the swaying teenage throng needed any further encouragement to unleash their hormonal frustrations, a girl wedged in three people across from Cassie starts to shout up out of the mêlée.

"Who do we want?" she yells, her turned-up mouth and mischievous glint displaying complete and utter defiance.

Cassie smiles, already a fan of her chutzpah. "Secret Oktober!"

The girl turns and winks at her, buoyed by her comradeship. "When do we want 'em?"

"Now!" roars Cassie.

The chant initially falls on deaf ears, but after a few more goes, the crowd begin to warm to the theme.

"Who do we want?"

"Secret Oktober!" comes the rousing response.

"When do we want 'em?"

"Now!"

Stoking impatient anticipation, the mob moves backward and forward, and Cassie is caught up in the ebb and flow of a wave that she can't duck out of. Screams rise as young girls get caught up in the electrifying expectations of pubescent dreams, and car horns sound from the boy racers who have brought their Fiesta XR2s up to London's busiest street to show off, only to be thwarted by a thousand scantily clad girls.

A single synthesizer note echoes from above and hysteria reverberates around the buildings, bouncing off the walls.

"Good afternoon, London!"

The microphone screeches and you can't even see the person speaking, but the crowd knows exactly who it is. At least, those who saw the full-page advert in last night's *Evening Standard* do. The other bystanders, bemused office workers on their lunch breaks and frustrated cabbies, are there against their wishes, hemmed in by a mass of overactive hormones.

"Whose bright idea was this?" yells a commuter into the side of a policeman's helmet.

The policeman grimaces. "We're trying to shut it down, sir, but it's going to take a while to disperse."

Cassie isn't going anywhere—not until she's seen and heard all that her idols have come here to deliver.

"Thanks so much for coming out today," says Ben Edwards, the static on the microphone gradually easing through the speakers. "I must say, you're all looking particularly . . . *hot*."

Cassie's sure that from up there on the rooftop he can't even see the hordes of girls hanging on to his every word; she certainly can't see him from down here, but still the teasing words garner the desired effect, and girls scream as they no doubt fantasize that the lead singer of the country's biggest band is referring to them alone.

The opening bars of their latest hit single start up and the crowd surges forward, toward the store, as if expecting to be let inside and up the four floors of stairs to where the band are performing. But a ten-strong armed barricade of policemen block the way, holding the baying mob back.

"Sod this!" says the chanting girl, who's now next to Cassie. "We're not going to see anything from here. You wanna try and get a closer look?"

Cassie nods, not knowing if this cool chick with her bleached-blond hair, cut asymmetrically across one eye, is talking to her or someone else.

"Come on then," she says, grabbing Cassie's hand then ducking down and slipping out of sight into the sea of bodies.

Getting out is even harder than being in the middle of the fracas—Cassie feels like she's being churned around in someone's gut, before being regurgitated and spat out onto the softening tarmac of the gridlocked road. But once she is, the relief is instant, her sweat immediately evaporating as much-needed air buffets her overheated body.

"Come on!" says the girl, pulling her by the hand through the double doors of the department store across the street.

"Where are we going?"

"Somewhere we can actually see their faces," says the girl, taking the escalator steps two at a time.

By the time they emerge at the fifth-floor restaurant, panting and gasping for breath, Cassie has cottoned on to what the girl is planning and can only imagine that a hundred other fans have also worked it out. But there's just a gathering of well-heeled individuals, most with perfectly coiffed shampoo and sets, wondering why their lunches have been disrupted by the bedlam on the street below.

"I don't understand why they're not at school," she hears one lady say to her friend, who tuts in agreement. "They're just running amok, like animals in a zoo. The parents have lost all control!"

Cassie doesn't disagree, and if her dad knew she was here instead of sitting in her timetabled history class right now, he'd have a fit. Especially if he also found out that her mum had given her permission to play truant. Well, it was more of a wry smile as she wordlessly handed Cassie the national newspaper advert announcing the "secret" gig, but the intimation was there; it was in the special bond they shared, and if *that* was "losing control," then Cassie loved her all the more for it.

"Go and grab that corner table over by the window," says the girl, with an assertive nod. "I'll get us a can of pop."

Cassie run-walks to the corner, praying that her new friend's intuition has paid off. When she gets to the booth overlooking Oxford Street below, any expectations she may have had are blown out of the water.

"Oh my god!" she squeals, causing the purple-rinse brigade to pull their mouths tight in abject horror. But she doesn't care, because just across the road, one floor down, her favorite band in the whole wide world are performing a concert, seemingly just for her. The sound isn't exactly clear, muffled by the double glazing, but it doesn't matter; she'd rather *see* them than *hear* them and she can't get much closer than this. Not today, anyway.

"You're a fucking genius," she says, as a bottle of Panda Pop is slammed down on the table in front of her.

"I have my moments," says the girl, taking out a JPS cigarette from a pack of tens and lighting one up. "I'm Amelia, by the way."

"Cassie—pleased to meet you. How did you even think of this?"

Amelia shrugs her shoulders. "I can't take all the credit," she says, keeping a watchful eye on what's happening on the rooftop below. "Ben gave me a heads-up."

Cassie thinks she must have heard her wrong. "Sorry—Ben?" she questions, assuming it must be one other than of the "Edwards" variety.

"Ben!" says Amelia, smiling at the frontman, who, if Cassie didn't know better, seems to be smiling back.

"You *know* him?" she asks, her voice high-pitched.

Amelia nods coyly, giving nothing away.

"Like, to actually *talk* to?" Cassie blurts out, her brain working too fast for her mouth to keep up. "And he knows *you? How?*"

"Well . . ." Amelia starts, basking in the adulation her admission has afforded her. "We've known each other since this crazy ride began two years ago. I was first on the scene, having caught up with them after one of their early gigs in Brighton, and now we're here, playing on top of the world's most famous music store."

She says it as if she's part of the entourage, but if she were, she'd have an *Access All Areas* pass hanging from her neck, instead of almost breaking it by racing up five escalators to catch a glimpse of her idols from sixty feet away.

Cassie casts a suspicious glare as Amelia waves at the band, half-prepared to exchange her skepticism for jealousy if Ben Edwards waves back. She doesn't know whether she's relieved or disappointed when her new friend's call for attention goes unanswered. Though it doesn't seem to bother Amelia, who jumps up onto the banquette and hands her an Instamatic camera.

"Make sure you get them in the background!" she says, posing with her hands on her hips.

As Cassie peers through the viewfinder, she thinks that Amelia would be a lot prettier if she ditched the heavy black kohl and dark burgundy lipstick. It's too much for her petite features and makes her look unnecessarily aggressive.

"Oi, get down from there!" shouts a voice from across the sedate restaurant.

Amelia smiles and sticks two fingers up, much to onlookers' disgust.

"You should be ashamed of yourselves," says a woman near them, her hairdo so stiff that it looks like she's got a dead ferret on her head. "Do your parents even know you're here?"

Amelia goes to issue a retort, but something catches her eye. "Oh my god, look," she says, pointing out of the window.

Cassie is rendered speechless by the appearance of at least twenty policemen making their way slowly across the rooftop toward the band. The bobbies move as if they're closing in on a hardened criminal, but Ben and the boys are defiantly playing on, only faltering when Michael, the drummer, is manhandled, sending his sticks flying.

Ben brandishes his guitar like a riot shield, while Luke stands his ground behind his keyboard.

"Come on!" says Amelia, as if issuing a call to arms.

By the time they emerge into the blistering heat outside, the crowd are growing increasingly unsettled. The music has stopped and the police have become even more combative.

"They'll come out round the back," says Amelia, grabbing Cassie by the hand again and heading in the opposite direction to everyone else. She ducks down a side street and they run with burning lungs around the block, but there's already a sizeable crowd surrounding the two black limousines that are parked there.

"Link arms and don't let go," says Amelia, throwing herself into the outskirts of the throng as if she were diving into a swimming pool.

Cassie follows hesitantly, not wanting to break the connection, but she closes her eyes, relying on Amelia's lead to take her to where she needs to be.

The horde moves forward, picking Cassie up and taking her with them. The noise rises, the screams of young girls piercing her eardrums.

"Ben! I love you!"

"Michael, over here!"

"Luke, marry me!"

Cassie's body slams into something hard and unforgiving, her feet leaving the ground as she's lifted over the back of a car. She calls out—not in pain, but in shock and confusion, her mind unable to work out whether Amelia is pulling her or the crowd are pushing her.

"Ben!" Amelia yells. "What's going on?"

Cassie jostles for position, trying to follow Amelia's voice, but the physical contact is lost and she doesn't even know which way is up, let alone where Amelia is. But suddenly, she sees *him,* and the cacophony surrounding her is silenced, the hysteria no longer audible. It's as if she's been anesthetized, her limbs falling victim to the effect before her mind has a chance to.

Ben Edwards is so close that if she were to reach out, she'd be able to touch him. But her arms are pinned to her sides; it's only her eyes that can move, tracking his movements as he is pushed and shoved even more than she is.

"Ben!" Amelia calls out again, somehow managing to catch his attention.

He looks up, sees her and offers a solemn smile. "Hey, Mils," he says, as he's bundled into the back seat of the limo.

"Get back!" barks an overzealous security guard, before slamming the door and hitting the roof with an open palm. "Go, go, go!"

Despite his urgent calls, the car is only able to jerk forward a few inches at a time, stopped by the crowd, who are banging on the windows and laying themselves across the bonnet.

"Give them some room!" yells Amelia, pushing back, as if *she* were their bodyguard.

Cassie pushes back too, trying to get herself out of the way, but although her body is clear, as she leans into the crowd for support, she's not quick enough with her foot, which disappears under a painfully slow-moving back tire.

Her face must say it all, her ability to make a sound lost to the pain that is wracking her body.

"Her foot!" yells Amelia into the tiny gap of the open window. "It's under the car!"

The wheel rolls forward another half a turn and Cassie feels her exposed toes flattening against the man-made sole of her roman sandal.

"Are you OK?" asks Ben, sticking his head out.

Cassie doesn't know what's causing her to be more dumbstruck: the pain or the shock of having her idol talk to her.

She nods numbly as everyone around her screams for him, delighted to be given a clear view of their idol.

"Ben, I love you!" someone screeches in her ear.

"Fuck!" cries Cassie as the window is wound up and the car moves off.

"Oh my god!" shrieks Amelia. "Are you all right? Can you walk?"

Cassie grimaces as she takes a tentative step, the thumping throb reminding her of the *Tom and Jerry* cartoons she used to watch.

"I . . . I don't know," she groans, as Amelia props her up and forcefully pushes her way through the crowd.

A few minutes later, as Cassie sits on a bench, she already knows that the shock of what happened far outweighs the actual damage. But a part of her feels she needs to keep up the charade, if only for the twenty or so girls who are crowding around her, eulogizing about how they wished it was *their* foot Ben Edwards's car had run over.

"Do you think it's broken?" asks one.

"Does it matter?" quips another.

Cassie looks up with a pained expression.

"Well, you could *pretend* that it's broken," says the second girl breathlessly, warming to the theme. "And that you had to go to hospital."

"Why would I do that?" asks Cassie, confused.

"Because it would be a surefire way of getting Ben's attention. A friend of mine told *The Sun* that one of Madonna's bodyguards had pushed her into the road and she'd hit her head."

Cassie leans in, her interest piqued. "*And . . . ?*"

"And two days later, Madonna turned up at her house with a bouquet of flowers and two VIP tickets to her Wembley Stadium show next year."

"Get out of here!" says Cassie. "You've got to be pulling my chain."

The girl shakes her head. "God's honest truth."

Cassie's stomach flips at the thought of Ben Edwards turning up on her doorstep, but the jittery sensation is short-lived. Because, as much as her mother would welcome him in with open arms, she already knows that her dad would most likely slam the door in his face.

She goes to get up and winces as her swollen toes attempt to take her weight.

"We need to get some ice on those," says Amelia.

"My sister works just around the corner," says Cassie. "She'll have something."

"OK, lead the way," says Amelia, before laughing. "Oh, sorry—you can't . . ."

5

Nicole's feet are on fire and if she could sit down and take the weight off them, she fears she'd stay there for a week. But there's no time to rest; there's still an hour left of her shift, with just enough time to grab a plate of Jim's loaded potato skins before heading to her second job of the day. Well, she calls it a job, but technically she'd have to be paid for it to be a job.

"Are you all done here?" she asks a table of four, who have been acting up ever since they arrived three hours ago—the wine wasn't cold enough, the meat not cooked enough, even though they managed to consume both with gusto. Now they've been taking up premium space for the past hour, without ordering a single thing, while a line of hungry diners, eager to spend, are queuing around the block.

"We'd like the steaks taken off the bill," comes the retort, with a dismissive swish of a hand.

"But you *ate* them!" says Nicole, well used to this ruse.

The mustached man nearest to her places a hand on her behind. "We're happy to leave a healthy tip though," he says, raising his bushy eyebrows suggestively.

"You really don't want to be doing that," says Nicole, her contempt masked with a look of resignation.

"Isn't it all part of the *service*?" asks the man as he slides his clammy fingers down her leg.

"Jim!" she yells over to the kitchen. "We've got a hot one!"

A big, bearded man wearing a bloodied apron looks up from behind the counter, his eyes ablaze. He raises a meat cleaver in the air and slams it down onto his chopping board.

Nicole turns to the man with an apologetic expression. "You might want to explain to the chef over there why you won't be paying for the food he's so lovingly prepared for you."

The man scoffs.

"*And* why your hand is currently on his girlfriend's arse . . ."

There's a sudden whipping-out of wallets as the four of them almost fight to be the first to put money on the table.

"Much appreciated!" Nicole calls out, waving their five-pound tip in the air as they fall over themselves to get out of the restaurant.

Jim's menacing look dissolves into the sweetest smile as he watches them go.

"Give me a sec and I'll get you seated," Nicole says to the next in line, a couple who don't look like they'll be giving her any trouble at all. She breathes a sigh of relief, knowing that it'll make the next hour easier to deal with. That's how she approaches her time at the diner—in short, bite-sized chunks that move her ever forward to what she really wants to be doing.

"Hey, sis!" comes a voice.

A smile plays on Nicole's lips before she's even turned around to see who it is—immediately followed by a deepening frown as she realizes it's two o'clock on a Thursday afternoon.

"Why aren't you at school?" she asks as her little sister hobbles in, supported by another girl of similar age. The question of why she's being held up by a stranger can be asked later.

"It's all right, Mum knows . . ." says Cassie, rolling her eyes at Nicole's maternal glare.

"But Dad doesn't?"

Cassie looks at her as if she's mad. "Er, *no!*"

Nicole shakes her head in admonishment, taking the top chair from a stack and putting it down for Cassie to sit on.

"What happened?" she asks, bending over to take a closer look at Cassie's foot; the second toe is clawed up and three times the size it should be.

"A car ran over it," says Cassie, blithely.

"A *car?*" shrieks Nicole. "Well, then it's probably broken—it *looks* broken."

"All the better," says Cassie with a mischievous glint in her eye that Nicole knows spells trouble. "Because it wasn't just *any* car . . ."

Nicole looks at her questioningly before the penny drops. "Oh, you've got to be kidding me . . ." she says, with an air of exasperation. "This has got something to do with those boys, hasn't it?"

Cassie grins.

"So, you've skipped school to come into town to see them and they've run over your foot in their car?"

"Yep, but it was worth every second of pain," says Cassie, still smiling. "Because Ben Edwards actually looked at me. He knows I exist, and he can break all *ten* of my toes if it means he knows who I am."

Nicole tsks condescendingly. "You think he's going to remember you for *this?* The only thing he'll remember you for is being the stupid kid who threw herself under his car."

"I don't care," says Cassie, sounding every bit the immature sixteen-year-old that she is.

"Dad is going to kill you when he finds out," says Nicole, taking a dishcloth to the recently vacated table and wiping it down. "Not only have you skipped school behind his back, but you've done it to chase these boys across town. You know how he feels about all this . . ."

"But it was with Mum's permission," whines Cassie.

"Well, that's even worse—you're going to get *her* in a whole heap of trouble too."

Cassie's hunched shoulders relax. "I don't know why he gets so bent out of shape around this stuff. I could be doing a lot worse . . ."

"Not in his eyes," says Nicole. "He can't bear to see you waste your time and energy on a fantasy that will never come true. He's been there, seen it—remember? All those years he spent trying to get a break, quite literally working his fingers to the bone on that bloody guitar, night after night, so convinced was he that he was going to hit the big time. But his commitment and sacrifices amounted to nothing."

"He met Mum, didn't he?" muses Cassie petulantly.

"Yes, and he dragged her around the country *with* him," says Nicole. "And that's something he's never forgiven himself for . . ." She looks away, quelling the desire to cry. "Especially now."

"That's not exactly his fault," says Cassie, her bottom lip softening.

"Of course it isn't," says Nicole, pulling herself up short as she looks at the girl with her sister, not wanting to air her family's issues in public. "But he doesn't want the same for you." She ruffles her little sister's hair affectionately. "And you shouldn't want it for yourself—you're worth more than that."

Cassie shrugs despondently. "But *you're* following *your* passion," she says.

"Oh yeah, I'm smashing it," laughs Nicole sardonically, not wanting to give Cassie false hope of a life she's not sure exists. She hopes it does—that somewhere out there in the universe is a spotlight just waiting to shine on her. But it hasn't happened yet, despite months of gigging up and down the country every night, and waitressing in Jim's every day. She's exhausted, and spends some days barely able to function, but she *has* to push on—not just because that's what you have to do if you want to earn your stripes on the circuit, but because time is running out.

Her father had allowed her to ditch college, to pursue a dream they once both shared, only on the strict understanding that if, after a year, she hadn't made significant inroads into establishing a career that was notoriously hard to conquer, then she was to return to her studies with not so much as a by-your-leave. But what they hadn't yet agreed on, with just two months to go, was *what*, exactly, amounted to "significant inroads."

In Nicole's mind, it can be gauged by the fact that she's able to support herself, although the lion's share of her income isn't coming from her singing. But still, she's set herself up in a rented studio flat in Islington and is managing to put petrol into her run-down Mini. Surely that has to be seen as a win?

Yet Nicole fears that her father's barometer is going to be set by whether she's played Wembley Arena, thus creating an impossible task that she can't help but fail. She understands his reservations; no one had tried harder to be a professional musician than he had, and most would argue that that's *exactly* what he was. But he'd been under-booked and underpaid, which didn't bode well with a mortgage and a baby on the way. So, he'd given up on his castle in the sky and believed that everyone else should, too.

But Nicole's not ready to return to her marine biology course just yet, because performing speaks to her soul in a way that the underwater world, however fantastical, never could. It's in her blood, as much as it was in her father's, and although he may well have developed a method of denying it, as one brutal rebuttal followed another, if you have something burning within you—a passion that you can't extinguish—you have to at least follow that light for as long as you can.

"But you're happy," says Cassie, not yet mature enough to understand the sacrifices Nicole has made in pursuit of a dream that may never be realized. "You don't have to listen to Dad droning on about how you're wasting your life. He doesn't get to dictate where you go or what you do anymore."

"It's only because he cares," says Nicole. "Being a grown-up is hard, and I imagine being a parent even harder, so go easy—try not to upset him with all your antics. He's got a lot on his plate right now."

"That doesn't give him the right to be even more of an arse than normal," says Cassie.

"Perhaps he has *every* right—what with everything going on with Mum," says Nicole, looking at Cassie questioningly as she wraps a bag of ice in a tea towel and carefully places it on her sister's foot.

"I wish you'd come back home," says Cassie. "It was better then."

"Me being home isn't going to make what's going on any easier," says Nicole, though she has to admit, it would certainly alleviate some of the guilt that makes her feel as if she has a ten-ton weight around her neck.

6

Despite the pain, Cassie is still riding high when she wakes up the following morning, her dreams having been interspersed with the reality of how close she came to her idol.

As if reading her thoughts, Ben smiles down at her from the ceiling directly above her bed, the poster's staple holes peppering his square jawline. She'd had to buy six of the same magazine in order to find one with the foldout of him. Each of the three band members had been photographed individually and *Smash Hits* had wrapped the inserts up like a Willy Wonka chocolate bar, so you didn't know who you were getting until you ripped open the silver foil.

Cassie's heart lurches as she looks at him, the secret they now share bringing them closer together. But the split-second euphoria is superseded by the maudlin compression of the oxygen cylinder in the next room as it pumps life-saving air into her mother's lungs.

Snatching up the Sony Walkman from under her pillow, Cassie slides the headphones onto her ears and turns the volume up to maximum. As well as drowning out the noise, the beat of Secret Oktober's last single also has the ability to transport her to another time—back to when she was just a normal girl, whose mother would meet her with a hug and hot buttered toast when she got home from school. Back to BC—*Before Cancer*—when they were all living a life that had felt impervious. How quickly the carpet can be pulled from beneath your feet, upending everything you know.

The music stops and the play button pops back up when the cassette reaches the end of the reel. Cassie hits rewind and listens to the reassuring shrill of the tape as it backtracks to the beginning of her favorite song. She's done it so many times now that she can stop it almost to the second.

The line *"Just give me one more night, to hold you how you need to be held"* keeps coming back to haunt her, the words of a number-one pop song taking on a whole new meaning now that her mother's future seems to be hanging in the balance.

Gigi had only been ill for eight weeks; or at least, that's when the cancer decided to rear its ugly face publicly. Before that, it had been silently ravaging her body, its deadly cells wrapping themselves around her organs, strangling them with their far-reaching tentacles as she slept, utterly oblivious to the fact her body was turning on itself. She'd since said that it felt like the ultimate betrayal; Gigi looked after herself as well as she looked after her girls, ensuring they ate well, exercised regularly, and stayed hydrated. It was a lifestyle that she was likely predisposed to as a dancer, and one that Cassie had often pushed back against. But she's now of an age when she's beginning to appreciate that if she'd been allowed to frequent the McDonald's in town as much as she'd wanted to, she'd most likely not be the healthy teenager she is today. Though that theory rather lost its value in the face of her mother's diagnosis.

"We need to talk to you," her father John had said when she'd returned from school on that Wednesday afternoon two months ago.

Cassie had immediately known that something was wrong—

she'd never seen her father cry before and she assumed something had happened to one of her grandparents. She was mentally prepared for that—after all, it was the natural order of life. But then, as he struggled to find the right words, she had the absurd thought that perhaps something was wrong with *him*. He didn't share Gigi's conviction that "an apple a day kept the doctor away," favoring a diet more weighted with fatty foods and alcohol, so it *was* possible, but still so far of left field that it was almost inconceivable. Though what was *entirely* unimaginable was that it had anything to do with her mother. Not only because Gigi was seemingly utterly invincible, but she had sat there, staring straight ahead, with a fixed expression of utter defiance.

It's still there today, though you have to look past the pain that's etched in the deeply furrowed grooves in her brow to see it.

"How are you feeling?" Cassie asks now, as she peers around her parents' bedroom door, pleased to see her mother awake.

"Good," says Gigi, attempting to pull herself up against the pillows.

Cassie knows the lie is for her benefit. "Here, let me get you comfortable," she says, unable to comprehend how her mother's arms have become so bony that they can no longer support her frail body.

Eight weeks. How had it caused so much damage and devastation in such a short space of time? And how had Cassie not noticed its evil path before it had done its worst?

She'd spent every night since lying in bed, willing with all her might to be transported back to a time before her mother's body had stopped being like everybody else's. If Cassie had her time again, would she be able to pinpoint the exact moment that had happened?

It wasn't before their day out in town at the beginning of the year—she was sure of that. She would have seen it in the photos of her mother moonwalking across the zebra crossing outside the famous Abbey Road studios. She would have noticed it as Gigi led the five-hundred-strong fan chorus of Secret Oktober's new single as they stood in line for six hours outside Wembley Arena waiting for their concert tickets to go on sale.

No, there was nothing to suggest that anything was wrong as they'd sung, danced, and laughed their way around the capital on what Gigi had called a pilgrimage—a homage to their idols. But maybe her mother had known something she didn't. Maybe she already knew what was going on, hence insisting on the mother–daughter bonding trip.

"Did you see them?" Gigi croaks, grimacing as she falls back onto the pillows Cassie has fluffed up.

"Mum, you're not going to believe it," she says, sitting down on the edge of the bed, careful not to disturb any tubes.

Gigi smiles as Cassie recounts what happened, her sharp cheekbones rising up to meet her hooded eyes.

"You're clearly a far better groupie than I ever was," she says, wheezing as she laughs.

Cassie giggles, remembering how her mum had spent the night at the airport to welcome the Beatles home from America. She'd stolen money from her grandmother's purse and bunked off school, only to see the very top of Paul McCartney's head among a sea of policemen's helmets. Well, at least she thought it was Paul, but it was difficult to be sure from her position behind a wire fence at the far end of the runway.

When Gigi's father had found out, he'd given her three lashings with a wooden ruler. It's not lost on Cassie that her own father would probably do the same to her if he knew where she'd been yesterday. But the high she'd felt when Ben had looked at her was worth the risk.

"They're on *Saturday Superstore* this morning," says Gigi, wincing as she attempts to reach for a glass of water on her bedside table.

Cassie hurriedly picks it up and holds it to her mother's dry and cracked lips. "Oh, are they?" she says, in faux surprise. "I'd better stick a tape in and record it then."

"Oh, have you got to go to work?"

Cassie hesitates, wondering what the harm would be in telling her mum the truth—she's sure she wouldn't disapprove. In fact, she'd positively encourage her rebelliousness—and remind her that you only live once. But to save her mother from having to cover for her with her father, she lies. "Yeah, I start in an hour," she says. But Gigi is already asleep, her body drained from the energy it had taken to smile.

Cassie bends down to kiss her. She hates saying goodbye, especially when her mum's eyes are closed, and she can't help but turn an ear to her mouth, willing herself to hear the breath that, up until now, she'd taken for granted.

A hundred or so girls are already congregating outside the entrance of the BBC Television Center on Wood Lane, and Cassie can't help but feel perturbed that Amelia's not the only one who has inside information.

"Hey, over here!" her new friend calls out. Dressed in a frilly pirate shirt and red leather trousers tied around the waist with a long white sash, she seemingly worships at the altar of the New Romantic revolution that Secret Oktober spearheaded two years ago. But whereas they, and everyone else, have moved on to shoulder-padded linen suits, she is still happily ensconced in dandy heaven. "You've just missed them," she says.

"Shit!"

Cassie hasn't come all this way, risking her part-time job and the wrath of her father, for nothing.

"It's OK," says Amelia, as if reading her mind. "If you don't get to see them on their way out, we'll definitely catch them at the airport."

"Airport?" questions Cassie.

Amelia nods. "Yeah, they're flying to Paris this afternoon, so we'll head to Heathrow after here."

"How do you know all this stuff?" asks Cassie, wishing she had the inside track on their movements. "And how does Ben know your name?"

Amelia shrugs, though her apparent nonchalance is laced with a smug superiority. Cassie doesn't blame her; it's clearly a powerful position she holds, both in the band's inner sanctum and that of the fans' world, though there's no doubt she picks and chooses who to share her valuable knowledge with. While other girls look at her with unbridled hope, praying that she sprinkles some of her stardust on them, it seems it's Cassie who is once again elected as today's lucky recipient.

"Come on," says Amelia, reaching for her hand and pulling her further along Wood Lane, away from the prying eyes of the ever-alert security presence.

"Where are we going?" giggles Cassie, already loving the adventure she knows she's about to embark on.

"We're going in," says Amelia as she gets a footing on the six-foot fence that runs around the entire perimeter of the TV studios.

Cassie looks up at the world-famous circular building, its curved walls stretching up seven or eight floors. "Are you completely mad?" she asks. "It'll be like a maze in there, and the security guards will be hunting us down like we're the IRA."

"I know what studio they're in," says Amelia, her eyes dancing at the idea of being rebellious. But then, Cassie imagines she spends her whole life refusing to live by the rules.

"This is such a bad idea," says Cassie as Amelia falls onto the grass on the other side in an ungainly heap.

"I bet you won't be saying that when you're face to face with Ben Edwards in ten minutes," says Amelia with a grin.

The thought makes Cassie's stomach somersault as she climbs up the railings and carefully lifts herself over the forbidding metal spikes. There's a snag, a pulling-up, and for a second she can't work out what's going on, but as her jeans get tighter and tighter around her bum, she realizes her belt has caught on a railing, giving her the wedgie of all wedgies.

"Oh no, you haven't?!" shrieks Amelia, her rounded cheeks looking fit to burst.

"I bloody have," replies Cassie, not knowing whether to laugh or cry as she hangs there helplessly, like a pig in an abattoir.

"Wait, hold on," chokes Amelia, struggling to contain her hysteria. "I need to . . ." She rummages in her bag and pulls out her Instamatic camera.

"Don't you dare," says Cassie in mock indignation.

"This is too good to miss," cackles Amelia as she reels the winder. "Say cheese!"

"Help me!" cries Cassie through tears of laughter.

Amelia wraps her arms around Cassie's knees and attempts to lift her. "Just a bit more," she says, breathless from giggling. She jerks her upward and suddenly the belt's released and the two of them are sent crashing to the ground, falling onto one another in a jumble of limbs.

"I like you, but not like *that*," says Amelia, laughing as their faces come uncomfortably close to one another's.

Cassie abruptly pulls away, the comment taking her back to last year when Suzanna accused her of leering at her when she was getting changed for netball. It had been wholly untrue, but an off-the-cuff remark has a habit of sticking, especially when it comes from the girl who everybody fears the most. So, Cassie had spent the past two terms going out of her way to prove that it was boys she was attracted to. Perhaps that's why Ben is such a big deal; it gives her a chance to demonstrate what really floats her boat.

"I don't fancy you, either," she says, scrabbling to get to her feet.

"You *don't*?" says Amelia, looking put out. "Well, I can't pretend that I'm not disappointed, because if I *did* swing that way, I would definitely fancy *you*!"

Cassie can't help but smile, buoyed by Amelia's devil-may-care attitude. She's everything Cassie wants to be, if only she could shake off the shackles that bind her to a life of conformity.

They cross the lawn as if they're in an Arnold Schwarzenegger movie, heading for a door that's held ever-so-slightly ajar by a block of wood. As they step into a dark abyss, it reminds Cassie of how she'd imagine backstage to be, with huge lights fixed to the heavily rigged ceiling and sound checks echoing around the underbelly of a seating stand. A frisson of adrenaline sets her nerves alight—the thought of how close the band might be, conflicting with the very real danger of trespassing and a vision of what her father will do if she's caught.

"Come on—this way," calls out Amelia, stepping over cables the size of tree trunks, each color-coded to mean something to somebody.

Following the draw of a white light, they push through some double doors, out into a corridor where a man is pushing a trolley piled high with film reels. A woman in red patent high heels sashays past him in the opposite direction.

"Good morning, Miss Francis. How are you today?" the man chirps. He looks disappointed but not surprised when she doesn't respond, and Cassie can't help but wonder if the same exchange occurs every day.

"Hi, Fred," says Amelia, reading his ID badge as she stops beside him. "I need to get this visitor to Studio Seven as quickly as possible." She nods in Cassie's direction. "What's the best way?"

What the hell is she doing? They should be using the shadows to escape detection, not stepping directly into the light. Cassie waits for the man to make a grab for the walkie-talkie attached to his belt, sure that they've reached the end of the road, but instead his face lights up.

"Well, if you go down those stairs, turn right and take the second left, you'll be able to sneak in the fire door."

"You're a star," calls out Amelia.

He smiles, more to himself than to Cassie as she passes by, happy to have proven himself useful to someone.

"Oi, where do you two think you're going?" comes a gruff voice from behind them.

Cassie's knees buckle beneath her. She's never had the law breathing down her neck before and she imagines that if she turns around, she'll see a burly policeman who'll handcuff her and march her off to the local nick.

Her heart races as they pick up the pace, their steps quickening as they follow the curve of the building.

"Stop!" comes the voice, as they get ever closer to the illuminated sign of Studio Seven.

Amelia sneaks a look back at Cassie, checking that she's with her, before swinging the door open. The minute she does, they're hit by a wall of sound—the drumbeat of Secret Oktober's latest hit accompanied by the squeals of what sounds like a thousand teenagers.

Cassie can hardly breathe, though whether it's because they're so close or about to be hauled out of there she can't tell. She's just cleared the back of the seating stand and emerged into the blinding lights of the studio floor when she's pulled backward off her feet. The last thing she sees as she's lifted up is the very top of Ben Edwards's head.

She can't help but smile. She's done her mother proud.

7

It's past nine by the time Nicole lets herself into the house she used to call home, and she's immediately unnerved by the disconcerting silence.

"Hello?" she calls out from the hall, the simple word so full of apprehension as she waits for a response. When none comes, she bounds up the stairs, two at a time, but then stops outside her mother's closed bedroom door, her bravado suddenly diminished.

She takes a deep breath, forcing the choking fear away as she pushes the door open.

"Hello?" she says again, into the darkened room, where only a dim light reaches out from beneath the tassel-fringed shade on the bedside cabinet. She can just make out the silhouette of her father, standing beside the bed.

"Leave us!" barks John, throwing an outstretched arm in her direction.

Another man is bent over Gigi with a syringe in his hand.

"Is-is everything OK?" Nicole stutters.

"Everything is fine," snaps John.

"M-mum?" Nicole calls out, feeling like a little girl who just needs to hear her mother's voice. She used to covet it for reassurance and to feel secure. Now, she realizes, it's to know she's still alive.

"I said go!" John shouts.

She softly closes the door and leans her ear to it.

"There must be something more we can do," cries John's pitiful voice. "Something else we can try."

The doctor's silence speaks volumes, and Nicole's heart breaks.

She tries to busy herself with making dinner, hoping that she's misconstrued her father's desperate words, but she accidentally puts raw sausages in a saucepan of boiling water and uncooked potatoes into a frying pan laced with oil.

"Shit!" she says, burning herself on the pan handle as she drops it into the sink, her mind clearly as mashed as the potatoes she was intending to prepare.

"What's going on? Where's Cassie?" asks John, coming into the kitchen. His voice may sound as forthright as usual, but Nicole only has to take one look at his face to see that inside he's a broken man.

"I guess she's not in from work yet," says Nicole.

"But it's after nine," says John, looking at his watch.

"Maybe she's clocking in some overtime," says Nicole, knowing it's unlikely.

He nods, temporarily assuaged, but the real elephant in the room looms large. Nicole knows that it's down to her to address it—if she's brave enough.

"So, what's going on with Mum?" she asks, avoiding eye contact by looking in the fridge for something she doesn't need.

John makes a strange grunting sound and Nicole waits to see if it's to stifle a sob or to clear his throat to speak.

"The doctor's wrong" is all he says, before roughly pulling open the cutlery drawer, noisily collecting knives and forks and taking them through to the dining room.

Nicole waits a beat. "What did he say?"

She watches through the serving hatch as her father's shoulders convulse, and she can't help but let out a whimper that escapes from deep within her chest.

"He . . . he thinks she's had enough," says John. "He thinks she can't take any more."

Nicole swallows the implication.

"But he doesn't know my Gigi," he says, laying the table with increasing vigor, as if he's attempting to power his wife's resilience with his own hands. "He doesn't know what she's capable of—the strength of her mind, what her body can do . . ." His voice breaks and Nicole instinctively wants to go to him, but knows he would rather brush her off than show any vulnerability.

"So, what's next?"

"We keep going," he snaps, as if she shouldn't need to ask. "We take the medicines. We do the treatments. We don't give up, because one of them is going to work and when that day comes, these doctors will realize that they have no idea who they're dealing with. Your mum's going to show them that miracles really do exist."

His jaw is set and his eyes are locked as he wills himself to believe his own sermon, but an unrelenting despair is etched into every crevice of his furrowed brow as the reality of losing his beloved wife bears down on him.

Nicole is grateful for the sound of the key in the front door, if only to bring him back from the brink of where she fears he's going.

"Hey," gushes Cassie, her curls bouncing as she runs to hug her sister. The sense of relief that she doesn't have to manage her father alone tonight is palpable. But it only adds to the weight of responsibility on Nicole's shoulders.

"You look like a stick of rock," says Nicole, forcing a laugh as Cassie stands there in her work tabard and striped blouse. "I bet if we cut you open, you'd have 'Woolworths' running all the way through you."

Cassie checks that their dad is still in the dining room. "It'd say 'Secret Oktober,'" she whispers, with a wink.

Nicole rolls her eyes. Sometimes her little sister displays such levels of maturity that she forgets she's only sixteen, but this whole obsession with a pop group, which seems to have ramped up a gear in recent months, makes her seem younger than her years. There's a part of Nicole that gets it—to a degree. It's a bond that she shares with their mother—an excuse to recall memories of a time gone by and an attempt to re-create them—and Nicole supposes that, right now, Cassie is looking to garner as much of that as she can. But to the detriment of everything else?

"I wouldn't push it tonight," she says.

"Why?" presses Cassie, seemingly oblivious to what's going on. Nicole wishes *she* was as blithely ignorant.

"It's not a good time, as you well know . . ."

"Has something happened with Mum?" asks Cassie, her eyes widening.

Nicole blinks back the sting of tears. How will life ever be the same if anything happens to her? Who will Nicole turn to when her mother's voice is the only one she heeds?

She would never have got through the past few months as unscathed as she was, if it weren't for her mother's unswerving support and heartfelt advice. While John was threatening to kill Nicole's ex-boyfriend Aaron for daring to cheat, it was Gigi's more measured approach that their daughter had harnessed.

"One day he'll wake up and his heart will hurt, and he'll not know why," she'd said, stroking Nicole's long hair as she lay on the sofa. "But eventually it will dawn on him that it's because he lost the best thing that ever happened to him."

It had only taken two weeks for the epiphany to present itself, but, thanks to her mother's incessant determination to drill into her that she deserved better than Aaron, Nicole was more than ready when he came begging for forgiveness. And every time she'd been tempted to capitulate since, it was her mother who lifted her onto a pedestal so that her perspective wasn't skewed by the empty promises he was throwing her way.

Nicole can't stop a tear from falling. How will she hold herself up without her mother? And more important, how will she be able to keep Cassie's head above water while she herself is drowning?

"There's no change," lies Nicole, under the guise of protecting her. "But Dad's not in a good place, so I would advise you to tread lightly."

The three of them sit at the dining table in silence, the *News at Ten* presenter the only voice in the room. The TV is on more often than not these days. In fact, it almost never gets turned off, as they attempt to fill the void of Gigi's absence, even though she's still upstairs.

"So, how was work?" John asks Cassie, as he pushes sausages around his plate with no intention of eating them.

"It was good," she says, nodding enthusiastically. "They put me on pick 'n' mix today."

John does his best to feign interest. "What does that entail, then?"

"Well, I'm on the scales, taking money, trying to stop everyone who walks past from thinking they can pocket a sweet without me noticing."

"What, *stealing* it?" asks John, with an expression of disbelief.

Cassie nods. "The pick 'n' mix is notorious for it. People seem to think it's one for the bag, two for the mouth."

John shakes his head. "And that's down to you, is it? To try and stop it from happening?"

"Yeah," she says. "It's a lot of responsibility, but I think I held my own."

He nods, as if he's almost proud of her. "So, they're beginning to trust you? That's good. It's important that you can be trusted—it goes a long way."

"Yeah," says Cassie absently.

"And finally," says the newsreader, cutting through the forced atmosphere, "Britain's boy-band sensation, Secret Oktober, were given a hysterical send-off at Heathrow Airport earlier today, when over one hundred screaming girls turned up to wave them on their way."

Cassie's face freezes and she jumps up like a cat on a hot tin roof from the table. "Let's get the washing-up done so we don't have to do it later," she says, taking her plate through to the kitchen bin and noisily scraping it clean.

Nicole struggles to swallow the lumpy mashed potato in her mouth as she dares to contemplate what might be about to ensue. She throws Cassie a questioning look through the hatch, hoping her fears are unfounded.

"Look at this," says John, derisorily. "All these girls making a fool of themselves over some fly-by-nights who they'll be embarrassed by this time next year." He tuts. "God, what must their parents think?"

Cassie clangs the cutlery even more loudly. "Come on," she calls out. "Come and help me."

Channeling Cassie's rising panic as if it were her own, Nicole races to turn the TV off, but it's too late.

"What the . . . ?" starts John, squinting at the TV.

Nicole closes her eyes and holds her breath.

"Please tell me I haven't just seen what I think I've seen," John bellows. "That that wasn't you throwing yourself all over those boys."

"*What?*" says Cassie, looking at him incredulously, as if the mere suggestion is so far-fetched that even *she* can't believe it.

"I saw you! You were hanging off some chump who looked even more embarrassed than I feel."

"I-I . . ." starts Cassie, desperately looking to Nicole for help, now that their mother can no longer stand up for her.

"So not only have you made a complete and utter fool of yourself, heaping humiliation on me and your mother, but you've also spent the last fifteen minutes telling me barefaced lies."

Cassie's nostrils flare. "If you're embarrassed to be my father, then that's your problem, but don't you ever suggest that Mum would be anything other than proud of me!" she cries, before storming out of the room.

"Come back here right now, young lady—"

"Don't!" Nicole warns her father as she holds him back from following Cassie. "I'll go."

"Well, you'd better talk some sense into her," he barks. "Because I will not have her behave the way she's behaving."

As Nicole climbs the stairs, her limbs weary with worry and fear, she wishes more than ever that she could slip in beside her mother like she used to. It takes her until she gets to the top that she realizes she still can.

8

"Hannah!" I call out, my throat hoarse. "Hannah!"

"We've checked the boathouse and the yacht club," says Joe, the current owner of Danny's, the bar where I used to work. "There's nothing."

Every time someone tells me they haven't found her, another little piece of my heart breaks. It's been almost two hours and night has transcended day, the reflection of the moon in the water of Glorietta Bay a sickening reminder. As small a town as Coronado is, what chance have we got of finding her if she's wandered off by herself, let alone if she's been led away by someone else? Someone I can't help but fear has a sinister motive.

"Over here!" calls a voice from somewhere beyond the *Naked Warrior* memorial.

I race toward the unnerving cry, willing myself to believe it can only be something positive. But Brad's there before I am, and his face says it all.

"It was tucked under the bench," says Justin, the chef from the Night & Day Cafe, as he holds up my little girl's Rapunzel backpack. I swallow the ever-present threat of bile that the reactive acid in my stomach has reduced its contents to.

Brad pulls my shaking body into his and holds me so tight that I can barely breathe. "This doesn't mean anything," he says, more to convince himself than me. "Apart from that she was here and we're close—I can feel it."

I look to the water's edge, just a few feet away, its inky-black surface sending shivers down my spine. How can something I have such a deep love and respect for suddenly feel so menacing? As if it's holding the secret to the rest of my life and won't give it up.

I will myself not to go there, but I can't help but imagine Hannah's tiny body lying motionless at the bottom. She's a strong swimmer—Brad had made sure of that—but even if she had gone in of her own accord, there's only so long her little organs would have been able to withstand the cold. An involuntary sob escapes from deep within my chest.

"Don't let your imagination get the better of you," says Brad, reading my mind.

"I just want her home," I cry into his chest.

"I know," he croaks, letting his guard down for the first time. "I just don't understand who would do something like this."

Hank appears at our side. "I think we're going to have to seriously start thinking about who *might* . . ." he says, with a grave expression.

"Do you honestly think this is someone we *know*?" asks Brad, his voice high-pitched. "That Hannah's been specifically targeted because someone has a grudge against one of *us*?"

Hank shakes his head and puffs out his cheeks. "It's something we're going to have to consider. This doesn't happen in a place like this for no reason. Have you fallen out with anyone recently? Is there anyone at work who's pissed at something you've done, something you said . . . ?" He's looking to Brad, whose vexed forehead suggests he's having to dig deep to come up with something. I will him to try harder, because not only might it lead us to Hannah, but it will also mean that this has nothing to do with me.

"There's no one," says Brad, looking between me and Hank, the glow of the streetlight giving his already ashen complexion a yellowing hue. "We do so much for this community—we're well thought of; at least, I thought we were . . ."

Hank puts a reassuring hand on Brad's back.

"What about you?" he asks me.

I wince at his abrupt tone—or maybe that's how he always talks, except now it suddenly sounds accusatory.

"You've got the city council hearing for the seals at La Jolla coming up—there must be quite a few disgruntled locals who think they've got as much right of way to the beach as the seals have." He looks at me with raised eyebrows. "Have you come across anyone who's been more vocal than most? Who's perhaps taken offense at what you're trying to do?"

I rack my brain, thinking of all the run-ins I've had since starting the petition to close the beach. But as much as I try to pretend that the old man who called me "an interfering bitch" might be riled enough to warrant kidnapping my daughter, I can't turn a blind eye to the woman who coincidentally turned up on my doorstep today, asking questions about what happened twenty-five years ago. I always knew I couldn't run from it—forever—that it would catch up with me in the end—but I never imagined that my daughter would be the pawn, punished for something *I've* done. How naive of me.

"Nic?" prompts Brad. "Can you think of anyone?"

My mouth opens and I go to speak, but there's too much to unpack here and now, and it won't go anywhere toward finding Hannah. So, I numbly shake my head instead.

"Right, we're going to work backward over toward the Del," Hank shouts out to the growing team of volunteers. "Make sure to

I WOULD DIE FOR YOU   51

check any tucked-away places—anywhere a child might think is
exciting to hide." He's still acting as if this is nothing more than a
case of Hannah having run off—at least to the locals—for fear that
the more sinister reality will elicit a panicked community.

"What about your boat?" says Justin. "Could Hannah have gone
there?"

In any other circumstance, it's highly probable. She loves going
out on the water, especially if it means she gets to spend special time
with her dad. The pair of them often head out at the weekends,
taking sandwiches and a flask to while away an afternoon on the
waves. Brad invariably fills her head with tales of his Navy SEAL
exploits and she'll come bursting through the door, desperately
needing to know if Daddy really used to be as brave as he said he
was, now that he has a desk job.

"He's even braver now," I'd said to her last week when they came
in from watching the military jets fly over North Island, just off
Coronado.

"But he doesn't do all that dangerous stuff anymore," she'd said,
looking at me all confused.

"No, but he gets to be your dad," I'd said, smiling. "And that's
way harder than anything a Navy SEAL has to go through."

She'd rolled her eyes and I'd laughed as if I was joking, but
watching him now, as his panicked eyes dart from side to side and
a tangible fear crawls into every crevice of his vexed expression, I
realize that I meant it.

"Nic, go and check the boat," says Brad, his brain clearly working at a million miles an hour.

"But . . ." I start, knowing that it's a waste of time.

"She might have gone there if she was scared," he says, as if trying to convince himself that the story everyone else is working to
might actually be true.

"She was *taken,*" I hiss under my breath. "She's not going to be
conveniently dropped back to our boat."

He fixes me with an unmoving stare, as if questioning why I wouldn't want to explore every avenue. "If she's been left somewhere by someone who has grown tired of this sick game, then the boat might be the place she'd go if she can't make her way home."

His rambling thoughts strike a chord I don't want to hear. "Is that what you think this is?" I snap, though my frustration isn't aimed at him. "That someone's playing a *game* with us?"

"I hope that's all it is," he chokes, as he runs a frantic hand through his hair. "Because the alternative doesn't bear thinking about."

I force both his alternative, and the resounding voice that this is all my fault, to the back of my mind as I race down the jetty, willing life into Brad's theory. He could be right; this could all be a bad judgment call instigated by a disgruntled resident who has bitten off more than they can chew. Maybe they wanted to teach me a lesson, to make me realize that I should be focusing more on my daughter's well-being than that of the seals. And as I near the boat, I don't doubt that they might be right, and vow that from this point onward that's exactly what I'll do. But as I rip the tarp cover off and catch sight of Hannah's pink windbreaker, I wonder if I'll ever get the chance.

9

Despite intending for them to go to the Secret Oktober concert together, Cassie had long since realized that her mother wouldn't be
well enough. Still, she'd refused to give her ticket to anyone else in
the vain hope that Gigi would somehow muster the energy at the
last minute. But as she peers around her parents' bedroom door,
keeping everything crossed, it seems that no amount of wishful
thinking could get her mother to sit up, let alone leave the house,
and Cassie can't help but feel crushed by an overwhelming sadness.

"I'm off," she says quietly, hoping she can't be heard over the rise
and fall of the oxygen cylinder.

But her mother is more astute than she gives her credit for.
"Where to?" comes a fragile voice.

Cassie sucks in a breath, consumed with guilt for something she
has no control over.

"I-I'm going to the Secret Oktober concert . . ." she starts, knowing that her mother's disappointment will match her own.

"*What?* Without *me?*" murmurs Gigi. "Pass me my pink suit and I'll meet you downstairs in ten minutes."

Whether it's her wicked sense of humor talking or a drug-induced confusion, Cassie isn't sure, but bizarrely she finds herself waiting in the hallway, part of her willing her mum to appear beside her so acutely that it seems impossible that it won't happen. But ten minutes later she solemnly gives up on a miracle and silently lets herself out of the house.

By the time she gets to Wembley Arena, the queue is already depressingly long, stretching around at least two corners of the huge building, without an end in sight. She scans the line, searching for Amelia's face among the crowd, hoping that she's nearer the front than the back.

"Cassie!" comes an ear-splitting screech. "Over here!"

Cassie ducks under the rope that Amelia is holding up, issuing hollow apologies as disgruntled moans ring out from those behind. Though they quickly dissipate when one of the windowless arena's doors begins to open. It's slow, painfully slow, as if even the staff are playing the game—ramping up the tension within an already restless crowd. High-pitched screams ring out as a random steward pokes his bald head out. Frustrated groans follow when he ducks back in and closes the door again.

By the time the whispers have reached the queue around the corner, word is that it was Ben Edwards himself who had appeared, which sends the line surging forward, forcing decisive action.

"No running!" the gatekeeper shouts pointlessly as the doors swing open and a thousand hysterical girls fight to get through the six-foot square entrance.

Amelia takes Cassie's hand and they sprint with burning lungs across the concourse, through the doors marked "Arena Floor" and out into the hallowed magnificence of the empty auditorium. Cassie momentarily falters, wanting to take it all in, but bodies are running at her like wild horses, threatening to trample anything that stands in their way.

"Come on!" shouts Amelia, pulling on her hand.

It's not until they've reached the barrier by the stage, gripping it with white knuckles, that it occurs to Cassie that they'll have to stand their ground for the next two hours until Secret Oktober come on—though having Amelia there makes the time go surprisingly quickly, with new friends being made thanks to her envy-inducing stories of hanging out with the band.

"How do you know where they're next going to be?" asks one girl, as Cassie flips through a photo album that Amelia has brought with her. Each slip-in pocket displays another picture of her with a band member at the airport, at the recording studio, at their hotel.

Amelia shrugs casually. "At the beginning, it was a game of cat and mouse. I had to keep reinventing the wheel, because they caught on."

"Caught on to what?" Cassie asks.

"To my genius," says Amelia, without an iota of irony. "They thought they were being clever, checking into hotels under false names, but they hadn't reckoned on me setting off the fire alarm."

Cassie's mouth drops open. "You set off a *fire alarm*?"

"It's easy," says Amelia, nonchalantly. "One night, I did three different hotels to find out where they were. And the looks on their faces when they all had to congregate on Park Lane so they could be accounted for!" She throws her head back and laughs. "That's how I found out they were using cartoon names because Ben said his name was Donald Duck."

"That is well impressive," says Cassie, in awe of her new friend's ingenuity and chutzpah. "But how do you get away with it with your parents? If my dad found out I'd done something like that . . ." She blows out her cheeks and shakes her head.

"Oh, my mum's the same," says Amelia. "I'm an only child and since she and my dad split up, it's just been the two of us. She loves me so much, but sometimes it can be suffocating . . ."

Cassie nods, remembering Nicole's words after the blow-out with her dad last week. "It's only because he loves you," she'd said, when Cassie had complained that he didn't give her room to breathe.

"But I'm sixteen," Cassie had answered back. "I know I shouldn't have bunked off work to go and see Secret Oktober, but wouldn't he rather me be doing that than spending time with a boy? I could be skulking around with someone like Aaron—would he be happier then?"

As soon as the barb about Nicole's ex-boyfriend was out, Cassie felt guilty, but her sister had swallowed the unintended insult. "So, would you rather have a father who didn't care about who you were with or where you were? Who didn't love you enough to make sure you were in school when you were supposed to be and get the best-possible grades you can to give yourself a better chance at life?"

Cassie knows that one day she'll see it like that, but right now it sounds like a broken record. "I know what you mean," she says to Amelia. "But you should count yourself lucky because I'd never get away with what you do."

"Believe me, if my mum knew half of what I get up to, she'd be down on me like a ton of bricks. She gets worried when I'm too long at the corner shop." She laughs. "I swear she puts her egg timer on the minute I leave the house and comes out looking for me when it goes off."

"So how do you do it?" asks Cassie, gesturing toward the photo albums.

Amelia shrugs her shoulders. "Like I say, I'm a genius when it comes to reinventing the wheel."

The lights go down, plunging the auditorium into darkness, and twelve thousand girls instantly lose their minds. Cassie looks wide-eyed at Amelia, the pair of them covering their ears in an attempt to protect themselves from the high-pitched screams that are raining down on them from every angle.

A single drumbeat sounds and the girl next to her throws her hands to either side of her head, as if it will somehow keep it from spontaneously combusting. Tears stream down her face, making it look like she's in pain rather than ecstasy.

Another beat, and butterflies take flight in Cassie's stomach, the anticipation shredding her nerves, pulling her chest tight. The person behind her presses forward, and she can feel the rounding of a stomach in the small of her back. She steels herself, pushing back to maintain a gap between her and the barrier, but the pressure increases.

Static crackles the huge video screens, sending an electrical current through the audience as tantalizing glimpses of each band member momentarily appear. They're gone before you can even work out who's who, but it doesn't matter to the hysterical crowd as they surge forward, desperate to get as close to the stage as possible, even though their idols aren't yet on it.

Unable to withstand the force any longer, the metal railing lodges itself under Cassie's ribs as she's pressed up against it. Her organs feel as if they're being slowly and systematically crushed under the weight of a thousand bodies.

"I can't breathe," she says, trying to lift herself, or at least her abdomen, above the unforgiving steel. But the more she tries, the more futile it feels.

Reaching out to the nearby security guard, she claws at his shoulder, but she can feel herself slipping. "I . . ." she starts, as a darkness descends.

He turns around to see her being swallowed whole, disappearing within a split second as the people she's spent the previous two hours confiding in step on her in their haste to move forward.

"Get her out!" he roars as he puts all twenty stone of his weight into lifting Cassie up. The crowd don't stop surging, but those around her slowly realize what's going on and do their part to help. Panicked and wide-eyed, Amelia watches her friend rise from the crowd like a phoenix.

"Where are you taking her?" she shouts over the ear-splitting crescendo.

"She'll just be backstage," the security guard booms into her ear. "The St. John's Ambulance crew will check her over and make sure she's OK."

The beat that Cassie knows so well—has listened to a thousand times—slowly infiltrates her befuddled brain. She knows where she is—or at least where she *was*—but she's lost all perspective on *when* she was there.

"Christ," comes a male voice. "Is she going to be all right?"

Cassie's eyes are assaulted by a blinding brightness as they're pulled open by a stranger with a concerned expression. Cassie instinctively flinches, but as she slowly becomes accustomed to the ring of light, she smiles. Because, blurred in the background, is a face that looks so much like Ben Edwards.

"Are you OK?" he asks, leaning in toward her with a worried frown. She manages a nod.

There are far-away drumbeats and screams that sound like they're trapped within a screw-top bottle. Cassie feels compelled to get up, to go toward the noise, but she doesn't want to ruin the best dream she's ever had.

"Make sure to look after her," says the voice, which is becoming more and more distant, though Cassie doesn't know whether it's him or her who's moving further away.

"Oh my god, where have you been?" screams Amelia when Cassie eventually gets back to where she started, wedging herself in between her friend and the barrier. "I've been so worried about you."

Cassie starts to tell her what happened, but Amelia has already turned her attention back to the stage, singing along to the rousing chorus of "Kissing Girls" with the rest of the twelve-thousand-strong backing band.

In the final throes, as the beat drops out and Ben delivers the last two lines a cappella, he kneels down directly in front of them. He's so close that Cassie can see the beads of sweat on his forehead and, just as the lights go out on the last note, he blows her a kiss.

10

"Are you sure they're going to let us in?" Cassie asks for the tenth time, as she and Amelia emerge from Charing Cross station.

Amelia smiles knowingly and drags her up the Strand, toward the Savoy hotel.

"Now, look as if you belong here," says Amelia, as they walk toward a top-hatted doorman helping a woman out of a white Rolls-Royce.

Cassie pats down her poodle perm and pushes her shoulders back, but every part of her feels like a fan, and every doorman of every hotel in London must be able to spot one. It's their job, when they have as many high-profile guests as they do. But the girls somehow manage to slip past as the doorman is busy unloading luggage from the trunk, only for Cassie to risk giving herself away when she stops, stock-still, in awe of the opulence inside.

Ornate pillars hold up a double-height ceiling hung with ten-foot-wide chandeliers that send shadows dancing across the polished checkered floor. Sumptuous green velour armchairs sit in front of dark mahogany paneling. Even the guests seem to move around as if they're in a 1950s movie.

"Close your mouth," laughs Amelia, as she confidently makes her way toward the lift.

By the time they arrive at the Royal Suite on the fifth floor, the party is in full swing. Whitney Houston's "How Will I Know" is blaring from the boombox, and trendy people dressed in mohair knits and baggy pinstripe suits are making the room look effortlessly cool. Cassie pulls at her shocking-pink shirt self-consciously and wishes she'd worn something edgier.

"Do you want a drink?" asks Amelia, with a nod toward the row of boxed wine taking up the entire length of the oversized dining table.

Cassie nods absently, feeling like she's outside of herself, looking in. This must be a mistake, a wind-up, because this doesn't happen to normal people—to people like her.

Her attention is pulled back into sharp focus when she hears the indomitable voice of Michael, Secret Oktober's drummer, booming from across the room. He's always the most vocal of the group, the first to answer an interviewer's question, the one seemingly without a filter.

It had got them into trouble more than once, when he'd questioned the need for a monarchy right before a concert for the Prince's Trust and commented that the borders between San Francisco and Britain needed to be closed if we wanted to stop the spread of AIDS in our country.

Luke and Ben had jokingly passed it off as a need for attention from a natural extrovert who had inadvertently been forced to hide behind a drum kit, saying that being in the dark, at the back of the stage, didn't come easily to someone who was clearly born to be a frontman. "Hence he feels the need to be seen and heard when he's *off*-stage," Ben was quoted in *The Sun* the next day, by way of apology.

"Did we just smash Wembley, or did we just smash Wembley?" yells Michael now, balancing precariously with one foot on the back of the three-piece suite and the other flailing for traction on the bookcase. "Does anyone have Duran Duran's number so I can tell them how it's done?"

The room concurs with whoops and cheers, but the flunkies will no doubt be brown-nosing Simon Le Bon this time next week.

Michael grins inanely as he shakes a magnum of champagne. "So, who's with me? Who wants to get this party started?"

People instinctively back away from him, knowing what's coming, but with little space to fill, there's nothing they can do to avoid the foam spray. A girl in a tight flesh-colored vest rushes forward and holds a glass up into the air, as if she's hoping to catch some of the bubbles. But all it serves to do is soak her top right through, exposing her braless breasts, as she screams in faux surprise.

"Micky Delaney, I'll get you for that," she shrieks, looking up at him.

"Not if I get you first," he says, jumping down and planting a kiss on her champagne-soaked lips.

"Who's *that*?" Cassie asks, somewhat indignantly. Michael may well be her least favorite member of the band, but she still doesn't want him to have a girlfriend.

"That's Kimberley Banks," says Amelia bitterly. "A model, supposedly. *She* seems to think they're seeing each other, but *he* says it's just a casual hookup whenever they're in the same room."

"Oh, I didn't know," says Cassie dejectedly, the girl's ample assets making her feel immediately inferior. "So is Ben with someone too?"

Amelia laughs. "There's no shortage, as you can imagine, but he's a little more selective than Michael—though that's not saying much."

"Oh my god, oh my god," wheezes Cassie when she sees Ben coming out of an adjoining room with his arm around a girl who looks like she's just stepped out of the pages of *Elle* magazine. With her glossy brown hair and legs that go up to her armpits, his taste in girls is obvious, and Cassie shrinks into herself as if to disguise the fact that she is the polar opposite.

"Hi, Ben, can I introduce you to my friend Bella?" purrs Kimberley, putting a territorial hand on his chest, much to the chagrin of the girl standing beside him. "She works with me and is a huge fan."

Bella giggles inanely as Ben takes hold of her hand and brings it slowly to his lips. "The pleasure is all mine, I'm sure," he says, charm dripping off every syllable.

"You were *amazing* tonight," she pouts, her eyes drinking in every part of him. "You had the crowd in the palm of your hand. I saw you in Birmingham last year and thought it was the best gig I'd ever seen, but tonight . . . ?" She shakes her head from side to side and blows her cheeks out. "Tonight, you knocked it out the park."

Cassie is unable to tear herself away from the pantomime playing out in front of her. If nothing else, the sycophantic display of cheap admiration teaches her how *not* to be, if she were ever to have a proper conversation with him. The fawning and stroking of both his body and his ego is so uncomfortable to watch that she's embarrassed for him—and even more embarrassed for the girl, who wouldn't give him the time of day if he were stacking shelves in the local supermarket.

"Well, thanks," he says.

"My friend's having a party on the other side of town," she continues, looking at him hopefully. "If you wanted to skip here?"

Ben considers the proposition and Cassie wills him to say no, though what purpose that will serve she doesn't know. She's dreamed of this moment and was convinced that if it were ever to happen, it would be the best night of her life. Except, now that she's here, it somehow feels like it would be less painful to be at home, in blissful ignorance, than to remain a wallflower who will never be noticed.

"I need another drink," she says, pressing the tap on the side of the wine box that is thankfully within reach.

"Hey, Curly, you're looking a lot better than when I last saw you."

Cassie almost drops her glass when she turns to find Ben standing there, his face as close as can be, breathing in the very same air as her. Her heart races, her body unable to withstand the surreality of what is happening.

Say something, she says to herself, but her throat constricts and her jaw locks.

Staring for far longer than is polite, she ticks off the checklist in her head that proves it's really him: the smooth skin that colors all too easily, the cheekbones that her mother says could slice ham, the cleft in his chin that his bandmates tease him about because they say it looks like a bum. That unmistakable smile.

Even if she *could* talk, she doesn't know what she could possibly say. This is a fantasy she's daydreamed about for so long. She'd predicted what Ben would say and she'd planned the perfect answer that would make him fall instantly in love with her. Except now, when he's right here in front of her—the pair of them face to face—her mind is blank of every feasible response.

"It *was* you I saw backstage on a stretcher, wasn't it?"

"I don't know if that's something I should admit to," she says eventually.

"Well, considering we hadn't even started our set, you certainly don't get any points for staying power."

"If you had any idea what it's like to have all your internal organs crushed, I'm sure you'd find your way to awarding me at least three."

His eyes crinkle with amusement. "I haven't seen you around before."

It's an open-ended statement that Cassie doesn't know what to do with. Should she pretend that a Secret Oktober concert is the last place you'd expect to find her; that she's only here by default? Or does she divulge her eighteen-month obsession with him that has affected not only her studies, but her relationship with her family, too?

"'That's because this isn't really my scene," she says, making the decision fairly quickly.

"Oh . . . ?" he replies, raising his eyebrows. "And what is?"

"I'm more of a Duranie," she continues, referencing their arch-rivals.

"You're funny. I like that," he says, as the edges of his mouth turn up. "I'm Ben, by the way."

He lingers awkwardly and Cassie has to stop herself from dissolving into a fit of hysteria. She hopes he doesn't kiss her hand—not only because it's sweaty, but because the charm offensive is somewhat lost now she's seen him do it to every other girl in the room.

As if able to read her mind, Ben leans in and gives her a kiss on the cheek. "Well, it's nice to meet you properly," he says. "When you're not unconscious."

A moment later and he's gone, flashing a smile as he looks back, though Cassie's unsure if it's at her or the legions of impossibly good-looking girls she's surrounded by. She pulls herself up short, hating the ever-present insecurity about how she looks and the belief that she'd never be deserving of his attention.

"You're as beautiful as the next girl," her mum would say whenever her self-esteem needed bolstering. "Even *more* so, because you're as beautiful on the inside as you are out."

But no matter how many times Cassie had heard it, she still couldn't convince herself to believe it, because what biased mother *wouldn't* say that to their child?

Amelia gives her a nudge, as if to alert her to how close Ben had been. But Cassie doesn't need telling; she could feel his arm as it brushed hers, smell the sweat he'd worked up onstage, hear the breath between the words she's already convinced she imagined.

But that's not what Amelia's trying to tell her. "They haven't come up for air in over five minutes," she says bitterly, as Michael's hand disappears up Kimberley's skirt.

"Babe, I've really got to go," squeaks the scantily dressed model as she makes a half-hearted attempt to get up from the sofa. "I've got work super early in the morning."

"But you can't," says Michael, pulling her back to him.

Kimberley giggles and playfully fights him off. "Call me when you get back from Manchester."

As she walks out, she gives Cassie and Amelia a cursory glance up and down as if assessing the threat level she's leaving behind.

"Hey," says Luke, the band's keyboard player, as he sidles up beside Cassie. "You OK?"

In any other universe, she'd be impossibly excited to have one of her idols single her out for attention, but she's holding out for Ben. She knows she's imagining it, but it seems that every time she looks to him, he's throwing a glance her way, as if checking she's still there. She wants to put it to the test by moving, to see if his eyes follow her, but she's scared that the delusional bubble that she's placed herself in—is happy to stay in for the rest of her life—will be unceremoniously popped by the truth.

"Fancy one of these?" says Luke, holding out a tiny white pill.

Cassie masks her shock. "Erm, actually, I was about to get going . . ."

"Well, I don't think you'll be going anywhere soon," he says, looking to the sofa, where Michael is gyrating against the girl lying underneath him.

"Oh my god," gasps Cassie, clamping a hand to her mouth, as a familiar flash of peroxide moves in time to Michael's thrusting hips. "Is that . . . is that *Amelia*?"

Luke looks at Cassie with a confused expression as Michael's hand disappears into Amelia's bra, exposing her breast. "Are you shocked by how quickly he moves on, or the fact that it's your friend underneath him?" he asks.

There's a part of Cassie that doesn't want to be associated with Amelia's sleazy behavior, but she can't deny that if it were *Ben* on top of *her*, she'd no doubt find a way to put her moral high ground aside.

"But he's got a girlfriend . . ." says Cassie, as if that were the only reason Amelia shouldn't be doing it.

Luke laughs. "Welcome to the world of Michael Delaney! This is what he does, but why *she* thinks so little of herself that she goes running every time he clicks his fingers, I don't know."

Cassie swallows the blatant disrespect for her friend, but it leaves a bitter taste and she suddenly feels strangely vulnerable, surrounded by people she'd convinced herself she knew well, yet doesn't really know at all.

"Relax," says Luke, as if reading her mind. "It's all par for the course."

She looks at him, desperately trying not to read too much into the implication.

"If you have one of these, it'll take your mind off it," he urges.

Ben catches her eye from across the room and she's sure he gives her a nod as he pops a tablet in his mouth.

"You'll have the best night of your life," Luke goes on, but she doesn't need any more encouragement; she wants to be in the same sphere as Ben, to experience the night, whatever it may bring, together.

It takes longer than she expected, but once the feeling starts, it wraps itself around her like a quilt. Everything is warm, everything is comfortable; the familiarity of everyone around her belying the fact they've only just met.

She wants to talk to them all, tell them her innermost thoughts, as she draws them near, desperate to feel their skin with her fingertips. Someone brushes past her with a silk shirt and she follows them across the room, fawning at the material, marveling at how it feels like liquid gold to the touch.

Twirling around, looking up at the ceiling, she wants this feeling of unadulterated freedom to last forever. With no one to answer to and no rules to abide by, she imagines that this is what it must feel like to be Nicole. Oh, what she wouldn't give to be her big sister right now. Independent, liberated, in charge of her own destiny . . .

She's still spinning, with a smile on her face, when a hand clamps down on her wrist. "Whoa, you're making me dizzy just looking at you," comes a man's laughing voice.

She stops, transfixed, thinking to herself how much he looks like Ben Edwards. She goes to tell him that, but the need to hug him is even more consuming. "You feel really good," she says, as she draws him into her, nuzzling her face into his neck, smelling him. "Dance with me."

He sways back and forth with her in his arms. "So, are you going to tell me your real name?" he says. "Or am I going to have to call you Curly forever?"

The suggestion that they might know each other for that long sends a frisson of anticipation along Cassie's heightened nerve endings.

"I think you might just have to call me Curly forever," she says, giggling, as Ben is pulled away from her by a faceless body.

"God, that's some good stuff!" says Michael as he goes for a second line of cocaine laid out on the glass tabletop.

Amelia laughs as she adjusts her top and takes the rolled-up twenty-pound note off him when he's finished. Cassie looks on in awe.

"Well, hey there, Charlene," says Michael, as if seeing her for the first time. "When did they let *you* out of Ramsey Street?"

Cassie looks at him perplexed, unable to see any resemblance between her and Kylie Minogue's character in *Neighbors*, but once it's been sitting with her for a few seconds, she puffs her chest out, bolstered by the compliment.

"You gonna join in?" he asks. She hopes he's referring to the drugs, as even in her utopian state she doesn't fancy sharing him with Amelia. Though she wouldn't bet that she couldn't be persuaded.

Amelia passes the note and Cassie hesitates before shaking her head. She doesn't want anything that will take away this feeling of utter delirium. There's no paranoia, no inhibitions, just a sense of wanting to love everyone around her—even Michael. He pats the sofa cushion beside him and Cassie sits down, as Amelia prickles with wary apprehension. Unperturbed, Michael moves closer so that their legs are touching, his breath hot on Cassie's bare shoulder.

"I'm horny as hell," he whispers in her ear, before swiping a finger across the glass tabletop, collecting the remnants of white powder that Amelia left behind. He rubs it on his gums and, without warning, grabs the back of Cassie's head, pulling her to him. His lips are just inches away from hers, his eyes wordlessly inviting her to open her mouth to share what's in his.

"Hey!" a voice calls out.

The single word is said with such conviction that Michael instantly releases his grip and looks up to see who would have the audacity to interrupt. When he sees Ben standing there, his mouth spreads into a satanic grin.

"Ah, sorry, mate," he says. "I've already called first dibs on her."

Ben's jaw twitches, as if he has a thousand words fighting to get out.

"You can have *her* instead, though," Michael says unkindly, offering Amelia as if she's discarded goods.

"Let's go," says Ben, authoritatively staking his claim as he takes Cassie by the hand and pulls her up.

"Where to?" she giggles, loving how loved she feels right in this moment.

"Somewhere we can be alone," he says, half dragging her across the suite and into another room.

With the drugs embedded deep within her nervous system, all the red flags that Cassie would usually rely on to forewarn her are stifled by her inherent need to see the good in everyone.

And as Ben locks the door behind him, she smiles, wondering what could possibly go wrong.

11

Nicole had briefly considered moving back home, the guilt of not being by her mother's side 24/7 laying heavy on her shoulders. But the row with Cassie and their dad last week only served as a reminder that the four of them all being under one roof again might not lend itself to the calm and harmonious environment her mother needs right now.

Nicole had tried to mediate, but Cassie is so deeply entrenched in the fantasy life that following that stupid band has seemingly afforded her that she can't see the wood for the trees. And their dad is so stubbornly stuck in his ways that he refuses to give her the leeway a sixteen-year-old needs to learn from the mistakes she makes. It seemed as if history was repeating itself and if something didn't change soon, Nicole wouldn't be surprised if his overbearing ways didn't drive Cassie away, just as they had done with her. Though the all-consuming threat of something happening to their mother in the meantime may cause a break with convention.

It's at times like this, when Nicole's conflicting emotions threaten to get the better of her, that she turns to the one thing that keeps her sane: music.

These lyrics have been in her head for years, gnawing at her subconscious like a dog with a bone, never quite letting go. But now they hold so much more resonance and she has to give them the space to breathe, if not to comfort herself, then to honor her mum.

She strums her guitar, easing into the four-chord melody. "*If you ever loved someone as much as I love you, you'd know there is nothing I wouldn't do . . .*" Her lilting voice drifts out of the open window of her studio flat.

She takes the pencil from behind her ear. "*I'd go to the ends of the earth if I had to . . .*" she chimes, writing it down as she goes. "*If it meant . . .*" She chews on the end of the pencil. "*If it meant . . .*"

"Nope," she says abruptly, before ripping the page out of her notebook, scrunching it into a ball and throwing it onto the pile of other discarded lyrics in the corner of the room.

There's a knock on the door and, knowing she hasn't buzzed anyone into the communal hallway downstairs, Nicole assumes it's a neighbor from one of the other tiny flats that the landlord had greedily carved out of the imposing Victorian building.

But as she swings the door open, standing on the threshold is Aaron, the man she'd once naively allowed herself to believe she might marry one day.

"Please, just give me a minute," he begs, as she goes to shut him out.

"What are you *doing* here?" exclaims Nicole, exhausted by his attempts to get her attention. "It's almost midnight."

"I need to talk to you," he says, his breath reeking of alcohol.

Nicole lets out a heavy sigh. "I've told you a million times, there's nothing you can say that's going to make any difference."

"But I can't imagine my life with anyone but you," he says.

"Well, you should have thought of that before you screwed Stacey Herriott."

"I've told you how sorry I am—I was drunk and it meant nothing. What more do I have to do?"

Nicole's heart momentarily tugs at the pained expression that stains his normally handsome face. It would be *so* easy to take him back; she misses the love they once shared and is still devastated that the life they'd planned was never going to happen. But she digs deep, remembering her mother's advice to hold on to the bitter disappointment she felt four months ago when he chose to toss their future aside in favor of a quick shag with a girl not known to be choosy.

"You'll never respect him again," Gigi had said. "And if you take him back, you'll not respect yourself either."

Back then, Nicole had refused to consider his pathetic attempts to win her over because she didn't want to let *herself* down. Now she won't fall for it because she refuses to let her mother down, and as she looks into Aaron's pleading eyes, Nicole feels nothing but a reinforced resilience.

"For the last time: I will *never* come back to you," she says. "Now will you *please* leave me alone and get on with your life."

A flash of something crosses his face and his top lip curls. "Is there someone else?" he snarls.

The turn of events takes Nicole by surprise. "*What*? No, of course not!"

"If I find out there is . . ."

Aaron had always been somewhat intense, but she could never accuse him of being jealous, so his twisted features unnerve her.

"You'll what?" she asks.

He fixes her with a steely stare. "If *I* can't have you, nobody can."

Nicole doesn't know whether to laugh or cry. A veiled threat, coming from a man she once adored, seems too preposterous to take seriously, but an irrational fear still creeps into her veins. Slamming the door shut, she catches her breath as she waits to hear movement on the other side.

The phone punctures the uncomfortable silence and Nicole almost doesn't want to answer it, knowing Aaron might still be there. Not because she's got anything to hide, but because she doesn't want him to get the wrong idea from a one-sided conversation, especially if he's going to use it against her.

"Nicole, it's me," says her dad, sounding panicked when she picks up.

Her stomach drops. "Is . . . is everything OK?" she asks, wanting to shut herself off to the answer.

"It's Cassie . . ." There's a pause. "She's not home yet."

Nicole raises her eyes to the ceiling, both in abject relief and pent-up frustration. Did he not realize that she was living on tenterhooks? Waiting, with her heart in her mouth, for the phone call that was going to change the rest of her life?

"Well, where did she go tonight?" she asks.

"She went off to that bloody concert, didn't she?" His voice is laced with hostility. "And if I find out this has got anything to do with those boys . . ."

Nicole considers the possibility but dismisses it out of hand. The closest Cassie would have been able to get was the stage door, and a band with Secret Oktober's following were likely to have got themselves out of there before the first fan even realized they'd left the stage.

"Who did she go with?" she asks, remembering that their mother had originally planned to accompany her. It pained Nicole, and worried her, that Cassie would surely have felt her absence even more profoundly than usual today.

Sometimes, she thinks both she and her dad take Cassie's strength of character too much for granted; they assume that what's going on at home isn't affecting her in the cruelest of ways. Because while she may come across as a sassy teenager who's got it all worked out, Nicole's sure that you'd only have to scratch the surface to see that she's perhaps not coping quite as well as it seems.

"She was going with some girl," says John, his anxiety rising with every passing word. "God knows who she is, or whether she even exists. Because, let's face it, Cassie's not exactly known for being upfront about where she is or what she's doing these days."

"Maybe we should cut her some slack," says Nicole. "Let her go do her thing, whatever that is."

John snorts. "Perhaps, when you're a parent, I'll remind you of the gut-wrenching nausea that comes when your children don't come home when they say they will. Because whether they're two or twenty-two, they're still your child, and that feeling never goes away."

Nicole rolls her eyes, accustomed to the well-used routine, but deep down, she knows that his frustrations are borne out of being a father to children he can no longer protect, and now a husband to an ailing wife he can't make better. And whichever way she looks at this, it doesn't sit right knowing that her little sister could be anywhere in London, feeling vulnerable and heavyhearted.

"She could be *anywhere*," John goes on, echoing her thoughts. "I shouldn't be having to worry about her, as well as everything else that's going on."

"I'm sure she's fine," says Nicole. "Probably just coming down from the high of the concert. How is Mum tonight?"

He sighs heavily. "Surprisingly good. I've been showing her photos of when we met and we've been laughing about the time we drove all the way to Cleveland in our old camper van, only to get to the venue and realize that we'd left my guitar in London."

Nicole can almost hear him smiling at the memory. Or is it because he's unexpectedly been able to have a conversation with his wife?

"Well, I say 'we,' but your mum was quick to remind me tonight that it was most definitely *my* fault." He chortles. "She was really quite determined to make the point; her eyes were shining and she had something about her that I haven't seen in weeks." There's a pause before he goes on to say, "Maybe a miracle awaits after all."

Nicole's chest constricts at his misplaced optimism, knowing enough from what she's read on death to know that a mysterious flash of vitality often occurs in the final days and hours.

"Maybe" is all she says, desperately trying to keep her voice upbeat. "I'll be over tomorrow, but if Cassie's not home in the next half an hour, call me back."

12

"We've found her!" cries a voice. "We've found her!"

A sudden rush of adrenaline and relief floods my entire body, and it takes all my strength to stop myself from falling to the ground. But Brad rushes to me all the same and holds me up, his crumpled face burying itself into my neck.

"Thank god!" he sobs, as his chest heaves up and down. "I thought we'd lost her."

I hold in the bloodcurdling fear that we still might have.

He takes hold of my hand and we race toward the Del, a seafront hotel that holds so much significance for the whole Coronado community; the place where marriages are celebrated and children's baptism parties held. But as I follow the pandemonium down to the beach, I can't help but wonder if it's about to take on a more macabre resonance.

"Where is she?" I scream, my lungs burning. "Hannah!"

"Mommy!" comes the tiniest of voices.

The inner strength that's kept me upright for the past two hours finally deserts me and I collapse onto my knees as she runs into my arms. I breathe her in, nuzzling her hair, never wanting to let her go. She looks the same, she smells the same, but I can't help but wonder if what she's been through will have changed something inside.

"Oh baby!" I cry. "My sweet baby."

"What are all these police officers doing here?" she asks, wide-eyed, their presence seemingly freaking her out more than the fact she's been somewhere I don't know about.

"It's OK, sweetheart," I say. "We thought you were lost, so Mommy and Daddy asked for help."

"Hey, Daddy," she says absently, as if it were just a normal day.

Brad's jaw spasms and every sinew in his body fights against the inherent need to scoop her up, for fear that making too much of a fuss will unsettle her.

"Hey, Bean," he says, his face lighting up as her nickname leaves his lips. If he's had any of the thoughts that I've had these past two hours, he'll no doubt have tortured himself with the possibility that he might never hear himself say it again.

"So, where have you been hiding?" I ask, careful to keep my voice level, even though I'm near to hysteria—with relief, anger, and a desperate need to know everything that's happened to my daughter since I saw her last.

"I've been with my auntie," she says, the innocence of her voice so at odds with the sinister words. "Did you forget that she was picking me up from school today?"

I bang my forehead with the heel of my hand. "I did!" I say, choosing to go with the story through her eyes, hoping it prompts her to disclose more along the way. "How dumb are we?"

She giggles. "Really dumb."

"So, did you have a nice time with"—my sing-song voice falters—"with . . . Auntie?"

She nods. "We went to see the fighter jets and I told her that's where Daddy works."

An involuntary shiver runs down my spine as I wonder whether the more information this woman has on my family, the more dangerous she is. But then I remember that, if it's the same person who appeared on my doorstep today, she already knows enough to put a bomb under our very existence and watch it explode.

"Did you tell her where *I* work?" I probe, gently.

"She already knew," says Hannah. "I told her I was going to be a seal doctor when I grow up."

In any other world, I'd revel in the impact my work has had on her—but not in the dark, dangerous one I'm currently being forced to live in.

I look to Brad, whose furrowed brow is questioning who this woman is and what she wants. I daren't tell him that I might already know.

"Do you fancy some ice cream?" I say, if only to stop the cold claw of terror wrapping itself around my heart.

"I've got a welfare officer on the way," says Hank. "Just to give Hannah the once-over and check she's OK."

I shake my head in an effort to force my stunned brain to understand how a stranger is better placed to know how my daughter is than I am.

"We'll be fine," I say, looking to Brad. "I just want to get things back to normal as quickly as possible. She'll tell us what happened in her own time." Though how I'm supposed to stop myself from asking a thousand questions until then, I don't know.

Hannah's taken hold of my hand and gives it a tug. "Come on," she says, taking advantage of my unusual offer of a sweet treat before dinner. "Let's go get that ice cream."

"We need to get to the bottom of this," Brad says to Hank. "I want to know *exactly* who this woman is and why she took our daughter."

Hank nods gravely. "I'll do my best to find out." Hannah swings between us as we walk away from the crowd, their relief as palpable as our own. But for me, the respite is brief as, among their smiling faces, all I can see are the twisted features of a woman who is intent on getting my attention. She's everywhere I look, throwing her head back as she laughs with thin lips, her eyes burrowing into my soul in desperate pursuit of the truth. And I can't help but shiver as I question just how far she's willing to go.

We eat our ice cream with enforced joviality, pretending it's just like any other day, but as soon as we get home, I'm unable to stop my brain from going into overdrive, desperately needing to know what Hannah knows.

"So, what did you and"—I stumble on the word—"*Auntie*, talk about?" I ask as I bathe her, paying particular attention to anything that looks out of place on her milky-white skin. There's a small bruise on her upper arm that I can't remember seeing last night, but that was back in another lifetime, when I wouldn't have thought to notice.

"I dunno," she says, shrugging as if it isn't important.

"Well, did she explain why you hadn't met her before?" I ask.

Hannah looks thoughtful for a moment. "She said that you all fell out . . ."

I quell the rising panic that's souring my mouth. "Did she say *why*?"

"I dunno, something to do with her boyfriend," she says, scooping the bath foam into her hands and blowing the bubbles into the air. She laughs when some land on the tip of my nose. Normally I would too.

"It was probably Daddy being overprotective of her," I say, inventing a sibling that has never existed. "They've always had a love-hate relationship."

"Well, maybe you should all try harder from now on," says Hannah, showing a degree of maturity I hadn't allowed for. "Because she seems really nice."

My jaw tenses and my throat tightens at the prospect of my daughter actually *liking* this stranger who has turned our world upside down. Yet I force myself to be grateful that the woman didn't do anything to make Hannah *dislike* her. It's by far the lesser of the two evils.

"What did she do that was so nice?" I ask, hoping my line of questioning will encourage her to open up without realizing she's being interrogated.

Hannah looks at me, sizing up whether she should say what she's about to say. "I'm going to the air show with her," she finally confesses. I suck in a breath, not just because she knows I can't take her this year, but because of the insinuation that this woman is intending to stick around.

"I told her you were going to be out of town and she promised to take me instead," she goes on, looking worried she might have upset me, even though I'm doing my utmost to force a smile.

"We'll have to see," I say, already mentally canceling my trip to the sea turtle convention in Michigan. I'm not taking any chances.

"Please, Mommy," she begs. "We had a really good time."

"You seem to be quite taken with her," I say, gritting my teeth.

Hannah smiles. "I think she's pretty."

"That doesn't make her a nice person," I snap, before I have a chance to stop myself. She looks surprised, not used to my uncharacteristic outburst. "Sorry, baby . . . I'm just tired. Tell me what makes her pretty." I wait for her to describe the woman who came to my door.

"Well, I like her hair," she says. "I want to grow mine long like hers."

I balk. Zoe didn't have long hair—but it's an easy mistake to make, I figure. "It's a nice color too, huh?"

Hannah nods thoughtfully. "Can people change their hair color?"

I nod. "To any color they want."

"Well, one day, when I'm a grown-up, I'm going to make mine brown like hers."

A shiver runs through me as I dare to imagine that we're talking about two different people. But that's impossible. Hannah must have gotten herself confused.

"Is she OK?" asks Brad, once I eventually stop watching her sleep and come downstairs.

"She thinks it's all one big adventure," I say tearfully.

He opens his arms and I gratefully fall into them. "We'll find out who did this," he says, with steadfast resolve.

"I just don't understand . . ." I cry.

He pulls me in even tighter and kisses the top of my head. "Don't beat yourself up—you're not to blame."

An incensed ball of anger fills my chest as I push away from him, nostrils flaring. "I never thought I was," I snap.

"I didn't mean . . ." he starts.

"Well then, what *did* you mean?"

He walks over to the drinks cabinet and unscrews the cap from the bottle of bourbon we'd been saving for a special occasion. Now, it looks like we're about to drink it to numb ourselves. The irony isn't lost on me.

He pours a double measure and knocks it back in one hit, as if to prove my point.

"I'm just saying that it's likely to be someone who's been riled by something you've done."

I fix him with a steely glare, daring him to go on. "Rather than anything *you've* done," I say, throwing it back at him when he doesn't.

He makes a strange gargling sound in the back of his throat, as if the suggestion is so absurd that it's laughable.

"So, you *do* think this is my fault?" I bark.

"That's not what I said." He puts his hands on his hips, looking exasperated. "There are a lot of fucked-up people out there who take great umbrage at the smallest of inconveniences. You're campaigning for one of the community's favorite beaches to be closed to the public for eight months of the year. Others don't think like we do. They believe they have more rights than those of an animal."

"They're *not* going to take my daughter to prove the point."

"Who knows what they might be capable of if they think they've suffered an injustice."

I blanch. No one knows that strength of feeling better than I do. But while I've spent years pushing that wasted emotion down deep into my subconscious, forcing it to a place where it is only a simmering ember, it seems that someone is desperate to reignite it again. And as much as I would rather it just be a disgruntled local resident, I only have to picture the woman's face at my front door to know it's so much more dangerous than that.

"I wouldn't be so quick to rule yourself out of this," I hiss, my tone accusatory to offload my own guilty conscience.

He looks at me as if I'm crazy. Right now I feel I might be, as my brain descends into a dangerous fight-or-flight mode, battling against what it knows to be true and the lies I have to tell myself in order to keep my past from catching up with me.

"Maybe you pushed someone too hard during Hell Week," I say, referring to the notoriously grueling SEAL training program. "Maybe they didn't make it through and now hold you accountable."

Brad shakes his head. "So, while *I'm* looking to condemn someone else for their unreasonable reaction to the good you're doing, *your* first port of call is to accuse me of not doing my job properly."

"They could be preparing to take a swipe at you," I say unkindly, in a misguided attempt to exonerate my selfish panic.

"I'm not even going to validate that with a response," says Brad, his brow furrowing as he snatches up his car keys and goes to walk out.

"So, that's how you want to deal with this, is it?" I yell after him. "Bury your head in the sand and pretend it's not happening."

The front door slams and I already hate myself for releasing my bitter vitriol on the one person who least deserves it. But that's what the weight of carrying this secret around makes me do sometimes.

"Mommy?"

My heart aches to see Hannah standing at the bottom of the stairs, bleary-eyed and holding the cuddly seal she calls Felix under her chin.

"It's OK, sweetheart," I say, going to her. "Everything's OK."

"Where's Daddy gone?"

I swallow the self-contempt I feel in this moment, hating myself for making my daughter feel even more insecure than she does already. "He had to go run a few errands."

Hannah looks out at the bright crescent moon whitewashing the front yard. "Why are you and Daddy fighting?" she asks, her voice so tiny.

"It's OK," I say again, whisking her up and holding her close to me, desperately needing to feel her heartbeat against my chest.

"But I heard you shouting," she says sleepily into my ear as I carry her back up the stairs. "And I told the lady you *never* fight."

I freeze two steps from the top, my blood turning ice-cold, but force myself not to jump to conclusions. I need her to tell me everything she's ready to tell me, but I don't know how to do that without my own fears bleeding out, feeding her own.

"Will I get in trouble for lying to her?" she asks, snapping me out of my stupor.

"Of course not," I exclaim. "You've done absolutely nothing wrong."

I lay her down in her bed and tuck the duvet up tight under her chin, as if it will create a shield that nothing, or no one, can infiltrate. "Did she ask any other questions about me and Daddy?"

Hannah shakes her head and I allow myself to believe that this woman isn't intent on tugging on the thread that will unravel my entire life.

"How come she didn't bring you back home?" I ask.

A sadness clouds her freckled features. "She said she was going to, but then she went to ask the other lady something . . ."

"What other lady?"

I wait two beats, suspended between the need to know and the need to let her tell me in her own time. When she turns onto her side and snuggles into Felix, I fear the latter is never going to come.

"Were there *two* ladies with you today?" I press.

Hannah closes her eyes as she shrugs her shoulders, too tired to respond.

I stifle a sob as I gently run my fingers through her copper-red hair, remembering Brad's shock when I gave birth. "Where in god's name did *that* come from?" he'd laughed.

If he'd thought to look at the regularly discarded boxes of hair dye hidden at the bottom of the garbage can, he'd be in no doubt.

When I think of all the lies I've told and the secrets I've hidden, I'd be a fool to think I could get away with it forever. If I'm honest with myself, it has always felt like the truth was close on my heels, snapping away like an alligator whose prey is just out of reach. But until now, I've always managed to stay one step ahead, distancing myself from the person I was back then, in the hope that it would eventually create a gulf so great that even my darkest memories couldn't traverse its narrowest point.

But in the dead of night, while Brad and Hannah are sleeping, those flashbacks come thick and fast, blighting the happiness I've worked so hard to find, convincing me that the only chance I have of defying the thieves of joy is to tell Brad who I really am. Yet by the first morning light this absurd thought has diminished along with the darkness, the reality of what the truth would do to him—to our marriage, our *life*—too much to bear.

Yet now it feels as if someone is gearing up to tell him *their* version—and that may well be so much worse than my own.

13

"Don't move!" yells a voice, shattering the fantasy that Cassie was living out.

Ben's hand freezes on her leg, the promise of what he was about to do immediately forgotten.

"What the . . . ?" they both say simultaneously, as a barrage of helmeted policemen rush into the hotel room.

"Stay right where you are," hollers one. "Don't move a finger."

Despite the instruction, Cassie finds herself lifting her arms in the air in shocked surrender.

"What have you got on your person?" barks the seemingly impatient leader of the pack, as his hands run roughly over Cassie's body.

"I-I don't have anything," she says, confused by the question and the invasion of her personal space.

"Hey!" Ben shouts. "Lay off her!"

Cassie smiles, not only because she's touched by his protectiveness, but also because for a split second she imagines that they're all part of a stripper troupe who are playing a prank on them. She remembers Nicole having a stripogram for her twenty-first birthday last year and Cassie had been as intrigued by his sleazy routine as Nicole had been mortified.

"Well, come on then!" she says now, standing up from the sofa. "If you're going to arrest me, can we make it quick?"

"What have you taken?" asks the policeman.

"Why, do you want some?" laughs Cassie.

"You'd better shut up," Ben tells her.

"Cuff 'em," barks the policeman as his colleagues rush toward the pair of them.

There's still a part of Cassie that's waiting for them to start taking their clothes off, but the force with which they snap the handcuffs onto her wrists makes her wonder through the haze of drugs if she's read this wrong.

"*Ow*," she wails, as two bobbies get on either side of her and manhandle her into the room where she'd left a party in full swing just ten minutes before.

The remnants of the good time everybody had been having are still very much evident. Empty beer cans are strewn across the floor, burning cigarettes are lying abandoned in ashtrays, and white powder residue sits on the glass top of the coffee table.

Cassie frantically looks around for Amelia, but all she can see are strangers' expressions mirroring her own as they struggle to comprehend what's going on. It's then that she realizes that this is serious, and the dreamy effects of the hallucinogenic wear off fast.

"Keep moving!" yells a policeman, shoving her from behind.

"What the hell do you think you're playing at?" Ben yells. She doesn't dare turn around for fear that he might be talking to *her*. How can this be happening? He'd been about to make all her dreams come true; he was just seconds away from kissing her, she was sure of it. Yet now they're being carted off by the police and he thinks it's her fault.

Tears burn at the back of her throat as she rues the loss of a once-in-a-lifetime opportunity. But as soon as she sees the open doors of a police van parked alongside the back entrance of the hotel, she starts crying for an entirely different reason.

"I can't," she says, as the fear of god strikes within her.

"Move!" barks one of the officers flanking her sides. She tries to dig her heels in to create resistance, but it's futile.

"If my dad finds out, he'll kill me," she sobs, her senses suddenly alert to the bigger picture.

The hold on her weakens a little. "How old are you?" asks the officer, his tone softer.

"I-I'm sixteen," she whispers. Hearing herself say it brings home the enormity of the situation. If her father finds out about this, she'll never be allowed out again, let alone to see Secret Oktober. "Wh-what are you going to do to me? Where are you taking me?"

"You need to come down to the police station," he says as he hoists her up into the back of the van, a little more gently now. "You've got some questions to answer, and then we'll no doubt have to give your parents a call."

"Can you at least tell me what I'm supposed to have done?" she calls out, but her voice is drowned out by the commotion of Ben being thrown in after her.

"You've had it in for us from the start," he shouts, banging on the van's metal sides. "Are you so bad at your job that you need to make an example out of us?"

He falls back onto the seated ledge. "Fuck!" he shouts, manically running a hand back and forth through his hair.

"What are we going to do?" cries Cassie. "I can't go to prison."

He looks at her as if seeing her for the first time. "Listen to me," he says, leaning forward. "You tell them nothing. You saw nothing, heard nothing, and took nothing."

"But I did . . ." says Cassie. "I took a—"

Ben puts a finger to his lips. "We stick to the story. You and I were in the bedroom, doing what young people do. We had no idea what was going on in the other room. We hadn't taken anything. We didn't even know there *were* any drugs at the party, let alone who might have brought them in."

Cassie nods her head vigorously.

"We need to nip this in the bud," he says. "I can't have the papers knowing about this."

"And I can't have my dad knowing about it," says Cassie, genuinely believing that he is the bigger problem.

"And he won't, *if* we stick together . . ."

Cassie allows herself a small smile, knowing she's prepared to do *anything* if it means they get to stick together. "It's ironic really, given the situation we're in, but my dad's wrong about you."

Ben's jaw spasms.

"He says you're just some fly-by-night pop star who's been blinded by fame and money, but I knew there was more to you than that. You really care about me, don't you?"

"Sure," he says hesitantly.

Cassie's heart feels as if it might burst. Maybe this was meant to happen. Maybe if they'd stayed in that bedroom by themselves, one thing would have led to another, and she would have become just another notch on his heavily engraved bedpost. But this has brought them together, bonded them in a way no other girl could even begin to get close to. He *needs* her, and she's not going to let him down.

14

As much as I tried, no amount of gentle persuasion or subliminal co-ercion could coax any more meaningful information from Hannah than she'd already given about the woman she called "Auntie." In fact, as excited as she seemingly was to spend more time with her, their lost afternoon together was all but forgotten by the following day, much to my chagrin.

But *I* haven't forgotten. Every second of every day is consumed with the same gut-wrenching fear and panic that coursed through my veins when I realized she was missing. In fact, sometimes the feeling is so overwhelming, I manage to convince myself she still hasn't come home. So, to prove to myself that she has, I've spent the past week sleeping on the floor beside her bed, watching her chest rise and fall, wishing I could carry her around in my pocket to keep her safe from harm.

Brad keeps telling me that my time would be better spent trying to narrow down the list of vengeful opposers to my beach-closure pe-tition, reminding me that in the past year we've had dog excrement left in the mailbox and a handwritten note delivered to the city council claiming that I'm misappropriating the funds of a grant I've not yet been given. But they're not the people we're looking for, because my work isn't the reason Hannah was taken.

I've wanted to tell him that, countless times, but it would mean being honest, and in all the varying hues that comes in, I'm *still* not sure I'm ready to progress to the next shade, even after what happened to Hannah.

I want to figure this out for myself, before I burden him with a past he doesn't know I had. I need to find out who this person is and what their end goal is. If it's to disrupt the life they don't feel I deserve, I can deal with that. But if it's to hold me accountable for something they think I've done, then that's another matter altogether.

"Mommy, Mommy, look!" cries Hannah excitedly, pulling me in the direction of the carousel ride. "Can I go on it?"

"Why don't we go and see the fighter jets?" I offer, desperately needing to keep her in my line of vision at all times. "We might find Daddy."

"He'll be busy," she says, knowing the drill on "air show day." "I want to go on the carousel. Please!"

"OK!" I relent. "But I'll come with you."

"I went on my own last year," she says, far too astute for her own good. "And I was only seven, so I can definitely go on my own now that I'm eight."

I want to tell her that that's not how it works when you've been kidnapped in between times, but I'm desperate to avoid offloading my own insecurities onto her. And besides, I reason with myself, what can possibly happen on a fairground ride?

"So, which one do you want to sit on?" I ask, assaulted by the kaleidoscope of color as we climb the steep steps. She runs around aimlessly, undecided between the horse and the carriage, before changing her mind at the last minute. I'm tempted to sit unnoticed on the mermaid behind her, but I know that she'll be looking out for me each time she comes round, expecting a wave and a big encouraging smile.

"OK, hold on tight," I say. "And if it finishes at a different place, wait for me to come round to you before you get off."

She smiles and shoos me away, the eight-year-old in her so desperately wanting to be independent without realizing what it truly means.

The organ music starts up and a shiver runs down my spine as I'm transported back to childhood Saturday nights when the theme tune of *Tales of the Unexpected* would send me scurrying behind the sofa. Mum would laugh and try to coax me out, but I would only emerge once the TV show had started, as it wasn't nearly as terrifying as the creepy music suggested.

One full turn and Hannah's waving enthusiastically. I wave back, pathetically relieved and grateful that she's still there. I don't think I'll ever take anything for granted again.

"Oh, hey, Nicole!" comes a voice from behind me.

I recognize the enforced joviality and force myself to turn around for fear of being rude. Eva may be the most interfering busybody on the island, but she has also ingratiated herself onto the mayor's voluntary team, so I have to go out of my way to humor her, as much as it pains me.

"Eva." It's an acknowledgment more than a greeting.

"I've been meaning to call you all week," she says, pulling me into her and suffocating me in a cloud of floral perfume. "Ever since I heard about young Hannah. What an absolute nightmare for all of you. How is she? Are you doing OK? Well, that's a ridiculous question, of course—how can you possibly be doing OK . . . ?"

The one saving grace with Eva is that minimal effort is required; she can have a conversation all by herself.

I wave as Hannah does another circuit.

"You poor thing," Eva goes on, without taking a breath. "I've not been able to stop thinking about you." Though not enough to warrant a phone call in the past few days, it seems.

"We're actually doing—" I start, before being cut off.

"Funnily enough, I thought I saw you and Brad in town a few days ago," she says. "Well, at least I assumed it was you because it was definitely Brad. But as I got closer, I realized it wasn't you at all." She pulls her mouth tight and widens her eyes as if needing to convey how awkward it was.

Hannah goes around again, but I no longer have the where-withal to raise my hand.

"What day was that?" I can't stop myself from asking.

Eva makes a show of trying to recall, but I can't imagine another's misfortune isn't ingrained on her memory. "Wednesday, maybe?" she says, far too quickly. "Yes, it must have been Wednesday because I had my hair done and went to Brewster's to meet friends after they finished work."

I bite down on my lip, remembering the night in question and how out of character it had been for Brad not to come home. But I reasoned it had been an intense few days and we were still silently blaming one another, even though I'd bet my life on him not having a single enemy in the world. Not even a pissed SEAL candidate.

When he'd appeared the next morning, having admitted to being drunk and falling asleep at his buddy Kelsey's house, it didn't occur to me to think he might have been lying. That's not the kind of relationship we have. At least, I didn't think so.

"Ah, that must have been his sister," I lie, aware of the bitter irony. "She was in town last week."

Eva eyes me with suspicion and I find myself wondering if she knows something I don't.

"Of course," she says, trying to sound convinced. "That would explain their closeness."

My lips pull thin, and I have an overwhelming desire to slap the meddling old cow in the face, but I restrain myself, if only for the sake of Hannah, who will be coming around again any second now.

I look up, my eyes furtively scanning the rise and fall of every horse that circumnavigates the 360-degree revolution. They all look the same, their colors bamboozling me, and I'm no longer able to distinguish between them. Yet I know that my red-headed daughter would be easy to spot if she were on one.

"Hannah!" I croak, taking four or five steps forward, as if it will help me see better. "Hannah!"

I spin around, my eyes no longer able to focus on my surroundings as panic descends and my legs threaten to give way.

"Nicole?" questions Eva. "Is everything OK?"

"She's not . . . she's not there!" I choke, the air to my lungs seemingly cut off at the pass. "She's gone!"

The carousel continues to spin, churning out its macabre music, and I'm struggling to breathe.

"Hannah!" I scream.

Concerned faces turn at my pitiful shriek; strangers give me a wide berth, while those I recognize rush to me with a look of "Dear god, not again" etched into their furrowed brows.

"Stop the ride!" I yell, my adrenaline-laced legs unable to decide which way to go first.

The galloping horses slow to a trot, and I jump up onto the first board, desperately trying to correct my balance as I crawl up the steps.

"Hannah!" I call out, weaving my way through the startled faces of young children suspended on mythical creatures.

"Mommy?" comes a voice.

It sounds like Hannah, but my brain is so convinced that she's gone that I dismiss it and allow the thousands of other noises in my head to run amok, goading me with a cacophony so loud that I put my hands over my ears to drown it out.

I see someone who looks a lot like Brad walking toward me on the platform and my blurred vision allows me to believe that he has our daughter's hand in his. I pull myself together, forcing myself to breathe, as I hold on to one of the candy-cane poles for support.

"Nicole!" he shouts, his voice sounding far away, even though he's getting ever closer.

I look down at his side and my little girl's silhouette slowly begins to come into focus. My chest convulses, letting out the fear that had been trapped inside.

"Hannah," I gasp. "Where were you?"

"Just here, Mommy," she says, looking between me and Brad, wondering what she's done wrong.

"But . . . but you weren't on the horse," I say, feeling like I'm losing my mind.

"I went in the mermaid," she says, pointing to the sickly pink tail fin that hides a seat within.

"But I told you . . ."

"Nic," says Brad sharply, taking hold of my flailing arm. "She's fine."

"She was supposed to stay where she was," I cry, my utter relief rushing out of me.

"But I wanted to sit with Auntie," says Hannah.

A knife plunges into my chest, twisting itself until I can't breathe. My head swivels, my eyes scanning the crowd below, who look on awkwardly, their desire to know what's going on at odds with the embarrassment they no doubt feel for me. I search for the features I vaguely recall from the woman at my door—the slim frame, the dirty-blond bob, the slight air of superiority about her—but my eyes still won't let me see straight. Whoever she is and wherever she is, I will *not* let her hold my family for ransom in this way. I would rather tell the truth than have her blackmailing me into living a lie.

"Listen, sweetie," I say, kneeling down to meet Hannah's eyes. "I know we may call her Auntie, but she's not really. She's a pretend auntie who isn't a part of our family, because Daddy doesn't actually have a sister."

Hannah screws up her face. "But she's not *Daddy's* sister," she says. "She's *yours.*"

15

"What if I'm not how he remembers me?" says Cassie, lowering the front of her crinkle swimsuit that she's paired with a neon-green puffball skirt and white stilettos.

"I'm not sure *anybody's* going to remember *anything* from the other night," says Amelia laughing.

"Apart from my dad," mutters Cassie acerbically.

"He'll get over it," says Amelia, proving that she doesn't know John very well. "I assume he doesn't know that you're here?"

Cassie looks at her incredulously.

"He would lose his absolute shit," she says. "I'm grounded and he's refusing to talk to me, so right now there's a me-shaped mound of pillows in my bed."

"Oh my god," squeals Amelia. "What if he takes a closer look and realizes that you're not there?" ·

The thought *had* occurred to Cassie, and for a split second it wasn't a risk she was prepared to take. But Ben was expecting her—

why else would he have given her an embossed invitation the other night? And she wasn't about to let him down.

"I'm sixteen!" she says. "He has to realize that he can't control my life anymore. I'm an adult now." Though as she walks into the vast entrance hall of the Natural History Museum, with the life-size skeleton of a diplodocus bearing down on her, she suddenly feels out of her depth. This isn't like the party at the hotel, with all its debauchery and excess; this is an event for real grown-ups, who, Cassie notes, are all power-dressed to the max. Men in pastel-colored linen suits, with shirts open two buttons too low, stare appreciatively at her and Amelia, and women who are too old to be dressed in lamé totter past on impossibly high heels.

"Bloody hell," mutters Amelia under her breath as they accept the offer of champagne from a passing waiter. "It's like *Dynasty* on speed in here."

Cassie almost chokes, sending bubbles fizzing up her nose. "Well, as long as we're not Krystle and Alexis . . ."

"If you stick to the agreement we'll get along just fine," says Amelia, more seriously than Cassie would like. "*You* stay away from Michael, and *I'll* stay away from Ben. Speaking of whom . . ."

"Oh god," says Cassie, unable to look, as pinpricks of anticipation make her fingers tingle. After five days of every eventuality going round her head, she still hasn't worked out how this is going to go down. What if he doesn't recognize her? What if he doesn't seem pleased to see her? *What if* . . . No, she can't bring herself to go there. "Where is he? Where is he?"

"Over there," says Amelia.

When she's brave enough to follow Amelia's gaze, Cassie can't help but be disappointed to see she's talking about Michael. His newly dyed peroxide-blond hair flops into his eyes as he leans in to listen to a man who looks like a headmaster lecturing one of his pupils.

"So, where's Ben?" asks Cassie, her excitement immediately

turning to abject desolation as she scans the expansive lobby. She can't contemplate the possibility that he's decided to swerve it and go somewhere else instead. She'd feel so stupid. She's risked so much, and it would all have been for nothing.

"Come on!" says Amelia, grabbing a couple more glasses of champagne as another tray goes by.

She pulls her shoulders back and sticks her chest out as she makes her way through the crowded space, smiling sweetly at the leering men in suits. The *same* men, Cassie imagines, that Ben had accused of stifling his career. "We haven't got as much freedom as you'd think," he'd told her at the hotel the other night, when she'd asked why the band hadn't performed her favorite song: the B-side of their fourth single. "They insist we go with the masses; follow the money," he'd said despondently. And as Cassie looks at their smug faces, she doesn't doubt that their greed represses his creativity.

"Hi, Micky," purrs Amelia, as she sidles up beside him.

The man he's with throws him a cautionary glance as he walks away, one that simultaneously says, *Be careful, but by god, if I had the chance, I would.*

"Well, hello there," says Michael, looking Amelia up and down, his dilated pupils coming to rest on her breasts. "I recognize those."

She giggles coquettishly and slaps him, reminding Cassie of a Barbara Windsor character from a *Carry On* film.

"What are you doing later?" she asks brazenly. "Fancy getting out of here and having some proper fun?"

He pulls a face as if weighing up his options, while Amelia waits expectantly. "We could go back to your hotel," she prompts, to fill the awkward silence.

Cassie clears her throat, embarrassed for her, but out of the corner of her eye she can sense a tangible excitement in the room, an uptick of energy that she knows only Ben could create.

She forces a deep breath in and out, wanting to look but unable to. Instead, she fixates on Michael, whose expression clouds over with utter contempt. His mouth pulls into a tight line, and he puts a hand on Amelia's behind and gives it a squeeze.

"Why wait till later?" he says, giving her a push. "Let's get the fun started now."

Left alone, Cassie alternates between watching them disappear behind a display case and staring at Ben as he holds court among a bunch of aging executives and what looks to be a gaggle of their wide-eyed daughters.

Wearing a red blazer over a black vest and a smile that could power the whole of South Kensington, Cassie's heart feels as if it's about to take flight—along with a hundred others, no doubt. But she'll wait her turn—play it cool while he works the room, getting to her when he's sweet-talked the suits and charmed every other girl along the way.

"A vol-au-vent?" asks a waiter, shoving a tray under her nose.

Too polite to refuse, Cassie takes a pastry cup and instantly regrets it, not knowing how she's supposed to negotiate a glass and an hors d'oeuvre while maintaining any degree of decorum.

Her face must say it all, as when she looks up, Ben is staring straight at her, smiling, as if he can read her innermost thoughts. Her cheeks flush with a red heat that grows hotter the more she tries to stop it.

"Oh, hi," comes a voice from behind her. "Weren't you at the party the other night?"

As much as Cassie is thrilled to be recognized—a sure sign that she's been initiated into the inner circle—she is equally horrified when she turns around to find Kimberley Banks standing there, holding a cigarette up to her painted pink lips.

"Oh," is all she can think to say, her brain feeling like a ten-ton truck has slammed into it.

"Have you seen Micky about?" asks Kimberley, looking around.

"Er, no," says Cassie, sticking to single words for fear that she'll inadvertently divulge that he's currently screwing Amelia behind the eight-foot-yeti exhibit.

"OK, cool," says Kimberley, turning toward the bar. "I guess I'll have to amuse myself until he is, then."

Cassie holds her breath as she watches Kimberley veer danger-ously close to the glass cabinet, before she's thankfully thwarted by Luke. Whether he does it because he knows what's at stake, Cassie's not sure, though she imagines the band are more than used to cov-ering for Michael's indiscretions.

By the time Cassie's turned her attention back to Ben, he's whis-pering to a girl with a blond poodle perm and too much electric-blue eyeliner. She knows he has to talk to people—it's a networking event, after all—but seeing the two of them being unnecessarily intimate makes Cassie's chest tighten.

She needs another drink and takes the opportunity to head to the makeshift bar closest to where Ben's standing, hoping she can catch his eye. If he gives her a sign, she'll happily go to his aid—he looks like he could do with rescuing. But just as he looks up, a glass smashes, shattering the atmosphere—and her illusion.

"What the fuck?" someone screeches.

There's a commotion across the hall, and as Cassie joins every-one else in looking to see where it's coming from, her heart sinks.

"You fucking bitch."

Cassie instinctively moves toward the fracas, needing to see what's going on while simultaneously hoping that she won't get dragged into the mêlée. A wail like a banshee rings out around the cavernous lobby, echoing off the brick ceiling that curves high above them.

Fists fly as Kimberley and Amelia fight for their man, while he stands by, watching them with an amused expression, his inflated ego enjoying the sideshow.

"Babe, it's not what you think," he offers half-heartedly.

Kimberley laughs sardonically as a security guard pulls her off a bedraggled-looking Amelia.

"You've just lost the best thing you'll ever have," she yells at Michael, her face contorted with rage and humiliation.

"Baby, *please* . . ." he begs, as if it's suddenly just dawned on him that she's serious.

"You're welcome to him," she spits at Amelia, who's struggling to right herself. "Good luck—you're gonna need it."

She slings her white handbag onto her shoulder with as much dignity as she can muster and storms toward the doors.

Cassie can't help but put herself in Kimberley's position, imagining what it would feel like if she were to discover Ben in such a compromising situation. She knows there's temptation around every corner, but she'd hope that he wouldn't sacrifice something so special for a sticky moment like Michael's just done.

"OK . . . testing . . . testing . . ." comes a booming voice through the speakers, a little sooner than Cassie would imagine was planned. "Ladies and gentlemen, if I could have your attention . . ."

The address pulls the eyes of rubberneckers away from the fray at the back of the hall to the stage, where a man is tapping the microphone head. "OK, I hope everyone can hear me. My name's Paul Jacobs and I'm the managing director of Tramline Records." He holds his hands up in faux modesty as a smattering of applause ripples around the room. "It's my honor to have Secret Oktober sign to our label and deliver an album that I believe is going to define their career. It has all the sounds you'd expect, but with an edge; it's new, it's exciting, and I just know that the world won't be able to get enough of it. But don't take my word for it, decide for yourselves . . . Ladies and gentleman, I give you Ben, Michael, and Luke—*Secret Oktober*!"

The boys make their way to the stage, Michael unsurprisingly the last as he straightens his shirt and checks his fly.

"Jesus Christ," wheezes Amelia, patting her hair down.

"You OK?" asks Cassie, as Luke fires up the opening chords of the new album's title track. She can't help but notice the look of disdain that Ben throws Michael as he heads to his place behind the drums.

"You could have given me a heads-up," says Amelia, before dissolving into a fit of giggles.

"That's not funny," whispers Cassie. She likes Amelia but she doesn't want to be associated with her sordid behavior. What she and Ben have got is poles apart from the shallow relationship that Amelia and Michael share.

Ben catches her eye and smiles, as if he's heard her thoughts, and as the bass guitar kicks in she wonders if he might sing this song to her. She flushes when he winks in her direction and happily imagines a hundred pairs of eyes burning like lasers into the back of her head, wishing they were her.

Girls sigh and swoon at the line, "*I want to lay down beside you, and do what we do so well.*" But he's only looking at one person and her insides have turned to jelly.

"That was incredible," breathes Cassie heavily into his ear as he comes offstage. She's praying they don't have to endure much more of this tireless sucking-up exercise before they can get out of here. *Where will we go?* she wonders, as desperate to be on her own with him as he clearly is to be with her.

"I'm glad you liked it," he says, brushing her hand with his, careful not to linger too long for fear that someone will see.

Now that she's in this position, Cassie can begin to understand why any relationships the boys have need to be kept under wraps. It would break the hearts of a million teenagers if they thought Ben had someone special in his life, though how she's expected to keep the secret to herself, she has *no* idea.

"I'll be waiting for you when you're ready to leave," she says as he goes to walk away.

He stops short and turns back to her. "What?"

"You know . . . I'm ready, whenever you want to go," says Cassie, hoping that he catches on this time. There are a lot of people jostling to get to him and she doesn't want to make any of the other girls feel bad.

He gives her a secret look—one that says *Be patient*—and her insides soar with a power so all-consuming that she feels as if she could grow wings.

16

"OK, this is the last song of the night," says Nicole, as she stares past the spotlights into the thinning crowd at Dallinger's. Being last on the bill means she's often playing to an empty room, the couples having long since retired to bed and the bigger groups having moved on to somewhere livelier. She doesn't mind, though—she'd only be singing to herself in her bedroom otherwise, and at least this place gives her a hot meal at the end of her set, which is more than she gets when she's at home.

"This is a song that's been in my head for a long time, but I've only recently got it down on paper. It's about the woman I love most in the world—and it means even more to me now than I could have ever thought possible." Her voice cracks on the last word, and she struggles to compose herself. "This is called 'I Would Die for You.'"

As soon as she starts singing, the emotion that had almost caught her out is swept up into the melody as she loses herself in it.

"There are things I could never teach you, no matter how hard I try
Because only you can decide how high you fly . . .
I can set you on your way and catch you if you fall
But only you will know . . ."

It's somehow a lot easier to sing your sorrow than speak it. And when Nicole strums the final chords on her guitar, a lone round of applause ripples through the darkness.

"Thanks," she says, smiling, always grateful for any appreciation shown, especially for a song that means so much.

"That was quite something," comes a voice out of the shadows.

Nicole holds a hand up to shield her eyes from the bright stage lights, but it doesn't help her much. "Thanks," she says, making her way down the steps to the floor. She gets ready with her excuse for what she fears is coming.

"Would you care to join me for a drink at the bar?" the man asks.

"I'm sorry," she says, without even looking in his direction. "I've been on my feet all day."

"We can sit," he says.

If she wasn't so tired, she'd smile. She hadn't heard that one before.

"I have to be up early," she says, hoping he doesn't have another suitable retort.

"*I* have to be on a 5 a.m. flight to Munich," he says, the amusement as prevalent in his voice as the sarcasm. "Where do *you* have to be?"

"Look, I don't mean to be rude—" she starts, stopping dead when she turns to face him.

His grimace seems to preempt her reaction, as if he's apologizing for the assumptions she's about to make. He has no idea.

"*You?*" she cries, her eyes widening in disbelief.

"OK, can we skip the part where you think you might know me, and throw any preconceived ideas you may have in the bin?"

Nicole goes to tell him that she *does* know him, that she's greeted by his face every time she goes into Cassie's bedroom, but that's more than she'd care to admit.

"That was a really beautiful song," he says.

She shrugs her shoulders, as if what he thinks means nothing to her, but she can't help but feel flattered. He may well be the latest teen-idol offering on the hit factory conveyor belt, but he's still the lead singer of the biggest band in the country right now.

"I guess it's about your mum?"

His recognition of the woman behind the melody takes Nicole by surprise and makes her feel suddenly vulnerable. But then, sharing your innermost thoughts with a roomful of strangers has a habit of doing that.

"Like you listened to the words . . ." she says, her need to let him off the hook before he embarrasses both himself, and her, ever present—at least when it comes to her songwriting.

"*If you ever loved someone as much as I love you, you'd know there is nothing I wouldn't do . . .*" His a capella voice flows like liquid gold, rendering Nicole speechless and inexplicably close to tears.

"Is that you talking to your mum or her talking to you?" he asks.

"I-I . . ." she stutters, struggling to regain her composure. "I'd always imagined it was a conversation between us . . ."

"I bet she sings her lines even louder than you sing yours," he says, his eyes seemingly burrowing deep into her soul.

"Well, thanks for the feedback," she says, reaching behind the bar to grab her bag, if only to distract herself from the pull at the back of her throat.

"Have you ever thought about recording it?" he asks solemnly.

She laughs, like *really* laughs, while he stands there with a questioning expression, waiting for her to finish. "Look," she says eventually, "while you may think that every musician has access to a recording studio, I'm afraid most of us will never get to see the inside of one."

"I might be able to help you with that," he says, sounding surprisingly sincere.

"Does this chat-up line usually work?" asks Nicole, with wry amusement.

"When the offer of a drink is refused, then yes," he says, his eyes smiling.

"And when the promise to make me a star *still* falls short?" says Nicole, raising her eyebrows playfully.

"Well, then I'd have to cut my losses and ask that if it doesn't work out for you over the next twenty years, that you meet me in Los Angeles in 2006."

Nicole laughs out loud. "Why Los Angeles?" she asks.

"Because that's where I intend to hang up my boots," he says, looking at her as if he means it.

"Well, until then," she says, turning to walk out.

"Wait!" he says, putting out a hand to grab hold of her arm. "Will you please just think about it? You can't be happy singing in here every night for the rest of your life."

She goes to tell him he's wrong, but only a fool would do that.

"Take my card," he says, rummaging around in the pocket of his chained cargo pants. "And if you change your mind, give me a call."

Nicole absently takes it, as if it means nothing, but it feels like it's burning a hole in the palm of her hand.

Despite her protestations, Ben accompanies her out of the club and onto the street. "Hey, Larry," she says to the disheveled man who's getting ready to move into the sheltered doorway. He manages a toothy grin as he pulls the shopping trolley that contains his entire existence closer to him.

"What you got for me tonight, missy?" Larry says, holding out his hand.

Nicole reaches into the bag that's hooked over her shoulder and pulls out a foil-wrapped parcel. "You got lucky: the kitchen put too many sausages on and were about to throw them out."

She says the same thing every night; the pair of them have an unspoken agreement to pretend that she doesn't pay for the food she takes away, even though they both know that she does.

"That'll keep the dragon at bay," he says, referencing the heroin he's always chasing.

"Well, try and hold him off for as long as you can," says Nicole, knowing that in an hour or so Larry will be barely conscious, having satiated himself with food *and* the potent drug.

"Which way are you heading?" Ben asks as they stand in the middle of the alley, each of them pondering their next move.

"The opposite way as you," says Nicole.

"Wow," says Ben, smirking and shaking his head. "You really don't like me, do you?"

She considers him, deep in thought as she taps her fingers on the outer edge of the card he's given her.

"Can I ask you something?" she says, her head cocked to the side and her eyes narrowed. "How come you're playing a sell-out Wembley Arena one week and in this shitty bar on the wrong side of town the next?"

He chews his lip, contemplating the answer. "Because I guess, sometimes, what you thought you wanted doesn't make you quite as happy as what you once had."

17

Brad and I have barely spoken these past two days, the unanswered questions festering between us, working their way under the impervious surface of trust and honesty our relationship was previously based on. While I can't help but blame myself for the turmoil that my family is being put through, I have to question why Brad would have lied to me about what he did last Wednesday night. And who he was with.

Eva *could*, of course, have been mistaken. It might not have been Brad she saw; he might not have been with another woman. It might all be a misunderstanding. But try as I might, I can't get past the possibility that it *was* him, and he was with the very person I'm trying so desperately hard to protect us from.

The doorbell rings and I'm unusually jumpy, nervous of who it might be. But as much as I don't want to answer it, hearing Brad's footsteps cross the landing above me forces me to rush to get there before he does.

"Hank!" My heart goes into my mouth, wondering what news he has, and I instinctively step out onto the porch and pull the door to behind me.

"We've got the CCTV from school," he says. "I thought you and Brad might want to take a look."

I suck in a breath. As much as I want to see the person who up-ended our world, there's a part of me that would rather not know.

"Of course," I say, reluctantly opening the door and calling Brad down.

In the living room, Hank puts his laptop on the coffee table and lifts the lid. "It's not the best picture. It's a little grainy, but you might be able to recognize something about her," he says.

I chance a glance at Brad and notice that he looks even more nervous than I do as the familiar corridor outside Hannah's classroom appears on the screen. I thought I'd have to squint to recognize anyone, so I'm taken aback by the clear picture of Freya's mom as she picks up her daughter's swimming bag from her peg and forces a smile at the woman behind her.

Hank hits the pause button on his keyboard. "There!" he says, pointing at the face on the screen with a stubby finger. "That's her!"

I peer in for a closer look and am comforted by the fact that I have never seen her before. With her long, dark-brown hair and indistinct features, she could be any number of people I pass on the street, but she isn't the woman who came to my house, which is as much of a relief as it is concerning.

But when I look to Brad, I'm sure I see a flicker of recognition cross his face. I chastise myself for looking too hard, trying to find something that isn't there.

"Have either of you seen her before?" asks Hank.

I look to Brad expectantly, waiting for him to reveal his hand. But all he offers is a half-hearted shake of the head.

"Me neither," I say.

You could cut the atmosphere with a knife once Hank leaves, disappointedly empty-handed.

"I think we need to talk," says Brad.

A searing heat overwhelms me as I allow for the possibility that everything that's happened has been orchestrated by a woman who wants something she hasn't got. Maybe this is about a woman scorned, an unrequited love for my husband. Did Brad know that his mistress was behind Hannah's disappearance? Was that why he met with her last week—to warn her off, to tell her she'd gone too far?

Maybe this isn't about me at all. Maybe it's pure coincidence that the woman at my door looking to dig up my past just happened to appear on the same day that Hannah was abducted. The idea works its way into my psyche, and I find selfish relief at the thought that this has everything to do with Brad having an affair, and nothing to do with me. I shock myself at the admission.

He looks at me with a deeply furrowed brow, as if waiting for me to bring him bang to rights. Does he know the game's up? That the net's closing in? Is he about to beg for my forgiveness, or just waiting for the right moment to tell me that the marriage I thought was rock-solid is over?

I shake my head, unable to believe that we would *ever* find ourselves in this position . . . but isn't that exactly what makes us vulnerable?

"What about?" I ask, needing to be put out of my misery.

"I don't want to do it here," he says, looking around the living room at the minutiae of the life we've built together. At the dominoes we brought back from Cuba after the locals had taught Hannah the basics. At the picture he commissioned my favorite artist to paint to mark our tenth anniversary. "I thought we could go into town."

"But we've got no one to stay with Hannah," I say, stalling.

"I've asked Barbara across the street to babysit for a couple of hours."

So, this is premeditated—he knows exactly what he's going to do.

I suddenly want to backtrack to this being about me, instead of it being the end of us—though I fear that once Brad finds out who I really am and what I've done, the outcome will undoubtedly be the same.

"I don't know . . ." I say, shaking my head. "What if she wakes up and we're not here?"

"That woman's not going to come into our house and take her again," he says brusquely. If his words are supposed to reassure me, they do the exact opposite. It's as if he knows for a *fact* that she won't. "Come on," he says. "I'll meet you in the car in five minutes."

I can't help but feel grateful that Tino's is unusually busy. The live band is so loud that customers are having to shout to talk over them. Orders are being called out from behind the bar and glasses are smashing against each other as they're being cleared from tables. Which all provide a myriad of distractions that I'm hoping will make it difficult for Brad to call time on our marriage.

"Hey, Nic," a voice calls out over the din of the band as they start up another number.

"Hi, Jules," I say, smiling and waving to Hank's wife, who's sitting in a booth with her girlfriends wearing what looks to be her husband's Stetson.

"You here for the karaoke?"

I bite my lip, chastising myself for forgetting that Tuesday is open-mic night. The first and last time we'd stumbled inadvertently into the sing-along was a couple of years ago, when I'd unusually had one too many drinks and been cajoled into taking to the stage with a group of moms from school. I'd momentarily lost myself as we hollered out Beyoncé's "Irreplaceable" and imagined I was back at Dallinger's in London. I allowed myself to dream for a second that instead of Brad looking up at me from the audience, it was Ben, on that first night when he came in and told me I had something special. I'd sung as if I were singing to him, without realizing that, one by one, the other girls had stopped and had all turned to look at me with their mouths agape.

The music had continued, but I'd immediately clammed up, fearful that I'd revealed more of my true self than it was safe to.

"When did you learn to sing like *that*?" Brad asked incredulously when I got back to our table, suddenly stone-cold sober.

"Wh-what?" I said, having hoped he was too drunk to notice.

"You sounded incredible up there," he said, looking at me with a renewed respect. If he had any idea of the trouble my voice had gotten me into, he'd know his pride was woefully misplaced. "How did I not know you could sing like that?"

"I didn't know I could," I'd said blithely, while vowing there and then never to let my guard down again—though that was recently put to the test when Hannah brought home a guitar from school. It had taken all my willpower to sit back and watch her as she clumsily strummed the chords, every fiber of my being itching to teach her how to play properly. But how could I explain why I was able to read guitar tablature and knew the difference between a major and a minor chord, when I'd never mentioned it before? So, I'd patiently listened as she tried to master the fretboard and gently encouraged her to practice her scales, then secretly inhaled the cedarwood to incite nostalgia once she'd gone to bed.

I shake my head, both in response to Jules's question and to rid myself of the pull to another time.

"Just a bite to eat," I say, ruefully.

"Well, good luck for tomorrow," she calls out. "We'll be there rooting for you."

"Thanks, I think I'm going to need it."

The thought of standing up in front of the San Diego community to appeal to their common decency had, up until now, filled me with unbridled passion and pride—nothing was more important to me than the petition to close La Jolla beach so that the seals would be able to thrive in their natural habitat without the constant threat of unwanted human interaction. But in the past week my world has changed on its axis and it's taking all my energy to keep my head above water, to save the life *I* had, let alone give the seals the life *they* deserve.

"So . . ." says Brad, heading into the shadows of the bar and putting two bottles of beer on a high-top table. "There's something I need to tell you."

I tip the beer back, desperate for the alcohol to anaesthetize my brain as to what's coming.

"I need you to listen," he goes on. "Before jumping to conclusions."

Tears immediately spring to my eyes and I grind my teeth together in the hope that it will go some way to stop them from falling.

"It's that woman on the CCTV, isn't it? You know who she is."

His jaw twitches involuntarily and I throw a hand up to my mouth to stop me from calling out. How could he bring me somewhere like this, to tell me something like that? That's almost as disrespectful as the act itself. How can he have so little regard for the twenty years we've spent together as to bring me here to tell me it's all been a lie?

I can't look at him, so instead my eyes focus on a woman walking across the bar toward us, with her hair falling around her eyes and an unreadable expression.

I force a tight smile as she gets nearer, sure that I know her from somewhere, though in my heightened state I'm struggling to place her.

"Hello again," she says, stopping in front of me.

Her eyes lock with mine and I feel like I've been electrocuted with a cattle prod. An unfathomable shock runs through me, from the top of my head to the tips of my toes. This can't be happening. She *can't* be here.

I look manically from Brad to her, my brain going into free fall as I wait for one of them to determine how this is going to go. But she stands there, on mute, making an already excruciating situation all the more agonizing. But I suppose that's the idea.

She smirks, as if enjoying my discomfort. "Well, isn't this a co-incidence?"

Isn't it just?

"I don't suppose you've had second thoughts about what we dis-cussed?"

"Er . . ." I bluster, feeling my mouth dry up. "I . . . not really, no . . ."

Zoe looks to Brad. "Sorry to interrupt," she says apologetically. "I was just hoping to convince Nicole to help with something."

"I-I don't believe we've met," he says, his voice sounding unlike his own.

"I'm Zoe," she says, reaching across the table with an outstretched hand.

I want to snatch it away, not wanting the man I love to be tainted by my past.

"You're English?" observes Brad.

Zoe nods. "Just visiting for a week or two."

The stilted silence that follows begs to be filled, but I don't trust myself, my brain unable to think fast enough to justify this woman's presence.

Brad looks to me, the cogs turning as he no doubt attempts to second-guess our relationship. I'm not surprised he's struggling; I'd not spoken about *anyone* from "back home." Over the years, I'd spo-radically thrown in an occasional mention of a Gina or a Caroline, both of whom I knew at school, though not well enough to remember their surnames; but they'd given me a footing in the past, an anchor on which to hang a superficial history that went some way to convince Brad that the woman he'd chosen to spend his life with had had a perfectly normal upbringing in England.

And I suppose I had, up until a point. But then it had all got turned upside down and the "normal" I'd taken for granted was destroyed, so that nothing was ever normal again. The life I'd had "before" was forcibly wiped from my consciousness, with no trace left of the person I'd been and the life I'd led.

Brad had often tried to get me to revisit the trauma that had so suddenly descended upon our unsuspecting family, even though he had no concept of what had really happened and how deeply scarred it had left me. "Perhaps if you went back to England, with me by your side, you could put the bad memories to bed once and for all," he'd say, believing that it was the death of my sister that was responsible for the cavernous wound that had left me hollow.

"You'll have your own family with you this time," he'd said in his efforts to convince me to face my demons. "And nobody can ever take that away."

I couldn't help but blanch at the empty promise. The people you love can *always* be taken away.

"We could visit your old haunts," he'd said during his latest attempt. "Give Hannah a sense of your life before us." He'd looked at me hopefully. "Perhaps we can even show her your sister's resting place?"

His naivety was dangerous.

"No!" I'd snapped, as the truth sat heavily on my chest. "I'm never going back there." I'd meant it both literally and metaphorically.

"What are you so afraid of?" he'd said, letting out a heavy sigh of resignation.

This, I answer silently now, as I look at Zoe, unable to believe that everything I've spent years running away from is about to catch up with me. Here, in this dirty, windowless bar.

"I'm writing a book," Zoe goes on, slowly and painfully perforating the life I've spent years building. "And I was hoping Nicole might be able to help me with my research."

"There's no one on this island who knows more about the seal colony than Nicole," says Brad, looking at me proudly. I glow in his pride for a split second, before remembering it's gravely misplaced.

"It's not about the seals," says Zoe.

"Oh?" says Brad, looking perplexed.

This is it. The weight of what she knows bears down on me, making it difficult to breathe.

After all the years I've had to tell Brad the truth, *my* truth, someone else has got there first. If *his* confession wasn't about to put a dagger through our marriage, this will surely be the death knell. My hand shakes as I struggle to hold on to my beer bottle, my clammy fingers feeling it slip.

"It's about the rise and fall of the biggest band of the eighties."

"Oh . . ." says Brad, his eyebrows shooting up in surprise. "You don't look old enough to remember it."

Zoe offers a wry smile. "I wasn't there myself, but I've always been interested in eighties culture, and this story has truly earned its place in folklore."

"So, who were they?" he asks, his interest piqued, or maybe he's just relieved that he can hold off what he was about to say to me for a couple more minutes.

"A band called Secret Oktober," she says, making me flinch, even though I knew it was coming.

"Oh yeah, I remember them," says Brad, as if it's of little consequence to him. It isn't. *Yet.*

"They would've gone on to become the biggest band in the world," Zoe goes on, even though every part of me is willing her not to.

Brad throws me a look, knowing that we're on uncharted territory. But, as if sensing that it might not be a comfortable place for me to be, he swallows the question he looked set to ask. For a moment, I'm relieved, but his reticence only opens the floodgates for Zoe to continue.

"If it hadn't all ended in such tragic circumstances, of course . . ."

"He was murdered, wasn't he?" asks Brad.

"Well, technically it was manslaughter," says Zoe matter-of-factly.

I can feel Brad's eyes on me, burning like lasers into my skin. "So, what's any of that got to do with *you*?" he says, his curiosity getting the better of him.

It's as if the whole bar has been put on pause and a single spotlight has picked me out, blinding me with its beam, as it waits for an answer I'm not prepared to give. My mouth dries up as I look at Zoe, imploring her not to light the fuse of the bomb she's about to detonate.

"Well, your wife was a suspect," she says.

18

"Nicole! Phone!" calls out Cassie, stirring her from a Sunday-morning slumber.

Nicole throws the duvet over her head, desperate to take advantage of the only lie-in she gets all week, but now that she's awake she can hear her dad's nine-bit drill as he embarks on what is no doubt another DIY job invented in his quest to keep busy.

Since Cassie took it upon herself to stay out until one in the morning after the concert, Nicole has all but moved back home in an effort to keep the peace. But her dad has spent the week incandescent with rage and Cassie has been confined to the house, sullenly shrugging off any of Nicole's attempts to reach out to her.

"Phone!" yells Cassie again, throwing open Nicole's door.

"Tell them I'll call them back," groans Nicole.

"Tell him yourself," says Cassie, turning away and leaving the door ajar.

"For fuck's sake," mutters Nicole under her breath as she reluctantly slides her feet into her fluffy slippers and descends the stairs, avoiding the pink flowers on the patterned carpet as she always does—a twenty-year habit that she'd hoped to have grown out of by now.

"Hello?" she says groggily, not knowing anyone who might call her here on a Sunday morning, least of all a boy.

"Hey, is that Nicole Alderton?" comes a voice, far too loudly for this time in the morning. She goes to put the receiver down, not needing her senses to be assaulted by a cold caller, but stops in her tracks once her brain has had a second to catch up.

"Jesus!" she says, taking the phone through to the dining room, stretching the coiled cord to its limit.

"Well, actually it's Ben," says the voice, laughing. "But people have been known to call me that."

A prickly heat wraps itself around Nicole's neck and her eardrums are banging so loudly that she can't hear herself think. She needs to break this down into bite-sized chunks; weigh up how to deal with this one piece at a time. The most pressing problem, she quickly ascertains, is Cassie.

"You can't be calling me here," she says breathlessly, cupping her hand over the receiver to avoid anyone else hearing. "How did you get this number?"

"Well, the man behind the bar happened to mention you were staying with your parents in Finsbury Park for a while," he says, sounding a little perturbed. "And thankfully there aren't that many Aldertons in the phone book, so I tried my luck and kept everything crossed."

"You can't call me here again," she says, her mind fast-forwarding to what her dad will do if he finds out that the man his sixteen-year-old daughter is infatuated with is now trying his luck with the other one.

"OK, I promise," says Ben resolutely, and despite herself Nicole can't help but be disappointed.

He waits a heartbeat before adding, "On one condition . . ."

She sighs for effect, while desperately trying to push away the part of her that's excited by what his proposition is going to be.

"I need you to listen to something."

Her heart skips a beat.

"I've got something down on tape and I'd appreciate your opinion."

"OK . . ." she says hesitantly, not wanting to appear too keen, but the thought of being asked for her musical viewpoint from someone of Ben Edwards's standing sends an electrical pulse through her nervous system.

"So, is that a yes?" he asks, with an excited lilt.

"I'm sure I can fit it in at some point this week," she says.

"Ah, no can do," he says. "I'm on a European press tour for the new album from tomorrow and not back until after the weekend."

"Well, it looks like you'll have to find yourself another muse," she says, at pains to keep the disappointment of a lost opportunity from her voice.

"Not necessarily," he says. "What are you doing today?"

"*Today?*"

"Yeah, what's the problem?"

There must be a thousand and one reasons why she can't meet him today, but she's hard-pressed to think of any of them.

"Be ready in five minutes," he says.

"Don't be so ridiculous," she starts, looking at the clock above the fireplace, the second hand moving ever so slightly out of sync with the loud ticking noise. "I'm not even dressed."

"So, get dressed, and I'll meet you in the black car that's parked on the other side of your street."

"*What?*" she says, rushing to the window and pulling the net curtains aside, though why she's falling for it, she doesn't know. What she sees snatches her breath away. "You've got to be kidding me!"

"Five minutes," he says, waving at her through the graffitied glass panes of the telephone box outside her house.

With her heart feeling as if it's about to burst through her chest, Nicole pulls on the first things she can find: a pair of baggy jeans and a tassel-fringed blouse with built-in shoulder pads. It's a little over the top for first thing on a Sunday morning, but her need to get Ben away from here before Cassie or their dad sees him is far more pressing than what she looks like.

"Where are *you* going?" asks Cassie, her tone accusatory, as she carries a plate of beans on toast back up to her room.

"I've just got to do a few things back at the flat," she replies, falling over herself as she pulls her pixie boots on.

"Is that code for a secret rendezvous with whoever was on the phone?" asks Cassie, dourly.

"No!" snaps Nicole, before instantly regretting it. She doesn't need to attract any more attention to the fact that a global superstar, who is as equally revered as reviled in this house, is sitting outside it . . . *like, right now.*

She half walks, half runs up to the car and past it, knowing that she daren't get into it while it's in sight of the house. Cassie could be looking out of the window right now, and knowing her, she knows the number plate of the vehicle Ben travels in off by heart. So, Nicole keeps walking, around the corner, as the soft purr of its engine follows her.

"What the hell do you think you're doing here?" she exclaims when it pulls up next to her and the window rolls down. Her burgeoning excitement has been replaced by a raging anger that he would be so arrogant as to expect her to drop everything to see him. *He wasn't wrong though, was he?*

"What's the problem?" he asks, seeming genuinely perplexed. But then, Nicole supposes he doesn't normally get complaints when he turns up at someone's house unannounced.

"This isn't on," she says, still not sure whether she's getting in the car or not. "I-I've got stuff going on at home and this doesn't make my life very easy."

"Oh, I'm sorry," he says, looking like a reprimanded schoolboy. "I just assumed . . ."

"Well, don't," says Nicole. "The world doesn't revolve around Ben Edwards."

He smiles. "You know my name, though."

She wants to tell him that the only reason for that is because her little sister has been obsessed with him for the past eighteen months; has spent every penny of her hard-earned cash on him, and every moment she should have been studying staring woefully at his face on her bedroom ceiling.

"You said you had something . . ." she starts impatiently, the need to give him the impression she has far better things to be doing at loggerheads with the spine-tingling anticipation of what he has in store.

"I want to play you something," he says, turning a cassette in between his thumb and forefinger.

She makes a show of getting in the back seat, rolling her eyes, as if she's doing him a favor.

"OK—you ready?" he says, pushing the tape into the slot of the car's radio cassette player that's mounted on the carpet-lined partition separating them from the driver. The mechanical spools grab hold of it with a satisfying click. "But I need you to stay open-minded."

The gentle strumming of guitar chords echoes in Nicole's chest, making her want to close her eyes and lose herself in the soothing melody.

"There are things I could never teach you, no matter how hard I try,
Because only you can decide how high you fly,
I can set you on your way and catch you if you fall,
But only you will know . . ."

Ben's voice reaches into every crevice of Nicole's being, its rawness making her fingertips tingle. In all the hours she's been forced to listen to Secret Oktober through the walls of Cassie's bedroom, she's never heard Ben sing like this. She wouldn't have thought it possible, and just when she thinks she can't be any more surprised, he sings the chorus in falsetto.

> *"If you ever loved someone as much as I love you,*
> *You'd know there is nothing I wouldn't do,*
> *And I promise you, I will never let you down,*
> *I'll make you proud of me, no matter where you are . . ."*

Nicole's eyes widen and she turns to face him. "That's *my* song," she says, the words catching in her throat. "That . . . that's . . ."

Ben grimaces, waiting to see which side of the fence she falls on.

"I sang that in the bar the other night. You were there." Her mind is a jumble of emotions that she can't separate. *What is he playing at?*

"I know, I know," he says, shifting along the leather seat. "It's such a beautiful song and I thought . . ."

"You thought what?" she asks, wondering why she suddenly feels so exposed and vulnerable, while forcing herself to silently repeat the mantra *They're just words*. But they're *her* words, written for only *her* to sing, and to hear them in another voice, no matter how beautiful, is beyond disconcerting.

"I just wanted to lay down some vocals," he says. "To get your mum's words on the page. It could be your love letter to each other."

Without warning, tears rush to Nicole's eyes and no matter how much she battles to hold them back, clenching her jaw, one escapes onto her cheek.

"Hey, I'm sorry," says Ben, going to put his arm out to comfort her, before thinking better of it. "I really didn't mean to upset you. I thought you'd like the idea."

Nicole goes to speak, but her voice deserts her, so she nods instead.

"It's OK, I get it," says Ben, falling back against the seat, deflated. "I don't know what I was thinking—I should never have taken your words."

"It's . . . it's not that," she manages. "It's just—"

"No, you're right," he says, ejecting the cassette in a fit of pique. "I overstepped the mark. I wouldn't have liked it if someone—"

"My mother's very ill," says Nicole, the words tumbling out before she can stop them.

An ominous silence fills the car, the atmosphere suddenly dark and foreboding as the gravitas of those four words and what they might mean circle the restricted space.

"I'm sorry," says Ben, as he presses a button to slide up the soundproof-glass partition.

"We don't know if she's going to make it."

She's crying now, and without saying a word Ben pulls her into him and wraps his arms around her so tightly that she feels as if she's being cocooned in a security blanket. As ridiculous as it sounds, she can't remember feeling this safe since her mother last hugged her, when she had enough strength in her arms to do so.

"I'm sorry . . . I don't know why . . ." She sobs into Ben's chest, though what she's going to say, she doesn't know. Bizarrely, in this moment, her overriding concern is not getting last night's mascara on his shirt.

"Is your dad around?" Ben asks gently, resting his chin on the top of her head.

Nicole nods.

"I'm so sorry—I never meant to hurt you," he says. "If I'd known . . ."

"It's fine," she says, pulling herself away from him, suddenly feeling embarrassed. "What you did was really special—I liked it a lot."

Every sinew in Ben's body relaxes with relief. "Maybe you'll want to record it one day."

Nicole snorts unattractively. "Right, like that's going to happen."

Ben smiles that smile of his and, despite herself, something flutters deep in Nicole's stomach.

"I have a friend who has a studio not far from here. We could go and fool around a bit." His eyes alight with mischief. "Play with some sounds, work on some lyrics—just see what happens, no pressure."

Panic and exhilaration engulf Nicole in equal measure. This can't be happening. This only happens to people in movies. "Are you for real?"

"So, is that a yes?"

"But why would you do this?" she asks, her usual cynicism creeping back with a vengeance; the thought of anyone doing anything without expecting something in return is alien to her. "If it's to get me into bed, it's a rather elaborate ruse."

Ben throws his head back and laughs. "No disrespect, but if I wanted to get laid, the fact that I'm the biggest pop star in the country right now is usually enough."

"That and your unswerving modesty," says Nicole with raised eyebrows.

"Exactly!" says Ben. "So, are we doing this or what?"

"OK," she says, hesitantly. "But I'm not going to sleep with you."

"And I wouldn't expect you to," he says, with a wry smile.

19

I'm inventing things to do in order to avoid having to go upstairs and get ready for bed. But I know that the longer I draw it out, the elephant in the room is only going to loom ever larger in Brad's mind. I hear him stomp from the bedroom to the bathroom, slamming the door.

I wonder if I've got time to run up the stairs, get into my nightgown, slip into bed and pretend I'm asleep before he comes back out. But even if I have, Brad has always been of the belief that we should never go to sleep on an argument—and although it hasn't happened yet, this has the potential to be the mother of all arguments.

We cross on the landing outside the bathroom, me having planned it with precision so as to limit the chances of him raising his voice since Hannah is within earshot. But I know I'm only putting off his inevitable wrath—and who can blame him? I deserve everything he's going to give.

It feels as if there's a boulder on my chest as I clean my teeth, an obstruction that's been growing day by day, for every month and year of marriage that I haven't told him my deepest, darkest secret. There's a tiny part of me, buried somewhere I'd never be able to reach, that's relieved it's all about to be cast out into the open. But I'd never choose to do it like this; I'm still not ready. Though if I were honest with myself, I'm not sure I ever would be.

Brad's making a good show of reading his book when I come out of the bathroom, willing myself to pretend that it's just a normal night. I switch off my bedside lamp and climb into the cool cotton sheets beside him. My head has just hit the pillow when he slams the book down, making me jump.

"Are you honestly intending to go to sleep without telling me what the hell she was talking about?" he exclaims, his hurt and fury so evidently close to the surface.

"I-I don't know what you want me to say."

He jumps out of bed and switches on the main light, making me feel as if I'm an unwilling actor onstage. *"Something! Anything!* You need to start talking because until you offer an explanation I can even begin to understand, we're going to have a huge problem."

I pull myself up against the headboard. "She came by a week or so ago."

"And you didn't think to tell me?" he seethes. "What does she want from you?"

"She was asking questions about what happened back then."

Brad's jaw tenses as he looks at me with narrowed eyes. "And what *did* happen back then?"

I swallow. "I-I was around the band at the time."

"Around the band?" he repeats incredulously. "Is that honestly all you're going to give me?"

"I-I was seeing Ben Edwards . . ." I falter, the memory of his smiling face flashing in front of my eyes. "Wh-when it happened."

"Jesus!" roars Brad. "I always knew you were running from something, but I never imagined it would be something like this."

I thought I'd prepared myself for every eventuality, getting ready every conceivable answer to the questions I knew he was going to ask. But this is a sucker punch I wasn't expecting, and I turn into my pillow to stifle a sob. He doesn't mean it, of course—he can't possibly have known that I had come to America for any reason other than that my sister had tragically been taken from us and, feeling alone and bereft, I wanted a new start somewhere far away, where no one knew me.

That's why I got on a plane to Los Angeles, took the Pacific Surfliner to San Diego, and then, when it still didn't feel quite far enough away from my former life in London, jumped on the ferry to the tiny island of Coronado. At least that's what Brad thinks.

"I wasn't . . . It wasn't . . ." I start, my rehearsed lines deserting me.

"Why wouldn't you have thought to tell me something like that?" He looks at me wide-eyed, expecting an answer.

"I should have been honest. I should have told you, but I was scared."

"Of what?" he says, still too agitated to sit down and talk it through calmly. "What have you got to be scared of?"

I disguise a shudder. If only he knew.

"It was a really difficult time that I wanted to put behind me," I say, matter-of-factly.

"So *that's* why you fled to America?"

"I didn't *flee* anywhere," I say, hurt by the suggestion, even though it's true. "After the trial, I just needed to get away for a while."

"And never go back?"

"I was always intending to, but then I met you, so . . ." I shrug my shoulders nonchalantly, but nothing about me is indifferent.

Brad's eyes narrow and he goes to say something before seemingly thinking better of it.

"Go on," I prompt.

He straightens himself up and runs a hand through his beard. "But you were a suspect?"

I suck in a breath. "Yes, but thankfully justice prevailed."

"So, what's this woman doing here now, then?" he asks, looking more worried than mad. "What does she want?"

"She was after some help with her book—I assume looking to fill in some blanks, but I told her I wasn't interested in being dragged back to the past."

"What day was she here?"

Bizarrely, it's the question I've been most frightened of. "Wh-what?" I stutter.

"What day was she here?" he asks again, slowly and deliberately.

"Erm, I-I can't really remember."

"Well, was it *before* Hannah went missing, or after?" His patience is wearing thin and I've run out of places to hide.

"I think . . . I think it was the same day . . ." My vagueness lends itself to someone who genuinely doesn't know, but it's etched into my memory, and I'm a fool if I think Brad doesn't know me well enough to see it.

His nostrils flare. "So, this has something to do with what happened to her."

"*What?* No, of course not. Why would you think that?"

He snorts derisively. "Are you honestly telling me it's pure coincidence? That our daughter going missing has nothing to do with your mucky past being raked up on the very same day?"

"Yes," I say, sounding far more forthright than I feel. "There would be no reason on earth why what happened twenty-five years ago would result in anything happening to Hannah."

"You'd better be telling me the truth," he warns, his features pinched.

20

The last four weeks have been as surreal as they've been testing, the juxtaposition of what's been happening outside the house
with the turmoil of watching her mother's slow deterioration ripping Nicole's emotions to shreds and scattering them in opposite
directions.

How is she supposed to feel? How is she supposed to imagine
what next week will bring, if she can't predict what will happen tomorrow? So much feels up in the air, like she's living in an unen-
viable limbo but where there's only one possible outcome. Is it any
wonder, then, that every time she's with Ben, she's consumed not
only with the guilt of forgoing precious time with her mum, but the
constant fear of Cassie finding out that the man staring out at her
from her bedroom wall is so much closer than she thinks.

But now that Nicole has temporarily moved back home, she
needs space to breathe, and spending time with Ben, writing songs
and making music, allows her to do that.

"I didn't know you were such a prolific songwriter," she says, struggling to hide her emotions as he plays her a new song in the studio she's come to feel surprisingly comfortable in. The meaningful words and soulful voice sound as if they belong to one of the Motown artists her mother used to listen to.

"Do you like it?" he asks, looking at her with nervous trepidation. "Honestly?"

"It's amazing! Have you recorded it?"

He shakes his head. "I'm trying to convince management to release it as our next single, but there's some . . . resistance, shall we say?"

"Who from?"

He laughs, but there's an uneasy edge to it. "The management aren't sure that it sets the tone of a Secret Oktober record. They think it's too melancholy and grown-up for our audience. I keep telling them that they're underestimating the angst of a teenage mind."

"But that line, '*Look at those before you, to know who you want to become*' will sing to the hearts of thirteen- and fourteen-year-old girls all over the country."

Ben shrugs his shoulders despondently. "But it's not just management I have to convince. Other band members aren't exactly ecstatic that I'm writing my own songs either."

"Why wouldn't they want that?" asks Nicole, knowing that to date the band's music had been penned by a hit-factory production team. It had led to the snobby music press labeling their records as just another tune on the conveyor belt of mediocre. "Surely it's a good thing."

"There's a lot of stuff that the public don't get to see," he says, his eyes downcast. "And a lot of it would surprise you."

"Like what?" Nicole can't help but ask.

"Well, life is not always easy with Michael. He has to be carefully managed and everyone walks on eggshells around him, not wanting to upset him. So, when he says he's not happy with something, people tend to listen."

"And he doesn't like that song?" she asks, unable to understand how anyone can fail to recognize its potential.

"Oh, he *loves* the song! He just doesn't like the fact that I wrote it."

"So, he'd rather the band lose out on a great song than see you get the credit for it?"

"That's about the sum of it," says Ben.

"How has it come to this? I'd assumed you were all as thick as thieves."

"We used to be, when we first formed the band," he says sadly. "Micky and I were best friends from school, but in the past year he's changed into someone I don't know."

"Is he not happy in the band?"

Ben shrugs his shoulders. "He's not happy with *anything,* and he's making bad decisions about the things he does and the people he mixes with. But I won't have him throw away everything we've worked for."

"What will you do?"

"Anything I have to, because the way he's headed, he's going to destroy us."

Nicole shakes her head knowingly. "I think your place in the public's affections is pretty well cemented."

"Until they find out what's *really* been going on behind the scenes," says Ben scathingly. "Then we're finished."

"You make it sound like you've done something illegal," says Nicole, half-jokingly.

Ben takes a deep breath. "We're terrifyingly close," he says, looking at her, as if questioning whether he can trust her or not. "A month or so ago, we had an after-party and it got raided by the police."

Nicole's brow furrows. She already doesn't like where this is going.

"The place was littered with drugs, and I was dragged down to the station and cautioned."

"How has that not made the news?" Nicole asks incredulously.

"Because we paid a lot of people to keep it off the books."

Nicole's eyebrows shoot up, her expression a mixture of surprise and disappointment. "Well, it sounds like you and Michael are as bad as each other."

He shakes his head. "But that's just it. I've been known to pop a pill every once in a while, but Michael likes it *all*, and lines it up as if it's candy in a sweet shop. *He's* the one who brings it in and *he's* the one who gives it out."

"So, did he get a slap on the wrist as well?"

Ben laughs acerbically. "If he'd been caught, he most likely would have been hung, drawn, and quartered."

"But . . ." prompts Nicole, feeling like there's one coming.

"But while the rest of us were being arrested, he somehow managed to jump out the window and do a runner down the fire escape."

"Oi, oi, what's going on 'ere then?"

They both jump at the sound of the gravelly voice, and Ben drops his headphones as if they're on fire. Nicole surreptitiously removes hers, too, not needing to ask who it is.

"So, this is where you've been hiding?" says Michael from behind a cloud of smoke. The intoxicating blend of marijuana furls its way up Nicole's nose, the heat burning the tiny hairs in her nostrils.

"What are *you* doing here?" says Ben.

"What's the problem, bro?" says Michael, the words at odds with his condescending tone. "You sound like I've caught you doing something you shouldn't."

"I'm just laying down my vocals for 'Friends Like These'," Ben lies.

"What, without the rest of the band?" snarls Michael, knowing, even in his stoned haze, that it's unlikely.

"Thought we'd try something new."

"So, who's *she*?" growls Michael, giving Nicole a cursory glance up and down to size up whether she's someone he might be interested in. As if he has a choice to make.

Ben bristles beside her as his brain no doubt fast-tracks to find the most acceptable answer. Just watching him is exhausting.

"She's the new studio assistant," he says, making Nicole feel even smaller than she already does. He turns to her to continue the charade. "We've got band-time booked in for when we get back from America, right?"

Nicole nods numbly.

"Well, you'd better make sure your sweet ass is here when we come back," says Michael, coming toward her and running a hand up her bare leg, the tips of his fingers feeling their way under the frayed hem of her denim shorts.

"Hey, cut it out," snaps Ben, reaching forward and swiping his arm away.

"Or what?" says Michael, his nostrils flaring.

"You're pathetic," says Ben, turning to walk away.

"Hey, don't you turn your back on me!" roars Michael, pulling on Ben's shoulder.

"Get your fucking hands off me," says Ben, attempting to shrug him off. But Michael's not having it and steps up to him, puffing his chest out like he has something to prove.

"Come on then!" he bellows, poking Ben in the chest with a provoking finger. "Let's have it."

Ben looks at him, his expression a mixture of pity and sadness as to how they've got to this point.

"Go home," he says. "Get yourself cleaned up, and I'll see you at the awards tonight."

Michael looks like he's been shot with a tranquilizer dart, as the realization sinks in that he's not going to get the fight he was looking for.

"Yeah, right," he says, suddenly sheepish, though Nicole doesn't imagine his subservience will last very long.

"I'm so sorry," Ben says, once Michael has left. "Are you OK?"

Nicole nods, though she can still feel Michael's clammy hand on her thigh.

Ben lets out a heavy sigh. "That's the kind of shit I'm having to deal with on a daily basis."

"He can't go around treating people like that," says Nicole.

"I know, but he's not in a good place right now, and it's a constant fight to keep him on the straight and narrow."

Nicole bites her tongue to stop herself from saying that he's a grown adult who's living a life that millions of others would kill for, so perhaps he needs to stop being treated with kid gloves and be given some tough love.

"I'll find a way to get through to him," says Ben, as if reading her mind.

She smiles, wishing him all the luck in the world, because she fears he's going to need it.

21

It's a military operation as one stretch limousine after another pulls up beside the red carpet that runs all the way from the roadside and up the steps to the Royal Albert Hall. The nation's press waits with bated breath as each foot appears from beneath the car door, second-guessing which legend from the music world is about to grace them with their presence.

Tina Turner steps out in a red leather minidress, her shaggy, supersized golden mullet instantly recognizable. Next comes Michael Jackson in his signature shades, waving to the screaming crowds with a crystal-gloved hand. But it's the bare foot that follows him out of the car that sends the flashbulbs into a frenzy.

The splayed toes of a hairy primate jump down onto the carpet, dressed as if he's going to a baseball game.

"It's Bubbles!" shrills the girl next to Cassie, taking her Instamatic camera and winding it on.

Once upon a time, Cassie would have killed to be up close and personal to the man who brought her *Thriller* and the dance routine that her mother had spent hours teaching her. But all she can think of right now is the promised arrival of Ben Edwards.

The band had gone to ground for the best part of a month, ever since the album launch, and the official word from the record company was that they were holed away, making bonus tracks. But Cassie and Amelia have been to the studio they usually frequent and there's been no sign of them. She only needs to see him *once* to know that what they shared on the night of the police raid still stands. That her pledge to stand by him is still deserved.

He'd disappeared so quickly that night at the museum—no doubt whisked away by security guards before he could say goodbye— that she hadn't had a chance to give him her phone number. And without being able to track him down since, she'd been left in an excruciating sense of limbo, knowing that *she* couldn't reach him, and *he* couldn't reach her.

How had *he* been managing, she wondered. Having to trust that she would eventually find a way to contact him—he must have felt so powerless.

There's an uptick in anticipation as girls on the other side of the red carpet become restless and agitated. From their vantage point, they get a sneak preview of a leg or an arm as the car door opens. Shrill shrieks ring out when a cowboy boot makes its mark on the ground. There's no other movement for what feels like a minute as the suspense is intentionally ramped up.

"It's Micky," says Amelia, an authority on the subject.

Butterflies take flight in Cassie's stomach. This has felt like such a long time coming, and her excitement is infused with a tangible relief that she and Ben are finally going to be together again.

The crowd goes wild as Michael lifts his six-foot frame out of the car, and he milks it for all it's worth. Despite the long line of limos queuing up behind his, he keeps them waiting as he ducks in and out of the blacked-out back seat, as if playing a game of cat and mouse.

"He's such a wind-up," says Amelia, smiling, while Cassie just wishes he'd move on so they can get to the main event of the evening.

"Ladies and gentlemen . . ." says Michael over-theatrically. "May I present Samantha Redgrave . . ."

Photographers fall over themselves to capture the coming together of one of the country's biggest pop stars and the current Page Three model of the year.

"What the . . . ?" says Amelia, as Samantha steps out in a full-length fur, despite the heat.

As soon as she's found the perfect spot on the red carpet, Samantha makes an elaborate show of peeling the coat tantalizingly slowly off her shoulders, before dropping it to the floor to reveal a sheer dress that leaves nothing to the imagination.

"I can't believe it," says Cassie, knowing that Amelia had held as high hopes for her and Michael tonight as she did for herself and Ben.

Though, if she were honest, the likelihood of Michael seeing Amelia as anything more than an easy lay was doubtful. But she would never say that to her friend, and they'd happily spent the past month fantasizing with great enthusiasm about how the four of them would secretly meet in London, giving the ever-present paparazzi the slip so they could nurture their fledgling relationships.

Amelia's lips pull tight and her nostrils flare. "Bastard."

"It might not mean anything," placates Cassie. "It might just be a publicity stunt."

"He's making me look stupid," seethes Amelia. "He can't just pick me up and put me down whenever he feels like it."

Cassie sucks in a relieved breath, suddenly grateful that she and Ben hadn't had a chance to do anything other than talk before the police burst into the hotel room. She may have spent every second since wishing that they had, but if she wanted to be different from every other girl and earn his respect, then she'd played it right. She didn't want to be a one-night stand; she wanted to be his girlfriend.

"I'm so sorry," she says to Amelia. "But I'm sure it's all for show. I'll have a word with Ben if you like—he'll know what's going on."

Amelia nods, biting down on her bottom lip, as if to hold back tears.

"Oh my god, here he is," says Cassie in a rush, any thoughts of her friend's heartbreak already forgotten.

Dressed in black-leather trousers and a chained waistcoat, Ben's eyes scan the crowd as if looking for her.

"Over here!" she calls out, jostling to the front, so that he can see her.

His whole face breaks into a smile, so delighted to be reconciled. He walks toward her and Cassie wonders if he might just kiss her here and now, in front of the world. She prepares herself for the eventuality and reaches out for him, but he stops just short to greet a woman with a microphone, kissing her on both cheeks before moving to stand next to her for the cameras.

"Alesha, good to see you again," he says, with a megawatt grin. "How are you?"

"All the better for seeing you," says the woman, blushing.

Cassie keeps the welcoming smile she'd proffered fixed to her face, but the corners of her mouth are twitching against the possibility that this isn't going to play out quite as she'd expected. The sexual chemistry between Ben and the other woman could power the entire evening's event, and Cassie can only assume that it's the consequence of a previous liaison. Because she won't allow herself to imagine it might be the prelude to an encounter yet to come.

"Secret Oktober are up for two awards this evening," says Alesha, losing herself in Ben's come-to-bed eyes. "Which is the most important to you? Best Album or Best Group?"

He strokes his square chin and throws a glance in Cassie's direction, but it's too quick for her to grab hold of. Still, she's sure he knows she's here; he just has to bide his time and work the floor.

"That's a tricky one," he says. "But I guess I'd be prouder to win Best Album, as we worked so hard on it."

"Michael's just made quite the entrance with Samantha Redgrave. Is that a serious relationship? Something the fans should be worried about?" Alesha laughs, as if it will make the question seem less incongruous, but Cassie can see Ben's jaw tense, even if the TV cameras can't.

"I wouldn't know about that," he says, with a saccharine-sweet smile. "You'd have to ask him."

Alesha tilts her head to the side coquettishly. "And what about *your* plus-one? Is there someone special you're having a clandestine meeting with inside?"

Ben laughs, and Cassie half expects him to turn to her and hold out his hand, inviting her to step under the roped cordon. But instead, he places a hand on Alesha's taffeta-clad behind. "Are you offering?" he asks.

Cassie swallows her contempt at the discourtesy, knowing it's all a game he has to play, a character he has to portray until they're on their own again.

The cameras stop rolling straight after Ben's fake laugh.

"If you want to hook up later . . ." purrs Alesha, attempting to be seductive. "I'll be done by ten."

"Ah, I'd love to," says Ben. "But I'm not intending to stay around for too long."

He reaches a hand out behind him and Cassie grabs it, feeling her heart soar as she squeezes tightly.

"Ben," she sighs, as he turns to look at her.

"Hey," he says, smiling. "How are you?"

Cassie fights back the happy tears that her nervous energy has spent weeks provoking. "I'm good; I'm so happy to see you."

"Ah, that's so sweet," he says. "Now, can I have my hand back?"

"Oh yeah, sorry," she says, releasing it as she ducks under the barrier to join him.

"Whoa, whoa, whoa," barks a security guard, stepping into action. "You need to stay behind the rope."

"It's OK," says Cassie, holding her hands up as she looks at Ben. "I'm with him."

The security guard furrows his brow dubiously, as he waits for confirmation and, for a split second, Ben looks as if he might not acknowledge her place by his side. But his rigid jaw suddenly slackens, and his narrowed eyes widen.

"It's all right," he says. "I've got this."

Cassie falls into him gratefully and slips her arm through his.

"OK, I'll tell you what we're going to do," he whispers into her ear. "You see that camera up ahead?"

Cassie looks ten feet in front of her to see a camera operator accompanying another earnest woman holding a microphone, ready to pounce.

"I'm going to walk with you until then and then I need to get on."

"OK," says Cassie, breathlessly. "Then where do *I* go?"

"Back to where you came from," says Ben, through gritted teeth, at pains to keep up appearances.

"But . . . but how will we find each other again?"

Ben turns to look at her with a vexed expression. "Why would we need to find each other again?"

An ice-cold hand reaches into Cassie's chest and tightly squeezes around her heart, but she fights against the remote possibility that she's got this all wrong.

"Look, it's been lovely meeting you," he says, dropping her arm. "But I really do have to be getting on . . ."

"But I thought we'd spend the evening together," says Cassie, her voice breaking. "I thought that's what you wanted."

The nod is almost imperceptible, but it's enough to summon security and Cassie feels herself being strong-armed away from Ben. "Wh-what are you doing?" she calls out. "Ben! Ben, help me!"

He turns away without a second glance, and Cassie finds herself being lifted up, carried behind the crowd, and ejected onto the concourse like a regurgitated nuisance.

She twists her ankle as she lands, but her wounded pride hurts her more than the physical pain ever could.

"Are you OK?" asks Amelia, running to her and helping her up.

Cassie goes to shrug her off, but the rejection stings so badly that she allows Amelia to take some of the weight, both literally *and* figuratively.

"They're fucking bastards," cries Cassie, feeling as if her insides have been hollowed out. "They don't give a shit about us."

"It's going to be OK," says Amelia, unable to hide the bitter vitriol from her voice. "I'm not going to let them get away with this."

And as Cassie looks at her twisted features, she doesn't doubt that she means it.

22

After last night, I'm not sure how I can possibly stand up in front of five hundred people and pretend that the seals and their welfare are at the forefront of my mind. The potential reward of getting this petition submitted and actioned has paled into insignificance now that the life I've tried so hard to create and preserve is hanging in the balance.

"OK, let's get you mic'd up," says a smiley woman coming at me, with no concept of what's going on behind my tired eyes. She rummages around the underside of my blazer, which I'd bought especially for the occasion, hoping it conveyed that I was friendly and approachable to the community while meaning business to local government, whose votes we need to sway with this one final push.

I peek around the side of the stage, my mouth drying out as rows and rows of expectant faces look through the booklet I'd so lovingly prepared, back when my life resembled the one I've spent the past twenty years cultivating.

"You're good to go," says the smiley woman. "You ready?"

I nod, but I feel I no longer know what I've signed up for.

"Ladies and gentlemen," starts the announcer, her voice booming around San Diego's revered convention center. "There's not a soul among us who doesn't love our city's seals, for all that they give *us*, and the world further afield. We're the lucky ones because they've chosen *our* beaches to live, play, swim, and birth pups on. But human intrusion on what should be a safe and protected environment is evermore prevalent, and it's fallen to one woman to be their voice. And thank goodness for her . . . Please welcome Nicole Forbes."

My ears fill with the whooping and hollering, but the noise still doesn't drown out the doubts and bewilderment that seep into my veins as I try to hold it together. A week ago, I would have been seen as an upstanding member of the community: a devoted mother, a loyal wife, someone who only ever wanted to do good. But now I crumble under the glaring spotlights as I hazard a guess as to how many of these well-meaning expressions are actually asking what kind of a mother loses their child. And I can't help but wonder to myself, *What kind of a wife has lived a life her husband doesn't know about?*

I scan the faces in front of me, paranoid that someone here knows more about me than I want them to. Or perhaps they know even more than *I* do. Do they know that my life is about to implode? Is there someone here who is going to be instrumental in that, and they're just waiting, biding their time, for the perfect moment to cut the strings and watch me fall?

I stumble through my well-rehearsed speech, hoping that my impassioned plea for just a few more signatures is better received than how it feels to deliver. My voice doesn't seem loud enough, and my eyes are fervently surfing the audience looking for Brad, my stalwart supporter, who up until twenty-four hours ago wouldn't have missed this for the world. Though now, that world has turned upside down, and I honestly don't know how it will ever be upright again.

When I finish, the floor is opened to questions and I numbly answer them, as if on autopilot, because all I can think about is getting home to salvage the wreckage of my marriage.

"I don't think you're being entirely honest about your motivations here," booms a voice over the microphone.

A collective gasp ripples through the audience before an awkward silence descends.

"Ex-cuse me?" I say, sure that I must have misheard, but also because I need to hear her speak again.

"I just think she should be honest, is all," reverberates the woman's British accent around the conference hall.

She's here. The woman who seems intent on destroying my life is here. *But where?*

My mouth dries up and there's a pull at the back of my throat as I frantically search the hundreds of faces, as if in a race against time.

"I'm sorry," I say, willing myself to focus. "I don't understand . . ."

"I had the pleasure of your husband's company the other evening," she goes on.

I grip the lectern as my insides twist against each other, fighting to control the swell of nausea.

"And he was telling me that if this petition is passed, you stand to get a grant from the city council . . ."

Where is she? Where is she? Her voice is bouncing off the walls, but I can't see her.

"And in order to get the petition passed, you need to prove that the seals need protecting."

"The seals *do* need protecting," I counter, resisting the temptation to jump down onto the floor and blindly run around the auditorium to hunt down the faceless voice. "There are, on average, three public assaults on them every week. It is causing them great distress and impacting how they interact with human beings and each other."

"But creating a petition gives you more impetus in the community and a better chance of proving the point."

"What exactly is your agenda here?" I ask, even though I'm terrified of the answer.

"I want to be sure, before I sign this petition, that the seals' best interests are being preserved and that this isn't all part of a shameless money-grabbing exercise by someone who could use a little windfall."

There's a sharp intake of breath, but I can't tell if it's from me or the audience.

"I don't know what you're trying to imply," I say, my voice wavering ever so slightly. "But any money we receive will go directly toward ensuring the welfare of the colony."

"So *not* toward the extravagant holiday you've booked to Barbados later this year . . . ?"

My knuckles turn white as I picture the marine biology bachelor's degree that proudly hangs in my office. I didn't go back to school for four years and dedicate my life to the preservation of sea life to have it be suggested that I have an ulterior motive.

"What I do in my private life has nothing to do with the conservation effort, and it certainly has *nothing* to do with you."

"I just want to make sure that everything's out in the open," she says cryptically, as I lock my knees in an attempt to stop my legs from buckling.

"I have nothing to hide," I say, though the tremor in my voice and the viselike grip around my chest, squeezing my rib cage, would suggest otherwise.

23

"OK, go from the top of the chorus one more time," says Ben's producer friend Vaughan through Nicole's headphones.

Ben strums his guitar on the high stool beside her, counting her in.

"There are things I could never teach you, no matter how hard I try,
Because only you can decide how high you fly,
I can set you on your way and catch you if you fall,
But only you will know . . ."

"That's great!" says Vaughan. "But can we just try something? Will you humor me for three more minutes?"

Nicole nods, happy to give him all the time in the world because there's no place she'd rather be than here in this converted spice mill, making music. *With you,* she says to herself, looking at Ben.

She immediately gives herself a shake, refusing to follow the millions of other girls down that well-traveled road. She's not one of *them*. She's not Cassie, who fantasizes about being with someone she barely knows, naive to the fact that the life she covets is barely a life lived.

Because being around Ben is exhausting. Just last week, he'd been desperate to see the new *Police Academy* film and, despite Nicole's protestations, he'd insisted that she go with him.

"It'll be fine," he'd said, when she'd told him it was too risky. "It's the midnight showing, so there'll be no one around."

"It's not other people I'm worried about," she'd said. "It's the paps. They seem to be able to sniff you out a mile away."

Ben had smiled that lopsided smile of his, which despite herself had made Nicole's insides flutter. "If they want to run a picture of us, put two and two together and come up with five, that's fine by me."

"Oh, well as long as it's OK by *you*," said Nicole.

He'd pulled a face at her sarcastic tone. "Sorry, are you embarrassed to be seen with me?"

Nicole sighed. "No, but it's not always about you. Other people have lives they don't want splashed all over the front pages of the newspaper."

"Have you got a secret boyfriend who doesn't know about me?" he'd teased, sailing a little too close to the truth to be funny.

Aaron had stepped up his efforts to win her back in recent weeks, even going so far as to sit in on her set at Dallinger's and follow her home, begging her to give him another chance. His pining made her nervous, the thought of him finding out about Ben ever-present, though it didn't cause her quite as many sleepless nights as the thought of Cassie finding out.

"There's nothing *to* know," she said to Ben, shutting down the thoughts in her head. "We're making music—that's it."

"You know, most girls would go out of their way to get photographed with me," he said. "Some have even leaked where we're going to be, just for the exposure."

"Well, I'm not most girls."

Ben had smiled. "You think I don't know that?"

So, against Nicole's better judgment, she had agreed to Ben dropping her off outside the cinema on Curzon Street, before having his chauffeur drive around the block a few times to give her time to get the tickets and popcorn. Then Ben had rushed through the foyer, careful to avoid eye contact with anyone, and they'd sneaked into the back row just as the lights went down.

They'd giggled about their subterfuge once they were inside, but getting back out again was a different matter. He'd left first, expecting to be able to put his head down and get straight into the waiting car outside, but it seemed that word had got out. Because by the time the film had finished, there was a baying mob in the foyer who the management were having trouble controlling.

The screams had echoed around the still-dark cinema as Ben had opened the door, and Nicole had instinctively slid down into her seat, frightened by the noise but even more terrified that her cover would be blown. Not to the population of 56 million, but to the young girl sitting at home who would feel so utterly betrayed by her sister's deceit.

"OK, so Nicole, how do you feel about Ben leading on your mum's lines?" asks Vaughan from behind the glass partition.

Nicole screws up her face. "Like a duet, you mean?"

"I just want to hear how it sounds with a dual perspective," he says. "Because the words can so easily lend themselves to any parent talking to their child."

"But . . ." starts Nicole, stopping when she asks herself why not.

"It's just an idea," says Vaughan. "We don't have to do anything with it, but I think it's worth getting it laid down, even if it's just for yourselves."

Nicole looks at Ben, who shrugs his shoulders compliantly. "It might be fun to give it a go," he says.

The difference between singing all the words herself and splitting the lines with Ben brings out emotions that Nicole wouldn't have thought possible. Her fingertips tingle as they share a microphone, the spark between them so intimate that it feels as if they've transcended boundaries she hadn't even known she'd put up. When they finish, there's an electrically charged silence that weighs heavy in the air.

"Wow!" says Vaughan, breathlessly into their headphones.

Nicole shifts awkwardly, avoiding eye contact with Ben, even though it feels like they've just seen each other without their clothes on.

"Did you *feel* that?" asks Ben, looking at her, awestruck.

"No," she says quickly, needing to nip whatever that was—this is—in the bud.

Ben sighs as he gives a nod to Vaughan, who discreetly lets himself out of his soundproof box, disappearing from view.

"What are you so afraid of?" Ben asks, standing up.

"*Me?*" retorts Nicole. "I'm not afraid of anything—only the things I can't control."

He nods knowingly. "And you feel you can control *this?*"

Nicole bites down on her lip, refusing to let him see the resolve, which she's tried so hard to uphold these past few weeks, from slipping.

"You can't be so blind as to not see what's going on here?" he says, his eyes burning into her, offering no escape.

She wants to scream at him that *of course* she can feel it. She's felt it ever since he spoke to her at the bar, ever since she heard his voice on the phone, ever since he pulled her to him in the car. But she won't give in to it—*she can't.*

"You're not like any other girl I've ever met," he says, coming toward her.

She instinctively stiffens as she barricades herself behind invisible walls.

"You've got a real talent," he says, tucking a stray piece of copper-colored hair behind her ear. "You're going places . . ."

"And I suppose *you* think you're going to ride my coattails?" she says, laughing sarcastically.

"There you go *again*," he says. "Using humor to deflect a compliment or ward off anything you don't want to talk about."

He's standing so close that Nicole can feel the heat of his body against hers.

"I value your friendship and I wouldn't want to do anything to jeopardize it, but I think we're both fooling ourselves if we truly believe that's all this is."

A breath catches in Nicole's throat as she watches Ben's mouth move toward hers, as if in slow motion.

"*No, no, no!*" screams her head. "*Yes, yes, yes!*" cries every other part of her anatomy.

As his lips meet hers, she vaguely recalls thinking, "*It's just a kiss, a one-off—nothing more.*"

So how come they end up in bed together, back at her flat?

24

"Where the hell have you been?" her dad roars as Cassie quietly lets herself into the house just after ten. She was hoping he would be in bed by now, but he's sitting on the bottom of the stairs, waiting and aggrieved.

"I . . ." she starts, not quite prepared with a plausible excuse.

"Let me guess . . ." says her dad, his voice simultaneously loaded with rage and resignation. "You're about to tell me that you went straight to work from school."

Cassie's head nods even though she knows it's probably the wrong thing to do.

"Except you didn't go to school today, *did you?*"

What? How did he know that? Amelia had sounded a dead ringer for her mum when she called the headmistress this morning, claiming her daughter had been up all night with a sickness bug.

"Or work. So where *were* you?"

Cassie chews on the inside of her cheek as she deliberates how many lies are going to get her out of this. She *could* say that the school had got it wrong; that of course she was there. She *could* say that Woolworths had begged her to cover a staff shortage. She *could* say that her mum had given her permission to go and study in the local library instead of the classroom. What she can't tell him is that she spent the day at Amelia's house—well, more of a caravan on blocks in the middle of a field. She'd discovered that the mother Amelia claimed worried about her if she went to the corner shop had actually been so high that she didn't even know who her daughter was, opting to chase the dragon with two unsavory-looking men on the couch rather than question why Amelia wasn't in school.

With every peach schnapps she'd drunk, Cassie had found herself marveling at how cool it must be to have parents who didn't care what you did. But as day had turned to night, and Amelia's mum had passed out in a drug-induced stupor, she had started to wonder if being loved was better than being ignored.

"I'm sorry," Cassie says to her dad, knowing by the look on his face that it's best to be conciliatory. "It was Sports Day today and I didn't want to miss out on a whole day of studying, so I went to Amelia's house with my books." She picks up her heavy school bag, as if to prove her point, praying that she'd not left any rattling empties in there.

"Well, while you've been wherever you've been, your mum . . ." His shoulders convulse and his head falls into his hands.

"Mum *what*?" Her voice breaks, fear rendering her speechless. She races up the stairs, without waiting for an answer, tripping over herself in her efforts to get to her mother's bedroom.

In the soft light of the shaded bedside lamp, Gigi looks like she always does when she's asleep, serene and peaceful. But her skin is sallow, reflecting the light instead of absorbing it.

"Mum, can you hear me?" cries Cassie, begging her to answer, or to at least see the flicker of her eyelids—a sign of recognition when she doesn't have the energy to open them. But there's nothing.

She forces a trembling hand toward her mother's face, willing her fingers to feel the warmth of her cheeks. But she stops herself just millimeters away, terrified that she'll be met with stone-cold porcelain.

"What's *wrong* with her?" she wails, as if the deterioration is unexpected.

Her father appears by her side, reaching a hand out to hold hers. "It's time" is all he says.

"No!" sobs Cassie, falling into him.

"Now listen," he says, peeling her away and holding her at arm's length. "I need you to go over to your sister's to see if she's there. Her phone's been off the hook for the past couple of hours, so I can only assume she is. I don't know if she was intending to stay there tonight, but I need her to come here straightaway." He looks at her as she nods numbly. "OK?"

Cassie can't remember making the two-mile journey, the route thankfully hardwired into her brain.

The communal front door is on the latch, as it so often is, and the hall is thick with the pungent aroma of what the Victorian building's twelve residents had for their dinner—people who, on this normal Tuesday night, have no idea that a woman is dying just down the road; people who will wake up tomorrow morning and get on with their day, while Cassie's life will never be the same again.

As she reaches Nicole's first-floor flat, there's a low, pulsating beat of music drifting up from under the front door. Cassie stands there for a moment, listening to the dulcet tones of the duo singing, wanting to give Nicole a couple more seconds of life as she knows it.

She knocks quietly, hoping that Nicole won't hear; but, knowing she can't put off the inevitable forever, she knocks again, louder this time.

"Shh, there's somebody at the door," Cassie hears Nicole say.

Cassie can't help but feel incensed that, while their mother's life is ebbing away, Nicole is entertaining a random man in her flat instead of being at home, where she belongs. The irony that Cassie also wasn't where she should have been until thirty minutes ago is lost on her.

"Nicole!" she calls out, banging on the door with an open palm. "It's me, Cassie!"

The ensuing panic can be heard over the music, as feet clamber on the wooden floor, no doubt shuffling away evidence. When Nicole eventually opens the door, her face is angst-ridden.

"What are *you* doing here?" she asks, her tone accusatory as she peers out through a crack.

"It's Mum," says Cassie, her chest collapsing in on itself. "Dad wants you to come straightaway."

The color drains from Nicole's face as she bolts away from the door, leaving it swinging in her wake.

"Stay there," she calls out from the bedroom. "I need to get dressed."

Cassie has no intention of crossing the threshold, knowing that doing so will give her a view into the tiny flat's bedroom. She doesn't need to see who her sister was about to screw, if indeed she hasn't already, though the white pixie boots beside the tape deck indicate he might be cooler than some of her previous mistakes.

So instead, she stands at the doorway, listening to the music:

"There are things I could never teach you, no matter how hard I try, Because only you can decide how high you fly . . ."

A lump forms in the back of her throat as the lilting melody reaches into her soul; the poignant words resonate as if they were her own. But there's something even more than that, something recognizable that she can't quite put her finger on. It's not a song she's heard before, but the voices—they wrap themselves around her like a security blanket she didn't know she needed, their familiarity so comforting that she could just lie down right here and travel away with them to a place where death doesn't happen—to where good people get to live forever.

She checks herself as a completely ludicrous thought occurs to her. It seems insane to suggest it—because how could it even be possible? But the longer Nicole keeps her waiting, the more Cassie is convinced that the voice belongs to someone she knows.

"Is . . . is that *you*?" she asks when Nicole appears, falling over herself to get her pumps on.

"*What?*" she exclaims, patting down her unkempt hair. "Of course not."

"But it sounds . . ."

"How would that even be possible?" says Nicole, pushing Cassie out of the door, clearly flustered.

"You're not going to leave him there on his own, are you?" Cassie asks.

"Who?"

"Jesus, Nic, I'm not stupid."

Nicole grimaces.

"So, who is he then?" asks Cassie, more because she doesn't want to talk about their mum than because she's nosy.

"He's just someone from work," says Nicole.

"Is it serious?"

"No," says Nicole, far too quickly. But Cassie sees something in her eyes that she's not seen before and can't help but wonder why Nicole would lie.

25

The tires screech as I turn the car into the driveway and hit the brakes just as the hood touches the garage door. The house is in darkness, save for the soft glow of the hall lamp, and there's a part of me that hopes Brad isn't home. But then I pull myself up, because if he isn't, I can't bear to think about where else he might be.

A tremor of panic ripples through me when I call his name and there's no answer. What if he's left? What if tonight was orchestrated by him, as his final revenge for living a lifetime of secrets? Would he go that far?

An ice-cold shiver makes me shudder as I stand paralyzed, looking up the stairs. *Would he?* My instinct is to race to Hannah's room, such is my sudden desperation to see that she's there, but I calm my breathing, forcing my overactive mind into submission. Still, every tread feels like a mountain, and I grip hold of the banister for support.

The bedside lamp that Hannah is too scared to turn off casts a glow through the crack in the door, which she likes to have open, though ironically its muted light casts sinister shadows on the walls. I stifle the sob that tries to escape as I gently touch the Hannah-shaped mound under the quilt. Her copper-red hair fans across the pillow, and I brush it away from her face, unable to imagine a world where I'll never see it again.

I desperately want to climb in beside her and wrap my arms around her tiny body, vowing to keep her safe from harm. But I can't make a promise I might not be able to keep, and the realization of what I stand to lose makes tears spring to my eyes.

"I love you," I whisper, leaning down to give her the lightest of kisses.

I pause by the closed door of the spare room, my feelings of resentment and anger matched only by the abject sadness and grief of what Brad and I have lost. I wonder if he's lying in that single bed, thinking of the woman who seems intent on ruining my life. Because he *does* know her—of that there's no doubt.

Is the conscience, which he must surely have battled with, eased now that he knows I've betrayed his trust as much as he has mine? Has he spent the past however long mired in self-loathing for what he was doing to our happy family, only to be glad to be given a get-out clause by the secrets of my past?

As I look out of the landing window, I'm blindsided by the thought of Brad parked up outside the house every other Saturday, waiting for Hannah to bound down the path with her Rapunzel backpack over her shoulder; the classic broken family, fractured by lies, crushed by deceit, and who, like everyone else, thought it couldn't possibly happen to *them*.

"Where did you think I might have taken her?" asks a voice as I descend the stairs.

"Jesus!" I yelp, scanning the darkened kitchen like a startled animal before I manage to hit the light switch. My fright turns to fury when I see Brad sitting in a chair, nursing a beer.

We stare at each other, jaws fixed, weighing up who's going to make the next move. I chance my arm, hoping it will give me the upper hand. "Why don't you put us both out of our misery and just tell me who the fuck she is and what she wants?"

His head tilts and he looks at me as if genuinely perplexed.

"She was intent on ruining me out there tonight," I hiss, forcing myself to stay calm, more for Hannah's benefit than Brad's. If we were on our own, I'd be hurling saucepans at his head around about now.

I look at him, wanting to see something, *anything*, that might offer an explanation, but his face is like stone, giving nothing away. "Whatever it is that's going on between you two, why wouldn't you want to do it behind closed doors? Use discretion, like most people, instead of having your sordid secret being played out in front of the whole city. At least for Hannah's sake, if not mine."

He tsks condescendingly and I ready myself, frightened that he's going to tell me what I already know. That this is some kind of payback for the secrets I've held on to for all these years, for never allowing him a glimpse into my past for fear that he'll see that I'm not the person he thought I was.

But that doesn't make sense, because Brad didn't know who I really was until Zoe told him in the bar the other night. Whatever's going on must have started *before* Zoe turned up—well before he'd been given a window into my truth—and that's an even more bitter pill to swallow.

"So that's the way you're going to play this?" he says, his mouth pulling into a tight line as if to stop everything he wants to say from spilling out all at once. "You think making this *my* problem means you don't have to account for *your* actions."

"I would never hurt you," I manage.

"You already have!" he says.

I smart at the rawness of his voice. All I want to do is run, knowing that no good can ever come from this confrontation, but I force myself to stand tall and relinquish the baton.

"It happened long before I met you," I offer. "You can't possibly believe it gives *you* cause to destroy everything we've built since? Our home, our family, Hannah . . . our whole lives."

"So, *you* forget to mention that you were implicated in one of the most controversial trials of the century . . . and somehow *I'm* the bad guy?"

"I'm not the one who's broken our marriage vows."

He laughs hollowly. "Do you honestly think I'm having an affair?"

If I could believe he was as aggrieved as his expression belies, I'd say it was almost impossible, but I'm not going to allow myself to be fooled so easily.

"Well, isn't that what you were about to tell me last night? Why else would a woman take another's child, knowing that it would strike the fear of god into any mother? And why else would she turn up tonight, taking a wrecking ball to my reputation?"

He gets up and goes to the fridge, painfully slowly, as if he's enjoying my unease, even though it should be *him* who's feeling the heat searing through his veins. I bat away the same oppressive sensation and chew the inside of my cheek as I wait for him to get another beer, open it, and sit back down again. His calmness unnerves me—it's as if he's waiting to reveal the ace up his sleeve.

"So, are you going to tell me who she is, or not?"

The way he looks at me sends chills down my spine. He looks nothing like the man I've loved unreservedly for the past twenty years. But then, I imagine I look very different to him as well.

"I met her in a bar in town."

My mouth immediately dries up, my throat feeling like it's lined with knives.

"She was on her own, looking for company, so I offered to buy her a drink."

The irony of his wedding band clinking against the side of the beer bottle, as he taps it thoughtfully, is not lost on me.

"And you somehow fell into bed together," I sneer.

"Do you want to stop talking and listen for a minute?" he snaps.

For a man who's been unfaithful, his demeanor is more accusatory than conciliatory. And after twenty years of what I honestly thought was a good marriage, I wouldn't have believed that he had it in him to behave this way, but I should know better. Because people always show their true colors when their backs are up against the wall.

"So how many times has it been? What does she give you that I don't? Are you in love with her?" The questions all come tumbling out in a deluge of insecure loathing—for myself as much as him. How had I not seen it? How could he do this to me? *To us?*

"Jesus! Will you just stop for a second?" he says, putting his hands on his head and turning to walk toward the French doors overlooking the yard we've spent our marriage lovingly cultivating. "I'm *not* sleeping with her."

I laugh cynically. "Well, you *would* say that, *wouldn't* you?"

I watch his back as his shoulders tense against the material of his shirt. "Not if it were true and I wanted out of our marriage, no!"

"So, what is it then?" I ask, confused. "What does she want?"

"I don't know," he says, turning to face me. "But she seemed more interested in talking about *you* than getting into bed with me."

I shake my head in an effort to sharpen the blurred lines. "Wh-what do you mean?" I dare to ask, as the foreboding sense that my past is coming back to haunt me returns with a vengeance.

"Well, we spoke for a while, passing the time of day with idle chat, and when I went to call it a night, she told me that my wife wasn't the person I thought she was."

I allow myself a smirk, as the first ripples of relief edge their way into my veins. "And you took that personally?" I exclaim incredulously. "It sounds as if she was horny, saw the wedding ring on your finger, and would say anything to ease your conscience."

"Mmm," he muses. "I thought so, too . . . until she mentioned your name."

My fingertips tingle, and I feel lightheaded as a rush of blood and adrenaline flood my body. "A lot of people know my name," I retort.

He nods, as if that would make sense. "Except she seemed to know more than just that, because she said you couldn't be trusted."

"Well, you know that's not true," I start, before remembering that I'm no longer living the life I was this time last week.

"And now, I realize that she had a point," he says, finishing the sentence.

The ground feels like it's falling away, the rock-solid foundations that I'd painstakingly built now crumbling around my ears. The years that I'd spent trying to be the best version of myself—the one I was always meant to be, *until Ben*—fall by the wayside, as I'm forced to admit that what happened back then *was* the real me. The good wife I've strived to be, and the perfect mother I've endeavored to mold myself into, is an imposter who has been hiding in plain sight. The realization crushes me.

"I'm still me," I offer. "I'm still the woman you fell in love with . . ."

Brad tilts his head to one side, looking at me as if questioning the validity of the statement.

"And who is *she*?" he hisses, scathingly. "Because she's certainly not the same woman that's all over the internet."

He laughs, as if berating himself for being so stupid, and it breaks my heart. "I mean, how could I not have known that my wife of twenty years was a redhead?" He shakes his head. "It's those secrets you kept from me that hurt the most. I thought we knew everything about each other, yet here I am, all this time later, with a wife who felt it necessary to hide her natural hair color from me."

"Brad, I wasn't hiding it from *you*, I was hiding it from myself. I didn't want to be constantly reminded of the person I once was."

"*And who were you, Nicole?*"

My jaw spasms involuntarily as I force myself to look at him. "Look, we can sit down and go through everything that you've read."

"It's not what's written about the case that I'm interested in—it's what's *not* written that bothers me. Because it seems that, despite you supposedly telling 'the whole truth and nothing but the truth' in court"—he floats speech marks in the air with his fingers—"the media didn't believe you."

"*I* wasn't the one on trial," I snap, unable to stop the barrage of images from battering my senses—the salacious headlines, the annihilation of my character in the courtroom, fans protesting, calling for justice.

"Well, maybe you should have been, because if you're able to keep secrets *this* easily . . ." He leaves the sentence there as he raises his eyebrows questioningly.

"You have *no* idea what happened," I hiss.

"I know that you were *there* that day—that you were treated as a suspect!"

"And quickly eliminated."

He shrugs his shoulders, but nothing about his body language is blasé. "I need to know what I'm dealing with," he says.

"Meaning?" I say, unable to believe the shift in the conversation. How am *I* being made out to be the villain here? *Maybe because you are*, a voice says in the back of my head.

"I've got Hannah to think about," Brad goes on.

"Don't you fucking dare!" I spit, restraining myself from taking the beer bottle from the side and smashing it over his head. Maybe he's got a point.

"I just need to make sure she's safe," he says, pushing me to my limit.

"She's as safe now as she's ever been," I seethe. "Nothing's changed apart from you finding out why I really left England."

"And so it has nothing to do with the tragic death of your sister?"

I eye him warily, unable to predict where he's going with this.

"Well, of course, that didn't help. It was a lot to take on, and it all happened within a matter of months."

He attempts to display a sympathetic expression, but its sincerity falls woefully short.

"It must have been so very hard for you," he says.

His tone has a biting iciness to it, and I shrug nonchalantly to offset the toxicity that's permeating the charged atmosphere. But inside, I feel like a fox being chased by hounds, and I almost want to give myself up so that I can be put out of my misery.

"It was," is all I feel safe saying.

Brad nods and puts his hands on his hips. "So, that's it? I know all there is to know; there's nothing more you need to tell me . . ."

My heart stops. *This is it.* This is my chance to put it all on the table, to be honest with the man I love so that I can stop running from the truth.

His eyes burrow deep into my soul, urging me to do the right thing, even though he can't possibly know if I don't.

Just tell him, I say to myself, taking a deep breath to bolster my wavering resolve.

"Well . . . ?" he implores, his impatience testing *him* as much as my abject fear is testing *me*.

I go to open my mouth, fully intending to tell him everything he doesn't already know, except . . . "That's it" comes out instead.

Brad's nostrils flare and his eyes blacken, turning his features into somebody I don't recognize.

"I gave you the chance to be honest."

"I have been!" I exclaim. "There's nothing more to tell!"

He glares at me as if I'm a stranger or, even worse, someone he's grown to hate.

"So, can you please explain why the very sister who supposedly died twenty-five years ago has just been on the phone wanting a reunion?"

26

"I'm *so* sorry," says Ben, when Nicole calls to tell him that her mother has died after three days in hospital. "Is there anything I can do?"

She considers the options, but knows that nothing and no one can bring her back. The realization floors her.

"I just feel so . . . so empty," she whispers, wrapping the phone cord around her finger as she sits on the carpet, resting her head on the dining room wall. "I mean, there's a physical hole within me that I can't ever see being filled again."

"I wish I was there with you," he says dourly. "I hate that you're dealing with this on your own."

Nicole sighs heavily, painfully aware of the Atlantic Ocean that stretches out between them.

"Have you made any arrangements for the funeral?"

"I'm supposed to be going with Dad to the undertakers tomorrow, but I don't know that I can face it. It feels too soon to be making decisions."

"I know this sounds crazy, but it might give you something to focus on . . ." he says. "Rather than torture yourself with your memories, you can put them to good use: Have you thought about singing your song at the service?"

The idea catches Nicole off guard. She's been biding her time, thinking she had some to spare in which to play her mum the song she's written for her. But the days and weeks have been cruelly snatched away, and the thought that she'll now never get to hear it crushes Nicole's insides.

"Are you going to accompany me on guitar?" she says, forcing a laugh in a bid to stave off the tsunami of tears that are gathering at the back of her throat.

"I'd be happy to," he says, without irony.

"Can you imagine?" says Nicole. "We arrange a classy, somber occasion, and then *you* pitch up and it turns into a media circus." They laugh, the pair of them equally more comfortable to explore this line of conversation than the alternative. "Mind you, knowing Mum, she'd probably revel in that. She was always very proud of her groupie status."

"I wish I could have met her," he says.

It's the simplest of statements—an auto-response for someone in his position—but the absolute impossibility of it ever happening makes Nicole's shoulders convulse.

"I'm sorry," says Ben, as she stifles her sobs. "That was insensitive."

"It's fine," says Nicole, sniffing. "Anyway, how's it all going over there?"

Seeing Secret Oktober take America by storm had been a welcome distraction these past few days. The ten o'clock news had eulogized about how Britain's latest export had the Yanks eating out of their hands, and yesterday's paper had pictures of screaming girls chasing the band's limousines down the street, one of whom had been rushed to hospital after her foot was caught under a wheel. It's on the tip of Nicole's tongue to tell Ben that he's beginning to make a habit of it, but she stops herself, not yet ready to share that her little sister proudly displays the same war wound to anyone who asks.

"It's pretty crazy," says Ben. "American fans are something else."

The line crackles and his voice becomes distant, bringing a lump to Nicole's throat. It has only been six weeks since he quite literally walked into her life, but she misses him beyond belief, though she's aware that her emotions are heightened to every sensation right now.

"Listen to this," he says. There are a few seconds of silence before a thunderous roar of hysterical screams rings down the line. "That's what happens whenever I stick my head out of the hotel window."

The juxtaposition of their lives has never been more apparent than right here in this moment, and Nicole wonders for the millionth time how anything can possibly come of the relationship they've convinced themselves they have. *His* days are filled with new experiences, new places, new people, while hers are spent grieving for the life that's been lost. While he's appearing alongside Madonna at Madison Square Garden, Nicole is waiting tables in a grotty restaurant. And as he revels in worldwide adulation, she can't even tell her own sister that she's met him.

"It sounds insane," she says, trying her best not to show the insecurities evoked by him having the pick of hundreds of girls.

"It's all a game," he'd said once, when she'd asked him how often he had sex with fans. "I might tease them, make them think they have a chance, that I would if I could . . . but I'd never go there."

"Don't you think that's a little cruel?" Nicole had asked.

"It works both ways. I'm under no illusions—I know that if I was working in the local pub, none of these girls would give me a second look."

"So, you've *never* taken advantage of your . . . situation?" she asked, for want of a better word.

He'd looked away, as if embarrassed. "I didn't say that! I used to—when we first started out, when I honestly believed that they were there because they liked me." He laughed. "I couldn't believe my luck: I'd gone from the geeky fella at school, who everyone thought was weird because I was in a crap band and spent all my spare time rehearsing in my parents' garage, to this stud muffin who was literally having girls throw themselves at him."

"I hate to break it to you . . ." Nicole had started with a pained expression.

"Yeah, yeah, I know," he said smiling. "It wasn't really me they were after at all. They just wanted the dream—the man they saw on stage—who I could never live up to."

"That, and the accolade of being able to say they'd slept with you," said Nicole.

"Exactly!" he exclaimed. "So, who was using who?"

He had a point.

"Is everybody behaving themselves?" Nicole asks now, knowing how keen Ben is to make a good impression on the American public.

He lets out a heavy sigh. "Michael's doing his usual: entertaining unsavory individuals, burning the midnight oil . . ."

"He needs to be careful," she warns.

"You think I don't know that?" he snaps.

Nicole can't help but be taken aback by his tone. While she can empathize with his frustration, she'd not borne the brunt of it before.

"I'm sorry," he says. "I didn't mean to . . ."

"It's OK," she says, letting him off just this once. She can't imagine how difficult it must be having to manage Michael, tiptoeing around him to avoid upsetting the equilibrium of the band.

"It's just exhausting," Ben goes on. "It's like babysitting a naughty toddler."

"Maybe something needs to give."

"What do you suggest?" asks Ben, glibly. "A media exposé? A spell in rehab?"

Nicole hadn't really thought about it. "Maybe sit down, as a band, and air your grievances once and for all. Get your feelings out in the open so that you're not constantly feeling like you're waiting for the hammer to fall."

Ben sighs. "I'm afraid that if I do something like that right now, I'll say something I'll regret."

"What can you possibly say that will make anything worse than it already is?"

There's a moment's silence. "That if he doesn't sort himself out, I'm going to leave."

There's a sharp intake of breath, but Nicole doesn't know if it came from her or him at the unexpected admission.

"But you love what you do," she says.

"I used to," he says. "But Michael seems intent on destroying everything we've created, and I'm not going to be left standing on a sinking ship."

"But you're on the precipice of cracking America," says Nicole. "You can't let him control your future—Secret Oktober is your life."

"I dunno," he says despondently. "Sometimes it feels like my only choice—that I'm going to have to take decisive action before somebody else does it for me."

If either of them had heard the click as the extension phone was put down, they would have known that it would happen sooner than they could possibly have imagined.

27

"Where's Daddy?" asks Hannah, coming into what used to be our bedroom. Our safe haven, where we hid from the world—at least until a week ago, when the world decided it was coming to find us.

"He had to leave for work super early," I lie, wondering if there's anything in the room that might suggest to an eight-year-old that he hadn't slept here at all.

I don't blame him for leaving. We both need time and space to get our heads around the secrets we'd kept and the lies we'd told. Well, the secrets *I'd* kept and the lies *I'd* told. But as he slammed the door, I doubted that he'd ever come back. Our problems seemed too insurmountable, our issues too deep-rooted to overcome. How can we move forward when he knows even less about his wife now than he did this time last week? This new version paints a very different picture to the original he's been admiring for all these years.

"M-my sister called? *Here?*" I'd floundered when he dropped the bombshell last night.

"Are you shocked because she got our number, or that she's come back from the dead?" Brad had said, his tone dripping with sarcasm and vitriol.

"I . . . I . . ."

"What the *fuck* is going on, Nicole?" he'd spat, unable to contain his fury any longer. "How is none of what I know about you true anymore?"

"Brad . . ." I'd said, going toward him with open arms.

"Don't!" he'd yelled, before storming out.

His bitter dejection still weighs heavily on my chest.

"What woke *you* up so early?" I ask, patting his side of the bed as Hannah climbs in.

"The phone in your office," she says, contentedly snuggling into the pillow. "It wouldn't stop ringing."

Confused, I reach over to my mobile on the nightstand and sit bolt upright when I see more than ten missed calls and voicemails. It must have been on silent.

On seeing Hank's name appear more than once, my stomach lurches and I instinctively turn to check that Hannah is, in fact, safely nestled in my bed. I head to the bathroom, quietly closing the door behind me as I wonder what could possibly have happened, because having the police chief call this many times at this early hour can only mean that something is wrong.

An all-consuming nausea threatens to overwhelm me as I force myself to recall the look on Brad's face as he left last night. It wasn't anger, it wasn't guilt, it was a gut-wrenching sadness and disappointment. Disappointment that I wasn't the woman he thought I was. The woman I'd made him believe I was.

I grip the sides of the basin as my phone rings again, its shrill tone reverberating around the windowless four walls.

"Nicole?" says Hank, when I eventually pluck up the courage to answer. "I need you to come up to La Jolla."

I can't bring myself to ask why. I can only numbly hang up, call

Barbara across the street on autopilot and pass her at the door as she comes in to look after Hannah.

The fifteen-minute drive is tortuous, as image after image assaults my senses, making me question everything I know about the man I married. Would he be so hurt that he'd do something so finite? Would he be so selfish as to leave a child who adored him? Would he be so malevolent as to do it *here*—in a place that has always been so sacred to both of us?

There's a small crowd looking on in horror from behind a cordoned-off area, keeping them off the beach; the irony that this was the very thing I was appealing for last night is not lost on me. I steel myself for whatever I'm about to witness, but nothing could have prepared me for the sea of red that assaults my senses.

"It's OK," says Hank. "It's not what you think . . ."

"Wh-what . . . ?" I start, as he gently steers me down to the once-golden sands.

"It's spray paint," he says, at pains to pull my tortured mind back from thinking it was the blood of slain seals. "We got a call at four o'clock this morning from a concerned local resident who was woken by the seals barking. She said it was much louder than normal and they sounded panicked."

"B-but . . . I can't even . . ." I stutter. "Why . . . why would anybody do this?"

Hank shakes his head. "It's the world we live in: The youngsters are bored and looking for entertainment, and some warped individuals think this is it."

Too angry to cry, a furious heat creeps up my neck and I clench my fists.

"I just don't understand who would do this," I say, imagining a crowd of students from the nearby college getting so drunk or high that they couldn't possibly account for their actions this morning.

"Well, that's the thing," says Hank. "The only way I can even begin to get my head around this is to believe that it must have been a moment of madness. That some louse, in his heightened state, thought it would somehow be a laugh."

"But . . . ?"

"*But*," says Hank, the unease etched into every furrow on his brow, "there seems to be a specific message they wanted to get across."

I follow him to a half-submerged rock, where four full-sized male seals perch on high-alert, the little trust they had for the human species now shattered once and for all.

"It's impossible to piece together, but there are random words that might mean something to someone, and if we can find out *who*, we might be able to track down the perpetrator."

Although the words daubed onto the animals' fur don't form a sentence, it doesn't take me long to see a pattern forming.

"*LIAR*," "*MURDERER*," "*FRAUD*" are just some that I can read, but it's not until a female seal hobbles to the water's edge that I catch sight of a capital "*B*" emblazoned across her back. I can't yet see the rest of the word. I half-run toward her, doing my utmost not to spook the colony any more than they have been already, but if we have any chance of catching whoever did this, I need as much information as possible.

"I've not noticed this one yet," says Hank, close on my heels.

"We've got to hope that something they've written will give us a clue as to what this is all about," I say. "Because someone clearly has an axe to grind and won't have gone to all this trouble for it to fall on deaf ears."

"Could it be political?" he moots.

"I would have thought it's going to have *something* to do with the city council decision next week," I offer. "I spoke about it at a conference last night, and it seems like too much of a coincidence for it not to be connected." I don't tell him that it's one of many.

"B . . . E . . ." Hank reads aloud as the seal nears the first wave-break. "Is that *BE-ACH*?" he questions, sounding disappointed. "Or *BE-WARE*? Maybe it's a threat of some kind . . ."

I attempt to get closer, knowing I only have a second or two to see what someone so clearly wants to be read. But when I see "*N*" as the third and final letter, my blood turns icy cold and, as the seal disappears beneath the surface, taking my secret with her, I realize that this isn't about the petition *or* politics. This is about me.

28

"What's wrong?" asks Nicole, as Cassie rushes into her bedroom, sobbing.

"I-I . . . just never thought . . ." she cries, as Nicole puts an arm around her. "I never thought he would do this."

"Shh, it's OK," soothes Nicole, sitting down next to her on the bed. "What's he done now?"

It occurs to Cassie that Nicole thinks their father is responsible for her tears. She shows her the newspaper to put her straight.

"*STAR LICKED COCAINE OFF MY BREASTS,*" the headline screams. "*Secret Oktober star in drugs rap—could this be the end of their world takeover attempt?*"

Nicole stares at the front page, her muscles twitching in an effort to keep her face expressionless.

"What's this?" she says, her tone clipped and abrupt.

"It's Ben," Cassie blurts out.

Nicole shakes her head. "Ben?" His name comes out as a throaty gargle.

Cassie nods fervently. "The guy from Secret Oktober who I've been mad about since forever."

Nicole's cheeks instantly flush as she goes to pick the newspaper up before seemingly thinking better of it. "What's he . . . What's he done?"

"It's a four-page blow-by-blow account of how he's screwed some model in America," cries Cassie bitterly.

Nicole gets up from the bed and walks across to the window overlooking the tree-lined avenue below.

"And that's a problem because . . . ?" she says eventually, after she's needlessly adjusted the net curtains.

"You just don't get it," says Cassie, as her head falls into her hands. "This could be the end of *everything*."

Nicole forces a laugh. "Don't you think you're being a little melodramatic? They're some crappy band who you've clearly developed an unhealthy obsession with."

"It's so much more than that," says Cassie. "I'd have thought you, of all people, would understand."

Nicole's jaw spasms. "And why would you think that?" she says through gritted teeth.

Cassie considers her, wondering how much she should share. If she tells her everything, the unbreakable bond she thought would forever join them will be severed, neither of them able to trust the other again. But isn't it already too late?

"Me and Ben . . . we . . ."

Nicole looks at her little sister with raised eyebrows. Cassie knew this would get her attention.

"We've got this thing . . ." she goes on.

"*Thing?*" questions Nicole.

"I know you think I'm just a kid living in a fantasy world, but what I have with the band has transcended that, and what I have with Ben is something even more—or at least I thought it was, until this!" Cassie picks up the offending article and slams it back down for effect. "I know there's always other girls hanging around him, trying their luck, but he promised me before he left that he wouldn't be tempted—that he wouldn't risk what we have . . ."

Nicole circles the tiny room and Cassie can almost hear her brain's cogs and wheels turning as she tries to figure out how best to approach this.

"What you *have*?" she probes. "What do you mean?"

"We've been seeing each other for the past two months," says Cassie. "It's been a bit on and off because it's really hard to hold down any kind of relationship when he does what he does—he's rarely here and, when he is, we can't be seen together because he's not allowed to be in a serious relationship, but we had something good going on behind closed doors." Her lips draw to a thin line, bitterness exuding from her with every syllable. "Or at least I thought we did."

An involuntary torrent of air rushes out of Nicole as she stands there, open-mouthed and poleaxed.

"Please don't be mad," begs Cassie. "I've got enough to deal with without having to go up against you as well."

"You're deluded," says Nicole. "This 'thing' you think you have is all in your head. It's not real, and the sooner you realize that the better. You should be going out with people your own age, meeting boys at school, not wasting your time pining over something that's never going to happen."

A searing heat prickles Cassie's extremities, her indignation at Nicole's poorly chosen words seeping out of every pore. How dare she? An inside force wants to launch itself across the room, to show Nicole who the deluded one really is, but Cassie uses every ounce of her restraint not to, knowing that it won't serve any purpose to let her sister know how hurt she truly is.

"You're wrong" is all she says, through gritted teeth.

Nicole snorts. "The likes of Ben Edwards don't live in the real world. They're fantasies created to give girls like you a warped perspective on what a normal boy is like, what a normal relationship is like. Just because you've got his posters all over your bedroom wall and his car once ran over your foot doesn't make him your boyfriend."

"I'm not a child," says Cassie, infuriated by her sister's patronizing tone. "And I'm not stupid. I know the difference, and what Ben and I have *is* different."

Nicole throws the paper a dirty look, as if the object itself has offended her.

Cassie picks it up and turns to the first double-page spread, where Ben is pictured, bleary-eyed, leaving a club with a scantily clad blond draped on his arm. "I mean, I can almost forgive him for the girl," she says, pushing it toward Nicole, who can't help but blanch. "But I can't get my head around the drugs. I don't understand why he'd take the risk, when he's already skating on thin ice."

"I thought they were the goody-two-shoes of pop," she says, as if fishing for information. "This is all news to me."

Cassie imagines it is. "It's not common knowledge, but Ben's already been cautioned."

"Has he?" says Nicole, her voice wavering. "When?"

"It doesn't matter," says Cassie, hoping her reticence to divulge any more information will make Nicole feel even more compelled to press. "I shouldn't have said anything—I don't want to betray Ben's trust."

"No, come on," says Nicole. "You obviously think you know something."

Cassie takes a deep breath, as if she's mulling over whether to say anything more. "OK, but you really mustn't tell anyone." She looks to Nicole, who offers a stilted nod. "So, a couple of months ago there was an after-party at the Savoy. There were lots of drinks and drugs and everyone was having a good time. But just after midnight, the police turned up and raided the place. Ben doesn't know whether they got a tip-off, but they hauled everyone down to the police station—those they could catch, anyway—to determine who supplied the drugs and who took them."

The more she says, the more deflated Nicole seems to become, as if someone has taken the valve out that keeps her upright. "That sounds like the rumor mill has gone into overdrive," she says. "You shouldn't believe everything you hear."

"I didn't *hear* it," says Cassie, pausing for effect. "I *saw* it."

Nicole laughs. "Right, so you were there the night it all went down, the night that Michael did a runner."

Cassie cocks her head to one side and narrows her eyes. "How do you know Michael did a runner?"

"What?" Nicole stops in her tracks and laughs nervously. "You just told me."

Cassie knows she didn't. She'd gone to great lengths not to. "Ben and I were there together, doing what young people do . . . until the police turned up, that is."

Nicole tsks as if it's of no consequence to her, but a blood-red stain is creeping up her neck, a sure sign that it means more to her than it should. "So, you reckon you've been seeing him since then?" she can't help but ask.

Cassie nods. "We have to be careful, as his reputation relies on him being single, but I was with him at his album launch, I went to the MCA Awards with him last week . . ."

Nicole blows out her cheeks and looks at her sister as if she's lost her mind.

"There'll no doubt be footage of us somewhere," says Cassie. "Because we walked the red carpet together before realizing there were TV cameras there."

"This is all a figment of your overactive imagination," barks Nicole. "You need to stop this madness right now, because if Dad finds out . . ."

"He already knows," says Cassie, almost enjoying herself.

"Wh-what?" splutters Nicole, her voice high-pitched.

"He came to the police station to pick me up."

29

There are a million reasons why Nicole won't take Ben's calls; she's even gone as far as unplugging the phone from the wall so as not to risk Cassie or her dad picking it up. But if she thought she could get away from the maelstrom that surrounded the tabloid story, she is sorely mistaken.

"I'd let him lick whatever he wanted off me," sighs a schoolgirl as she stands over the newspaper in the corner shop on the fourth day of revelations.

"Imagine looking down and seeing those eyes staring back at you," says her friend.

"Yeah, he's got fuck-me eyes if ever I saw them," giggles another.

"Ten JPS, please," says Nicole to the newsagent, biting her tongue to stop her from telling the girls how ridiculous they sound, even if everything they're saying is true.

She pulls herself up short, furious that she's still unable to hate Ben for what he's done. She's not yet allowed her emotions to fully comprehend how far his tentacles of deceit have reached, or what hurts her the most. But what she *does* know is that she is so bitterly disappointed in herself for allowing him to reel her in—enticing her with a shared love of music; then, just as she'd lowered her defenses, he'd pounced when she'd been at her most vulnerable. Much like he does with every girl he meets, she suspects—even her own sister, whose far-fetched story she still refuses to believe, though she can't get away from the fact that if it could happen to her, it could happen to Cassie.

As soon as she'd left her flat the other day, Nicole had ripped the newspaper into pieces, her fury knowing no bounds, until an hour later when she pathetically taped it all back together again.

Every single word of the girl's story had felt like a dagger in Nicole's heart. She'd boasted about how she and Ben had shared lines of cocaine after a drink-fueled party, bragged that they'd had mind-blowing sex three times, and that he'd called her again the next day for a repeat performance.

Minute by minute, step by step, every intimate detail had been spread across four pages, but as much as it hurt, Nicole kept reading, so sure that, by the end, it would be apparent that the liaison had happened months ago, before she and Ben had met.

She wasn't delusional enough to think that someone like Ben hadn't had more than his fair share of lovers and encounters; he'd told her as much. And it was unrealistic to believe that one or two of those wouldn't crawl out of the woodwork as soon as he hit the big time, desperate to claim their fifteen minutes of fame and a two-grand payday.

But ever since he'd held her that first night they'd made love, promising to keep her safe and telling her that he will always come back to her, she's believed that they would each forgo all others. That's the pact they'd made. That's the promise he'd given her. Yet now it seems there are most likely a horde of "special" girls, including the one he slept with on the very first night he was in America.

"I met him once," says one of the girls in the newsagent's, her voice infiltrating Nicole's eardrums despite her doing everything to keep it out. "A couple of years ago, when he was just starting out and signed to the record company that my dad worked for. And even then, he had that look in his eyes . . . like he could get anyone he wanted."

"He wouldn't be wrong though, would he?" giggles her friend as they make their way out of the shop, unaware of the profound effect their banal conversation is having on Nicole.

Ben had denied all the accusations pitted against him in an interview a couple of days later. But the die was already cast. The six o'clock news ran a segment on the golden-boy-band's "fall from grace," citing the fact that there were more police than fans at the airport to send them on their way back to England. "Perhaps it was to make sure they got on the plane," joked the newsreader, who had been fawning all over them in the studio just a few days earlier.

John's nostrils had flared as he'd shot a warning look at Cassie, leaving Nicole's overactive imagination to wonder if her little sister's claims were true, as preposterous as they were. She'd wanted to ask her dad what he knew, because there was no doubt that *something* had happened the night of the concert, the night of the drugs raid. Cassie had stayed out late, their worried father had needed to call Nicole, and Cassie had been grounded. But Nicole didn't want to reopen old wounds, and besides, she didn't actually want to hear the answer because she was happier in denial.

But it still doesn't stop the "what ifs" and "maybes" from playing on a loop inside her head, laughing in the face of her insomnia as she tosses and turns each night. The more she tries to rid herself of the picture of Ben and Cassie together, or him snorting cocaine off the kiss-'n'-tell girl's body, the more graphic the image becomes.

Even though they'd only been together for six weeks, it had felt like years, such was the bond they shared. But if it had meant nearly as much to him as it had meant to her, he wouldn't have done what he did. And if he *didn't* do it, she should know him well enough to know that too. But she doesn't, and that is perhaps the most painful realization of all.

Giving in to a sleepless night, she reaches over and switches on her bedside lamp. But instead of the peach-tinted lightbulb calming her with its warm tones, it casts a light that makes her feel more alone than ever: Everywhere she looks, there are reminders of Ben, even though his face is nowhere to be seen. The locked diary they'd written lyrics in sits redundantly on her bedside table, and the bottle of Poison perfume that he bought her stands on her dressing table. When she looks down, she sees that she's wearing his T-shirt—she can't even remember putting it on—but although she so desperately wants to sniff it, to breathe in the smell of him, she denies herself the pleasure, knowing it will be painfully short-lived.

A tapping noise makes her sit up, her ears more finely tuned after having to endure the cries of her mother calling out in the middle of the night as she pushed her way through the pain barrier. As selfish as it seems, Nicole wishes that she could still hear those anguished sobs, instead of the never-ending silence that has permeated every corner of the house since her mother has been gone.

There's another tap, against the window, as if the branches of the tree outside are reaching across and gently knocking on the glass. But there's little wind and as Nicole gets up and pulls the curtain aside, she finds the tree standing perfectly still.

The darkness of the road below is illuminated by the amber glow of the streetlight, and as she peers out to see past it she jumps as another *crack* makes it sound as if the glass is splintering.

It's then that she sees him, waving his arms above his head in the shadows.

"What the . . . ?" she says aloud, before snatching up her dressing gown from the chair.

She gently pulls the door to her father's bedroom closed and tiptoes down the stairs, taking care to avoid the creaking third tread.

As she studies the blurred silhouette through the frosted glass of the front door, it occurs to her that she may have jumped to the wrong conclusion. Surely Ben wouldn't have the gall to come here in the middle of the night.

"Nic, open up," comes his instantly recognizable voice, much too loud for Nicole's liking. "Please—just give me a minute."

She *has* to let him in for no other reason than not to wake Cassie and her dad, but moreover, she has to hear him out, if only to satisfy the sadistic streak in her that needs to be told that the relationship she thought they had was never anything more than a sick ploy by him to take advantage of her. He's clearly used to getting what he wants, however debauched, and she's almost grateful that he hadn't asked her for anything more than to love him the only way she knew how.

"You can't be here," she hisses, keeping the chain on the door.

"Just give me two minutes," he begs.

"I can't do this," says Nicole. "I've got way more important things to be thinking about than you."

"I know, and I'm sorry that you're having to deal with this on top of everything else. But if you'll just give me a chance to explain . . ."

"There's nothing you can possibly say that will justify what you've done," she says, close to tears.

"None of it's true," he says. "You have to believe me—I would never do that to you."

She laughs acerbically. "You've done it to yourself," she says. "And you'll never know how much it's cost you."

"I don't even know the girl who's said this stuff," he says.

"You looked pretty cozy in the pictures."

"The photos were of an ex-girlfriend who I haven't seen in over a year," he says, his voice cracking. "That's what the papers do—put words with pictures of people who have nothing to do with the story."

"So, the article is completely made up, is it?"

"Well, whoever it is hasn't been brave enough to be photographed, has she? Anyone could say that shit if they're not going to be identified. It could be a disgruntled fan, it could even be a journalist having a slow news day—they don't have to be held accountable, yet my life can be ruined. How is that fair?"

Just for a moment, Nicole gives him the benefit of the doubt, knowing that if he takes enough rope, he'll only hang himself if he's lying.

"I didn't do it," he says, looking at her imploringly. "You have to believe that I would never do anything to hurt you."

"You haven't just hurt *me*," says Nicole, her voice breaking. "Look what you've done to yourself—to the band. The woman is one thing, but the *drugs*."

He looks at the floor, shaking his head. "I haven't taken cocaine in over a year and I haven't slept with another girl since meeting you."

Nicole tsks and turns away, needing to gather herself. Even if the kiss-'n'-tell is a lie, what about Cassie? And every other girl she doesn't know about?

"After the article dropped, the police turned up at our hotel with a warrant to search our rooms. It goes without saying that despite their best efforts, they didn't find anything in mine."

Nicole looks at him, wide-eyed with expectancy before the penny drops: "Michael." His name comes out in a rush of breath.

Ben sucks on his teeth as he looks away, his pent-up frustration oozing from every pore.

"So . . . so, what's going to happen to him? To *you*?"

"They were going to make an example of him, that's for sure. But our manager spoke to them and they came to a compromise."

"How many times are you going to let him get away with this?" asks Nicole, knowing it's not really her place, but finding it increasingly difficult to understand how Michael is seemingly able to run roughshod over everything Secret Oktober has set out to do.

"It won't happen again," he says. "This is the last time, and he knows it."

Nicole doesn't suppose it matters—at least not to her. She was a fool to think that this could ever work. The odds are so heavily stacked against them, the obstacles so high to climb, that she convinces herself it can't possibly be worth it.

"I can't do this," she says, going to shut the door. "I don't want you to contact me again."

"Don't say that," he says, putting his foot out to stop her. "You're the best thing that's ever happened to me."

She bites down on her lip to stop from calling out as a visceral pain tears through her. It feels like her heart is bleeding and her blood is being pumped around her body in the wrong direction, sending her organs into shock. She tries to reason that nothing can possibly be physically wrong with her, but how can it not be, when everything hurts so much?

30

The onslaught on social media is brutal. Faceless keyboard warriors are questioning my motivation for setting up the foundation, while others are posting quotes from my speech at the convention center last night, calling for an investigation into my business practices and eligibility for a government grant.

"Only *she* would have something to gain from doing this," posts an anonymous-sounding account. While another responds with an audio clip of me saying "*I have nothing to hide.*"

The injustice of it all rips through me, but even more terrifying is the thought that whoever did this isn't quite finished yet.

The front door slams and I close my eyes, wishing I could press the rewind button, back to a week or so ago, when my husband and I were the same people we've been for the past twenty years.

"I heard what happened at La Jolla," says Brad, coming into the kitchen. "Are you OK?"

I nod stoically, but all I really want to do is fall into his arms and have him tell me that everything is going to be all right.

"Do you think . . ." He lets out a heavy sigh. "Do you think it's got something to do with everything else that's been going on?"

"I don't think we can rule it out," I say honestly.

"So, it might have something to do with your sister?" he asks, drawing quote marks around a word that up until last night he thought didn't apply to me.

"It would be too much of a coincidence for it not to be."

"Do you think she's the woman on the CCTV at Hannah's school; the woman I met in the bar?"

"And the woman at the conference last night . . ." I say, adding to the list.

He looks at me and my chest heaves, buckling under the weight of the monumental burden I've unwittingly brought to our door. "It's impossible to tell. I haven't seen Cassie in over twenty-five years—she was only seventeen when I left, and I wouldn't know what she looks like as a forty-two-year-old."

"But what reason would she have to come for you now?" asks Brad. "After all this time, and with such . . . such vengeance."

"It got really messy," I start, without knowing where I'm going. "There was a lot of finger-pointing, lots of unanswered questions. She felt I was to blame, in part, for what happened . . ." I swallow the pull at the back of my throat as a picture of Ben flashes in front of my eyes.

"And *were* you?" he asks, his eyes narrowing, as if afraid of the answer.

"No," I say with conviction, but the lie burns a hole in my tongue.

"So, if this *is* your sister, you have no idea what she wants, or how far she's prepared to go to get it . . ."

A shiver runs through me. "I assume she'll let me know all in good time," I say dourly.

He manically runs a hand through his beard, his eyes darting from side to side as his ravaged brain slips into fight-or-flight mode. "Well, then, I think under the circumstances, Hannah should be our priority."

"She always is."

He nods thoughtfully. "So, I'm going to take her to my parents' place, until we know exactly what's going on."

A guttural sob escapes from deep within my chest. "We're supposed to be a family," I choke. "I need you here with me."

His jaw tenses and I can't see any part of the man who vowed on our wedding day never to do anything to jeopardize my need to feel safe in a world that I could only remember being anything but. It took me a long time to believe him, but any misgivings were immediately eradicated when Hannah came along. Because seeing Brad step up and be the dad that our little girl deserved lit up my world in a way I never thought possible. And together, we'd carved out the perfect family life, becoming a symbol of respect within our community. I'd lulled myself into believing that nothing could ever upend our standing, but I hadn't reckoned on someone coming in with a wrecking ball, set on destroying everything we'd created. It turns out karma's a bitch.

"I think Hannah needs me more," he says bluntly.

"She needs her *mother*," I counter.

"But her mother can't keep her safe," he says, cruelly.

"This isn't my fault," I cry, feeling as if my heart is being ripped out of my chest.

"I don't care whose fault it is. I only care about keeping Hannah out of harm's way and it seems I can't do that here."

A wave of paranoia suddenly overwhelms me, its current dragging me into a bottomless vortex. "Is this all part of the plan?" I ask.

His brow furrows. "*What?*"

"Is this what you intended all along? To make me look like an unfit mother so you could take Hannah away from me?"

He looks at me wide-eyed. "Are you completely *insane?*"

"Well, it would make sense," I say, no longer able to control my rambling thoughts. "Maybe you're in this together, you and this woman . . ."

"Can you hear yourself right now?" he says, throwing his hands onto his head. "This is utter madness."

"I won't allow you to take my daughter and play happy families with another woman," I cry. "You're not going to use my past as an excuse to justify what you're doing."

"If you'd been honest about your past, then perhaps none of this would be happening," he barks.

There it is. All the proof I needed to know how far my husband will go to exonerate his own actions. "So, you *did* set this all up?" I accuse. "You dug around and found out what you could use on me to make me believe that I was being punished by my past."

His eyes stare straight through me, as if I'm nothing more than a stranger.

"Did you think you could unsettle me enough by sending someone to my door—*our home*—sniffing around for information under the guise of writing a book? Or were you hoping that our daughter being taken by someone claiming to be her aunt would send me over the edge?" I glare at him, digging my fingernails into my palms to stop me from lashing out. "How long have you been sitting on this minefield of information? You and your fancy woman must have been delighted to know you had so much ammunition to use against me. Have you had fun, the pair of you, watching my life fall apart?"

I will him to give me something, *anything*, but he stands there open-mouthed, caught out.

"You should have got out while you could," I go on. "Cut your losses and ridden off into the sunset together. But you wanted it all, didn't you, and you thought by taking me down—ruining my reputation, my standing in this community, bringing into question my ability to be a mother—you'd take my daughter with you . . ."

He turns and moves toward the door, wordlessly picking up Hannah's Rapunzel backpack from the kitchen island as he goes.

"Put that back *right now*."

He freezes, holding it in mid-air.

"I swear to god, if you go anywhere *near* Hannah, I will track you down and make your life a living hell."

He turns painfully slowly to face me; his skin ashen-white. "Is this the *real* Nicole Alderton I'm seeing now? Is this who you've been hiding for all these years?"

My jaw spasms, fighting to stop the truth from coming out.

He nods, as if he's finally seen the light into my past. "Maybe the media had every reason not to believe your version of events."

I fix him with a steely glare. Maybe they had.

31

Cassie's sure she can feel the tip of the knife in her rucksack as she's pressed back against the doors of the Tube carriage. She looks through her fringe at the evening commuters jostling for position as they make their way home, none of them aware of what she's about to do—and, if she goes through with it, how close they are to the story on tomorrow's front pages.

She's practically lifted off her feet in the mêlée at Oxford Circus, her feet scrabbling for purchase as she's carried into the passageway, shoulder to shoulder with the other passengers. Most of the bodies veer off to the Central Line, but Cassie follows the welcome draft up the escalators and out into the open air.

Even though she's been here several times before, once she's at street level she's momentarily disoriented by the chaos of London's busiest junction. A kaleidoscope of brightly colored cars veer in front of one another, double-decker buses battle it out with black taxis and hundreds of heads bob along the pavement, marching toward her in C-3PO fashion.

"Excuse me," she says to the news vendor on the corner, trying to catch him between his indecipherable hollers. "Do you know where the Langham hotel is?"

"Two minutes up there, darling, on the left."

Cassie walks through the opulent hotel lobby as if she's been there a million times before, her eyes furtively scanning for the ladies'. Once inside, she puts her bag onto the countertop and carefully takes out her Afro comb, working its teeth through her curls. She's forgotten her blusher, so pinches her cheeks to give them an instant boost of color and coats her lips with a metallic pink gloss that makes her eyes pop.

If she'd stopped to think about what she was doing, perhaps she would have talked herself out of it, but there's no time for that now—she's past the point of no return. Her fingers are tingling, and her heart is thumping so loudly that if she doesn't act on what the voices in her head are telling her, she'll never forgive herself. She *has* to do this, if not only to prove that she can.

There's a momentary pause after she's knocked on the door of room 628, and she shimmies down the front of her body suit, allowing her assets to be shown off to their best advantage, albeit heavily assisted by her padded bra.

"Hey," says Ben, swinging the door open with a wide smile. Though his high spirits last only a split second before his face clouds over with confusion. "Oh," he says, looking Cassie up and down.

"I heard this is where the party's at," she says, waiting for him to recognize her.

"Er, I think you've got the wrong room," he says, looking down the corridor as if hoping he can telepathically summon security.

"Oh," says Cassie, unable to disguise her hurt. "I'm sure Michael said it was in 628."

Ben's jaw spasms involuntarily.

"I'm with Samantha Redgrave," says Cassie, hating him for making her fall back on Plan B. "We're meeting here."

"I'll see if I can find out where you're meant to be," says Ben, turning his back and making his way to the phone beside the bed. Cassie follows him in and heads straight for the minibar, where a bottle of vodka sits unscrewed on the countertop.

"Hey, the party's not in here," says Ben, before he's even had a chance to pick up the phone.

But Cassie ignores him and smiles as she pours three-inch measures into two glass tumblers. "I think that's what you said last time, just before we got off our faces at the Savoy after your Wembley gig."

"You were *there* that night?" Ben asks, with more than a hint of suspicion, though whether it's because he doubts her or because he knows she may have a story that will cause shock waves in the wrong hands, Cassie can't quite make out.

"Yeah, it was wild," she says, going to the door and kicking it shut with the heel of her white stiletto.

"Look, I've got somewhere I need to be," says Ben, as Cassie hands him a glass.

She smarts at how easily he can lie to her. "No worries—I'll get out of your hair just as soon as I've finished this." She smiles, because he has no idea how long it's going to take her.

"I don't remember seeing you there that night," says Ben, eyeing her as he nervously sips his drink.

She shakes her head, still unable to understand how he could have forgotten who she is. The hackles on the back of her neck stand up at his lack of respect, but as she moves slowly toward him, she softens at the thought of being able to show him all over again why she's going to be the best thing that's ever happened to him.

"We were drunk and high," she says. "But from what I remember, we were having a good time." She raises her eyebrows, waiting for him to catch on, but he looks at her blankly.

"I'm clean now," he says, by way of excuse.

"Not quite," she says, clinking his glass with hers. "Another?"

She tops his glass up without waiting for a response. It feels like she has an advantage over him if he's drunk.

"So, I see you've been keeping yourself busy . . ." she starts, falling onto the over-plumped floral settee, "if the papers are anything to go by."

He rolls his eyes and sighs. "Just another wannabe chancing her arm for a turn in the spotlight . . . It's all bollocks, and I intend to prove it."

His strength of conviction takes Cassie by surprise. "What are you going to do?" she asks.

"I've got someone on the case," he says, pacing up and down. "People can't be allowed to make shit up about me and get away with it. They need to be exposed for the charlatans that they are."

"I get that," says Cassie. "But you might open yourself up to even bigger problems . . ."

His brow knits with confusion and his eyes are filled with apprehension, as if waiting for her to reveal her hand. "How so?" he says, hesitantly.

"Well, there's no point in protesting your innocence in one corner, only for them to find out that you were hauled to the police station on suspicion of drug offenses in another."

"And how would they find *that* out?" he asks. "It was over two months ago."

"Yeah, but there were quite a few people there when it happened, and it only takes one of them to spill—I'm surprised they haven't already."

"*Most* of the people there were trusted friends and colleagues," he says, pointedly.

Cassie shrugs her shoulders nonchalantly, but her words are anything but. "Well, then, you'd better make sure you don't piss any of them off," she says with a smile. "Now come and sit down with me."

"I really can't," he says, looking at his watch. "Let me give Michael a call to find out where you should be."

He goes to make a move toward the phone, but Cassie catches

hold of his hand. "Come on," she says, pulling him down onto the sofa. "Why don't you relax for a bit?"

He loses his footing and half falls onto her. "So, you want to finish what we started, do you?" she says, giggling.

He tries to right himself, but she makes a grab for him, one hand on his shoulder and another on his cheek as she pulls him closer. She wants him to give in to the inevitable, relinquish all others and allow himself to be caught up in the moment, but as her mouth moves in on his, she senses a resistance.

"Look, you're great, but I can't do this," he says, taking hold of her hand and moving it away from him.

A clap of thunder sounds in Cassie's head as the realization that she's not going to get what she came for—at least not willingly— hits home.

"Nobody needs to know," she says, her free hand going to his crotch. "This can be our little secret."

He pushes her away and stands up. "I'm sorry, but you need to go," he says, looking as if he's already done something he can't forgive himself for.

Cassie doesn't move, choked by an anger so raw it paralyzes her. "You can't treat me like some groupie who you can pick up whenever you feel like it."

"I-I wasn't aware that I was," he says, running a hand through his hair.

She gets up and goes to him, pulling at his fly, to give him one last chance to save himself.

"I mean it," he says, shrugging her off. "If you don't go, I'll call security."

Cassie laughs caustically. "Are you absolutely sure you want to do that?"

Ben looks at her uneasily. "Is that some kind of threat?" he asks, going to the door.

"I could *ruin* you," Cassie hisses, narrowing her eyes.

"What, you think you're going to blackmail me?" says Ben, smiling inanely, making Cassie feel small and stupid. "You think you've got a hold over me for what happened at the Savoy?"

"I'll tell everyone that you're exactly who the papers say you are," says Cassie. "A sex-mad, drug-crazed egomaniac."

"And to stop you from doing that, I have to *sleep* with you?" he asks, disbelievingly.

Cassie's lip wobbles, though she doesn't know if it's because when he puts it like that, it sounds ridiculous, or that she's going to have to follow through on her plan if he doesn't.

"It would definitely be the easier of the two options," she says, reaching into her bag on the floor. "You don't get to do what you do without consequences."

He puts his hands on his hips and shakes his head. "You make it sound as if I've somehow mistreated you or promised you something I've failed to deliver."

"You were *everything* to me," says Cassie, unable to stop a tear from falling. "And I thought I meant something to you."

As if sensing a tip in the wrong direction, Ben throws another glance toward the phone, no doubt assessing how quickly he can get to it and call for help.

"But I've never met you before," he says gently. "At least, not that I can remember. And I'm sorry for that, really I am, but I meet a hundred different people every day."

It sounds like a well-rehearsed speech and Cassie can't help but wonder how many times he's used it before. How many other girls has he made to feel special, only to discard them when someone better comes along? But he's done it to the wrong one this time.

"And they all want a piece of me," he goes on, "thinking they own me, but it's all part of the job. This isn't real life."

He looks at Cassie imploringly, as if willing her to understand, but she's not going to fall for it. "I really thought we had something," she says, wrapping her fingers around the handle of the knife and pulling it out of her bag, its five-inch blade catching the light.

There's a sharp intake of breath.

"You made me believe that I was special," she says, digging the pointed end into her palm. "That you'd picked me out for a reason."

Ben looks at her wide-eyed, as tiny pinpricks of sweat glisten on his upper lip. His mouth opens wordlessly as blood drips onto the cream-colored carpet. If it hurts, Cassie can't feel it, the emotional pain of his deceit far greater than any physical discomfort.

"But if you're telling me that I can't have you . . ."

She lifts the knife up and in one swift rush of air brings it down.

"No!" roars Ben, lifting his arms to intercept it, but it's too late. There's a sickening ripping sound as the blade penetrates flesh, and they hold on to each other as they both fall to the floor.

32

As Nicole walks through the plush lobby of the Langham hotel, she questions for the hundredth time why she's come. It's been a week since Ben turned up at her house in the middle of the night. A week since she told him never to contact her again. And a week of regretting it. But with everything else going on, she knows it was the right decision. So how come she's allowed him to talk her into coming to see him?

She spent the entire train journey trying to convince herself it was because of the music they made together. They've created something special—of that she is sure—and, for her part, she's not prepared to give that up just because he can't control his roving eye.

And as she walks along the corridor, her pumps sinking into the deep-pile carpet, she reasons that that's *all* she's here for. They should never have crossed the line into a personal relationship; it was a mistake and one that she's berated herself for ever since. She only hopes he has come to the same realization.

Taking a deep breath, Nicole flicks her hair behind her shoulders and stands tall, as if hoping it will give her all the resolve she needs. She must not allow herself to be distracted by the magnetic pull of Ben's captivating presence, as irresistible as she finds it.

Checking she's at the right room, she knocks on the door, her stomach somersaulting at the rush of movement from the other side.

"Oh, hello," says a girl, raising her eyebrows expectantly as she stands there in a white toweling robe.

Nicole is momentarily frozen, looking between the number on the door and the girl's Cheshire cat grin, as she tries to recall where she might have seen her before. Because she's sure she has.

"Are you room service?" asks the girl, looking Nicole up and down impertinently before she even has a chance to construct a sentence.

There's no doubt that it's the right room, but the sight of the messy, unmade bed that she can't help but picture Ben and this girl rolling around in suggests that nothing about this is right at all.

"Erm, no, sorry . . ." she says, her brain racing to catch up to her mouth. "I was told to come to 756, but you're not who I was expecting to see." She laughs awkwardly. "I must have been given the wrong room number."

"Oh, are you here for Ben's suit alterations?" asks the girl.

His name on her lips hits Nicole's windpipe like a sucker punch. She instinctively wants to buckle under the girl's intense gaze, but she'll be damned if Ben is going to make a fool of her a second time.

"He's just in the shower," says the girl, who with her asymmetric haircut reminds Nicole of Cyndi Lauper. "Come on in."

Nicole can hear the rush of water from the bathroom, see the rise of steam escaping from underneath the closed door. "I-I don't think . . ." She starts backing away.

"Come on, don't be shy," says the girl, taking her by the hand. "He's honestly just a normal guy, and he really needs his trousers taken up, otherwise I won't be seen dead on his arm tonight."

Her laughter gets lost in the kaleidoscope of emotions that assaults Nicole's senses—confusion, anger, humiliation—but there's something else: a sound that's trying to penetrate her ears, even though she knows she doesn't want it to.

It's not the girl knocking on the bathroom door or her calls of "Babe, hurry up!" It's not even her coy insinuation that they're running behind schedule because they've just got out of bed. It's the distant strum of a guitar, the lilting voice of a woman singing about a lost love, the thundering realization that it's *her* song playing on the stacked mini hi-fi in the corner of the room.

"Is that . . . ?" she starts, the words catching in her throat as she looks at the speakers that seem to be goading her.

The girl looks at her wide-eyed. "Oops," she says, rushing to turn it off. "I don't think Ben will want anyone listening to the new single."

"Th-that's his new single?" Nicole says hoarsely, the words feeling like razors on her tongue.

"It's coming out in a couple of weeks," says the girl, putting a conspiratorial finger to her lips. "But it would be more than my life's worth if you tell anyone I've told you."

Nicole stands there, clutching at her chest, trying to stop her heart from feeling as if it's being ripped out.

Ben had obviously forgotten how hard he'd had to beg her to come and see him three days ago, having taken a better offer in the meantime. She thinks back to every empty promise he made to her then; his reassurance that he'd not looked at another girl since they'd been together, that she was the only one for him, that he wanted to make music with her for evermore . . . How fickle his heart must be; how quickly he forgets. But then she remembers how his assistant had called just this afternoon to let her know that he was running late and had changed rooms.

So, he couldn't have merely forgotten; he must have brought her here on purpose, with the sole intention of causing maximum hurt and humiliation. How could he be so cruel? And what had she done to deserve him treating her so badly?

Storming to the hi-fi, she claws at the tape deck, hitting every button in an effort to eject the cassette.

"Hey," shouts the girl, attempting to pull her back. But Nicole's not leaving here without her tape, and if Ben thinks he's going to use *her* music, *her* voice to further *his* career, he's got another think coming.

She has to tug, the head of the machine still engaged, and as she yanks the cassette out of the hi-fi the tape unwinds, spilling ribbon from its plastic casing. Nicole catches her breath as the heartfelt harmonies she and Ben had pored over lay tangled on the floor—much like their relationship, she supposes.

"What the fuck do you think you're doing?" shrieks the girl.

Nicole's nostrils flare, her sense of shame knowing no bounds. "Do you know that your boyfriend in there is screwing everything that moves?" she spits.

The girl laughs. "Oh, darling, were you one of them?" she asks, her tone beyond patronizing.

Nicole swallows her dented pride and the bitter taste in her mouth.

"If you think you're telling me something new, I'm afraid a hundred other girls just like you have beaten you to it."

"Well, if you're still here to tell the story, then more fool you," snaps Nicole, her anger at odds with her compulsion to get on her knees and gather up the spooled tape.

"It's just sex," says the girl. "I'm not so naive as to believe that someone like Ben Edwards wouldn't need to get it from *somewhere* when I'm not around." She makes it sound as if it doesn't matter where that somewhere is.

"Just so you know, what *we* had transcended that," says Nicole assuredly, as if trying to convince herself.

"You keep telling yourself that," says the girl. "While *I'm* the one lying in bed beside him tonight."

The thought of another girl nestling into the nook of Ben's neck, their bare skin touching, makes Nicole feel sick, but worse than that it makes her feel stupid and foolish to have ever believed his hollow undertaking that *she* was everything *he* needed.

"Now, if you don't get the fuck out of here, I'm going to call security."

Nicole throws a glance toward the closed bathroom door, where the shower is still running and Ben is no doubt blissfully unaware of what he's lost—if he even cares.

Is she really going to walk out of here and let him off that easily? Is she honestly going to slope off into the shadows, as if she never existed?

"If you go anywhere near my music," she yells, going to the bathroom door and slamming her open palm on it, "I'll dedicate my life to making sure you regret it."

The girl hurriedly meets her there, taking ownership of the handle. "I'm calling security," she says, wide-eyed.

"I hope you're happy living your sad, vacuous life, with sad, vacuous hangers-on," says Nicole through the door as she throws the girl a look of utter contempt. "You deserve each other." She turns to leave. "I was always too good for him anyway . . ."

As she walks down the corridor, devoid of the hopeful spirit she'd come here with, she pretends that it means nothing, that Ben is inconsequential to her. But deep down she knows that if she had the chance to kill him right now, she would take it.

33

The shrill ring of my phone pierces the bubble I'd inadvertently put myself in, foolishly believing that it would protect me from the past.

"Hello?"

"Mrs. Nicole Forbes? Formerly Nicole Alderton?"

"Who wants to know?" I bark, my suspicions so close to the surface that it feels as if I'm giving away the keys to Fort Knox every time somebody asks me a question.

"My name is Jack Adams and I'm a solicitor here in London."

Blood rushes to my extremities, making my toes curl and fingertips tingle. Clearly Brad didn't take my threat seriously enough. "I know what's going on here," I say. "You're wasting your time."

"I-I'm sorry," says the man, who I imagine sitting in an office down the road, faking a bad British accent. "I don't understand."

"I know what Brad's been doing, but he won't win, so you can stop playing this vicious game."

"I'm afraid this isn't a game, Mrs. Forbes; I have some rather bad news . . ."

I wait, silently, for him to dig his own grave.

"It's about your father."

I swallow the lump that has immediately formed in my throat as it sinks in that maybe this doesn't have anything to do with Brad, and that the man I've been grieving over the past twenty-five years is now dead.

"I'm sorry to pass on such sensitive news over the phone, but you've proved very difficult to track down."

"H-how did you find me?" I ask.

"I'll have to admit, you were one of the trickier cases," he says. "But I had a few clues to go on and I'm not one to give up easily." He laughs. "And besides, your father wouldn't have let me. He was most insistent that I was not to rest until I'd tracked you down." I can almost hear him smiling to himself at the memory.

I choke back tears at the thought of Dad and the fanciful belief that we would one day be reconciled, that the universe would find the right time to bring us together so that we could tell our truths and try to forgive each other. The realization that this will now never happen catches in the back of my throat, but then I remember that this could all be another sick ploy to undermine me.

"How do I know you're who you say you are and that you're telling the truth?"

"Well, I don't really know how to prove that to you," says the man, "other than I've been left very specific instructions to carry out on your father's behalf."

"Which are?" I ask, allowing myself to believe, for just one second, that he really might be my father's voice from beyond the grave. I hold my breath, imagining all the possible scenarios, though none—*none*—could have prepared me for what he was about to say.

"Your father's last will and testament expresses that you are the sole beneficiary of his estate."

There's a lengthy silence as I wait for him to finish the sentence in a way that will make sense.

"Mrs. Forbes? Did you hear me?"

I laugh inanely. As inappropriate as it is in these circumstances, it's the only expression my body will allow.

"I can understand you might be shocked," he says, having clearly experienced this reaction before.

"I-I'm sorry, b-but that's . . . I mean . . . that's . . . how can that be?" I can't even string a sentence together.

"It was his last wish that everything should come to you."

"Th-that's impossible," I choke. "I haven't spoken to him in almost twenty-five years."

My mind meets itself coming backward as it traverses all the ways in which this man could possibly have made a mistake. He's a stranger to me; he might not even have known my father. He could easily have got his paperwork mixed up and called the wrong number on the list. Might he think he's talking to Cassie?

"I have a sister," I offer, giving him a get-out clause; a chance to realize his error. "She lives in England."

"I know," he says gently. "But she was not bequeathed anything in your father's will."

What? My brain feels as if it might explode.

"I'm sorry, but none of this makes any sense," I say. "Why would he have you go to such lengths to track me down? Why would he leave me anything at all, let alone all of it?"

There are so many questions—none of which I'd normally ask a stranger, but he's the only chance I have of getting any answers. And I *need* answers, not only to help me put the past to bed, but to safeguard my future.

"Perhaps that's why he felt the need to write you a letter," he says.

"Letter?"

"Yes, he was even more insistent that the letter reached you than the money."

I fall silent as I imagine what he could possibly have to say to me in death that he couldn't bring himself to tell me while he was alive. The thought terrifies me.

34

"What the hell's gone on *here?*" asks Michael when he shows up in Ben's room to find Cassie bleeding and Ben near-hysterical.

"You need to help me," Ben cries, as Cassie stares into space with a deep self-inflicted gash on the inside of her wrist. "She needs to get to a hospital."

Michael smirks, seemingly amused by Ben's inability to control the panic that's consuming him. "She can't be going anywhere, mate," he snipes.

"*What?*" says Ben, disbelievingly. "Look at her! She needs medical attention."

"Who even *is* she?" asks Michael.

Ben manically runs a hand through his hair. "I don't know; she just turned up here looking for you and started getting all weird."

Michael raises his eyebrows. "Don't be putting your bad shit on me, bro," he says. "This ain't got nothing to do with me."

"Actually it does, and you're going to help me, the way I helped you."

Michael kisses his teeth and rolls his eyes. "Taking the rap for a drug habit is slightly different than taking a fan to hospital dripping in blood."

"I have done *so* much more for you than that," spits Ben. "You're the one with a car—we need to get her to a hospital."

Michael looks at Cassie as if weighing up the options. "I want to know what I'm getting myself involved in first. What did you do to her?"

"I haven't fucking touched her," exclaims Ben, his frustration evident.

"Well, she could say that you have," says Michael, playing devil's advocate. "She could say anything . . ."

"If you're going to be an asshole and not help me, then I'm going to get Luke. Stay here with her until I get back."

"Yeah, whatever, man."

As soon as Ben leaves the room, Michael wraps a towel around Cassie's wrist and throws one of Ben's shirts over her shoulders. "Come on," he says, lifting her up and guiding her toward the door. "I'll take you to hospital myself."

As they ride the lift to the underground car park in silence, Cassie's sense of abject rejection is ever so slightly buoyed by the change of events. Despite her best efforts, and as much as she doesn't want to acknowledge it, Ben had made it plainly obvious that he didn't want her. But as she watches Michael stick his finger into a foil packet and rub white powder on his gums, she wonders whether Ben's loss might be *his* gain.

"I don't need to go to hospital," she says shakily, as he opens the passenger door of his Ford Escort.

He waits until he's in the driver's seat to say, "Good, because I'm not taking you there."

As they drive south across Waterloo Bridge, listening to Aerosmith at full volume, Cassie wonders where they might be going instead.

"So, I guess Secret Oktober is going to split up," she says, knowing it will stoke the fire.

"What?" he says, distractedly. He clearly has other things on his mind. "Why would you think that?"

"Well, if Ben is writing and recording with other people, I just assumed . . ."

Michael gives a false laugh. "Where the fuck did you hear that from?"

"Ben just told me. I thought you of all people would know about it."

The car very nearly drives straight over the side of the bridge, throwing Cassie into the dashboard as Michael performs an emergency stop.

"I knew it!" he yells, slamming his hands on the steering wheel. "The son of a bitch."

"Well, maybe it's nothing," says Cassie, in a lame attempt to backtrack, though she can't deny she's enjoying the power in her hands. If she can create a little discord between the two of them, it's the very least Ben deserves after everything he's done to her. But all it actually serves to do is make Michael see red.

He drives another half a mile, the unspoken tension in the car mounting with every red light, while Cassie not only tries to second-guess what he's thinking, but also where he's taking her. She looks at him questioningly as he turns into an unlit narrow street and pulls up alongside a derelict warehouse.

"Where are we?" she asks, looking up at the metal gantries suspended between the buildings on either side of her.

Michael turns off the engine and, without warning, lunges across the seat at her. He mauls at her top as his mouth clamps onto hers.

"Wh-what are you doing . . . ?" she manages, pressing herself into the seat in a futile attempt to get away from him.

He doesn't say a word, just keeps forcing himself onto her as he attempts to lift himself over the handbrake.

Cassie's flailing hand searches for the door handle and as she releases it she pushes herself out of the car, falling onto the pavement. She scrambles to her feet, her legs feeling like jelly beneath her as she tries to run, but she's not quick enough. Michael is a second behind, slamming himself into her and bundling her into the open doorway of a disused building. Disturbed by the unexpected invasion, pigeons flap and fly out of the holes where windows should be.

"Get off me!" she cries, desperately trying to dig her heels into the loose rubble under her stilettos, but she can't get any traction, her feet seemingly skating on ice.

"Shut the fuck up!" he sneers, his eyes hollow and devoid of empathy.

"Stop!" she cries, as he pushes her onto the ground, his crushing weight falling on top of her. "Get off me!" She pushes herself back, feeling the sting of tiny particles of loose stone leaving their imprint on her skin.

"Don't pretend this isn't what you want," Michael snarls, pulling at her underwear until it rips. "It's what you *all* want."

"No!" she mumbles, the word lost as his hand closes over her mouth, making her feel as if she's suffocating.

She takes herself to another place and another time, back to when she'd been sitting on the roundabout in the park. She must have been only six or seven, but as her mum had turned her back to her to get an ice lolly from the kiosk, a group of older boys had come along and started pushing the roundabout. Hollering as they ran around and around, Cassie had held on to the bar until her knuckles turned white, but the faster they went, the more she could feel herself sliding from her seat. She wanted to call out to them to stop, but she didn't want them to know she was scared, so she allowed herself to be thrown off, at what felt like forty miles per hour, onto the unforgiving tarmac. Her skin felt much the same as it did now, the sense of burning getting ever hotter as the grit worked its way into the open wounds.

And however brave she'd forced herself to be then, she has to dig even deeper now as Michael pushes himself into her, and his smothering hand cuts off the last semblance of air.

35

"It's me!" comes a frantic voice as soon as Nicole accepts the reverse-charge call from the operator.

"Cassie?" Nicole gasps, her sisterly instinct immediately telling her that something's wrong.

"Where are you? What's happened?"

"I-I'm in town," sobs Cassie. "But I haven't got any way of getting back home."

"What? Why?"

"I-I just need you to come and get me," pleads Cassie. "Right now."

"Where are you?" asks Nicole, her impatient tone more a sign of frustration that she isn't already with her than anything else.

"I'm on Tower Bridge."

"OK, stay in the phone box," says Nicole.

"Pl-please hurry," cries Cassie.

"I'll be with you as quickly as I can," she says, slamming down the handset and running out of the door.

In the twenty minutes it takes to get there, Nicole runs through every possible scenario that would result in her normally streetwise sister being stranded in town and sounding terrified. But when she pulls up outside the phone box, with the lights of the bridge's grand piers shining onto the filthy windows, nothing could have prepared her for what she sees.

"Jesus!" she cries, as Cassie falls into her arms, bloodied and bruised. "What the hell's happened?"

"I-I . . ." starts Cassie, before her chest convulses and her shoulders wrack with vicious sobs. "He . . . he . . ."

Nicole's blood feels like it's stopped pumping. "He *what*?"

"Everything . . . everything was fine," cries Cassie. "He was bringing me home; he was looking after me, but then . . ."

It's taking all of Nicole's restraint not to shake it out of her.

"But then he took me somewhere I didn't want to go and made me do things I didn't want to do."

Hot bile rushes to the back of Nicole's throat as she can't help but picture the horrific events unfolding.

She takes the blanket from the car's parcel shelf and wraps Cassie's shivering body in it before gently lowering her onto the back seat of the car. She slides in beside her and takes Cassie in her arms as the turmoil of what she's been through seeps out of her.

"I kept saying no, over and over, but he wouldn't listen, he was like a man possessed." She manically rubs at the bloodied skin on her arms. "I can still smell him on me. Can you smell him?"

Tears spring to Nicole's eyes as she pulls her sister in even tighter. She knows what she's about to say will have little bearing on the here and now, but she also knows that time is of the essence.

"Cass, we need to go to the police," she says quietly.

"No," says Cassie, pushing herself away from Nicole as if she's reliving it all over again. "No, I don't want the police involved. You have to promise me that you won't tell anyone. Not the police, not Dad, not anyone."

Nicole closes her eyes and takes a deep breath. She knew this would be Cassie's first reaction, but she has to make her see the importance of telling the police and telling them *now*. "I know it feels too raw to go over it again straightaway, but it'll be too late in a day or two's time. They need to get the evidence now, so they can lock the bastard in a cell and throw away the key."

"They'll say I deserved it," says Cassie.

"This *isn't* your fault," says Nicole, hating whoever did this to her for making her think it is. "There's nothing you could ever do to make it your fault."

"You don't know what I did," says Cassie, bowing her head as she sobs.

"I don't *care* what you did," says Nicole. "A man has taken advantage of you, and you have to make him accountable for his actions."

Cassie shakes her head vehemently. "I'm not going to report him."

"I'll be with you every step of the way," says Nicole. "We'll do it together."

"I can't," says Cassie, sounding terrified. "My life will never be the same again."

"He can't hurt you anymore, Cassie. I promise you that."

"You don't know who he is," she says, making Nicole pull up short. She holds Cassie away from her and looks at her in the half-light.

"Who is he, Cassie?" she asks, careful not to sound accusatory.

"Do you swear not to tell anyone?"

Nicole swallows her indignation at having to make a promise she doesn't want to keep. And if she'd known the name Cassie was going to drop, she would never have agreed to it.

36

The doorbell rings, but I make no attempt to move. My mind is too worn out from the conspiracy theories that have been railroading through it for the past day, desperately trying to separate fact from fiction. Despite everything pointing toward Brad being complicit in what's been going on, I still can't believe that the man I've loved for the past twenty years could be capable of something so hateful. But if the woman he met in the bar is the woman who took our daughter, is as much of a stranger to him as she is to me, then I have to face the very real possibility that it *was* Cassie who called and spoke to him. And that he's just as much a pawn in this game as I am.

The bell rings again and I suddenly think of Hannah, a myriad of possibilities flooding my mind as to why I shouldn't leave it unanswered. What if she's gone missing again? What if she's been hurt? What if she's walked out of school because other kids are being mean to her?

Of the thousand scenarios I dare to imagine, finding Zoe on the doorstep isn't one of them.

"No, absolutely not," I say, shaking my head.

"Please," she says. "Just one minute."

With her blond hair and impish face, she suddenly looks younger than I remembered, more naive than the savage Rottweiler I'd thrown out of my house and more innocent than the calculated journalist who'd accosted Brad and me in Tino's last week. God, that felt like another lifetime ago—when I was oblivious to the damage that could be done in just a few days.

"I don't know what you're looking to gain, or who you're working with, but I'm done with it."

"I understand how you must feel to have this brought to your door after all this time," she says.

"You have no idea." I seethe.

She looks awkward, no part of her seeming as if she'd be involved in a sick ploy to destroy my life. But until I'm convinced that this isn't what's happening here, I'll not be giving her the benefit of the doubt.

"I just have one question," says Zoe. "And then I promise you'll never see me again."

I want to tell her to go to hell and slam the door in her face. But there's something holding me back—a need to know what the question is. Because knowledge is power, and I've got a horrible feeling that I need all the power I can get.

"What is it?" I ask tersely.

"I don't want to take up any more of your time than is absolutely necessary," she says, rooting around in her bag. "So, I'll get to the point."

She takes out an old Sony Walkman, the kind I had when I was a struggling singer-songwriter. The kind I'd listen to my mixtapes on.

She presses the rewind button and I hold my breath as the shrill of the tape backtracking sends every sense into high alert. I used to find the sound exciting—a clean slate for new possibilities—but now, as I wait to see what's coming next, it just sounds like the scrambling of my brain.

The opening chords of a guitar filter through the muffled speaker, and my knuckles turn white as I grip hold of the door-frame. I want to snatch it from her and turn it off. I want to cry out loud to silence it. But instead, I grit my teeth and keep my eyes fixed firmly ahead as a voice from a bygone era fills the room.

"I would go to the ends of the earth if it meant I could keep you safe,
I would die for you if it meant I could keep you here with me . . ."

"Is that . . ." Zoe begins. "Is that you?"

"You need to tell me where you got this from." My voice is hoarse, strangled by regret.

"And I would do anything for your love," cuts in Ben's dulcet tones, singing in perfect harmony. *"Because your love is all I need."*

I can't breathe, my lungs closed off to air, as a voice I haven't heard in twenty-five years wraps itself around my vital organs, making them feel as if they're being systematically shut down.

The grief that I naively thought had been laid to rest rips through me, shredding the layers of resilience it has taken me years to construct. It's as if I'm being sucked back into the vortex of 1986, and despite gripping on to the here and now with all my strength, my fingers are being pried away, one by one, as I'm finally forced to face the past I thought I'd left behind.

"Excuse me . . ." I manage, fearing that if I don't remove myself from this situation, I'll not be able to mask the guilt that is running roughshod through my nervous system, about to tip me into terri-tories unknown.

She watches me as I run to the bathroom, my behavior only courting more suspicion, but there's nothing I can do. Of all the pieces of evidence I imagined she might have, that song is the only one I couldn't possibly have prepared for.

I lean back against the locked door, willing the incessant noise in my head to stop. Most days, I'm able to convince myself that I deserve to be happy, that I'm as worthy of a loving family as the next person. But on days like this, when the drums reverberate so loudly that I can't think straight, I'm reminded that nobody who's done something as unforgivable as I have is *ever* forgiven.

The tears threaten to fall, but I swallow them back down and force long, deep breaths in and out of my lungs. I need to focus, stay levelheaded.

My ashen complexion reflects back to me in the mirror, my eyes spooked and panic-stricken. If my world hasn't already imploded, then this is the detonator that will blow everything to smithereens.

I splash cold water onto my face, hoping it will kick-start my brain. But all it manages to achieve is to make me realize that perhaps Zoe knows even more than I do.

She offers a watery smile, giving nothing away, as I walk back into the hall on unsteady feet.

"So . . ." she starts, eager to continue, despite my obvious discomfort. "Is that you on the tape?"

"You need to leave."

She sidesteps my unease and pushes her shoulders back, as if the action will reassert her standing in what is essentially the hollowed husk of my life.

"Just tell me if it's you on that tape, and I promise I'll never darken your door again."

I suck in a breath, wondering what difference it would make if I told the truth, but then I stop myself. Why change the habit of a lifetime?

"Who *are* you?" I ask.

She shrugs, but her eyes widen, making her look like a deer caught in headlights. "I told you, I'm writing a book on the demise of Secret Oktober."

I shake my head in an effort to dislodge the doubt in my mind, but I can't shift the feeling that she wants more from me than just a story. I clasp my hands together to stop them from shaking.

"Where did you get that tape from?"

"I found it," she says, all too blithely.

"Where?"

She bites down on her lip, as tears spring to her eyes.

"Where?"

"My mother gave it to me," she says quietly.

I suck in a breath, the squeeze on my chest making me feel as if my heart is being stamped on. As much as I've dreamed that one day this song would somehow find me again, I've gone out of my way to make sure it wouldn't.

"I-I don't understand . . ." I start. "This wasn't supposed to happen. Not like this."

"I'm sorry," says Zoe. "I didn't know how else to do it."

"B-but how . . . How did you know it was me?"

"I didn't," says Zoe, looking at me with an expression I can't read. "But I was always aware of the tape because it used to be in a box in the attic. I'd have great adventures going up there as a kid and looking through everything." She ejects the cassette and runs her thumb across my scrawled handwriting on the label. "The idea of something being on here, hidden from the naked eye, was something of a fascination for me. It held a secret promise, an unknown entity that you couldn't open unless you had the right tool."

I dare to allow myself a smile as I listen to the musings of the post-Walkman generation, unable to imagine what it must have felt like to be presented with a reel of magnetic ribbon and be told that it had revolutionized the music industry.

"But when I was about ten years old, my mum gave me this machine to play it on," Zoe goes on, clutching what is now considered a piece of history.

"What did she tell you about it?" I ask, unsure of how much I want to know.

She shrugs. "She just said that one day it might be *really* important and that I was to take great care of it."

I stifle the urge to sob, my throat closing in on itself. "So that's why you're here?"

She nods self-consciously. "I guess. I don't want anything from it. I just wanted you to know that I had it. You know, if you ever wanted to . . ."

I shake my head aimlessly, because I honestly don't know *what* I want anymore.

37

"There's some bacon for you under the grill," says John as Nicole pads into the kitchen, bleary-eyed from being up all night. "I'm just going to take this up to Cassie."

"I'll take it to her," says Nicole hurriedly, snatching the butty from him and turning to leave as quickly as she came in. She needs to see Cassie before their father does.

Knocking gently on her sister's bedroom door, she tiptoes her way into the darkened room, eyeing the clothes she'd carefully laid over the dressing-table pouffe, imagining the evidence that may have imprinted itself between the fibers. She's hoping that, in the cold light of day, Cassie will reconsider whether she wants to go to the police, and Nicole wants to preserve every one of Michael's abhorrent cells in readiness.

"Hey, are you feeling up to eating?" she asks quietly, not wanting to rattle Cassie's already fragile state. "I've got one of Dad's specials."

There's a groan, like the one Nicole is used to hearing on the mornings she's unfortunate enough to be the one to wake Cassie for school. She opens one eye, stretching like a cat in the sliver of sunlight that's bleeding around her festoon blind, and Nicole can't help but be in awe of how Cassie's holding up. But a split second later it's as if she's been hit by a ten-ton truck, looking around wide-eyed and curling up into the fetal position, as if protecting herself all over again.

"It's OK, I'm here," says Nicole, going to her as her shoulders convulse.

"I thought for a second it was all a nightmare," says Cassie, crying into her. "I thought I'd dreamed it."

The rage that Nicole had battled with all night, that very nearly saw her hunt Michael down, returns with a vengeance. She imagines him waking up in his king-size bed this morning, no doubt flanked by one, if not two, girls, reveling in his prowess. He'll not give a second thought to what he did to Cassie, believing it's his right to take whatever he wants, from *whoever* he wants, with no consequences.

If Ben were more of a man, he would have taken Michael to task well before now. But instead, he's allowed a monster to manifest right in front of his eyes, disregarding rules and people. He wasn't much better himself, his self-professed honor and loyalty falling spectacularly short last night.

"Shh, it's going to be all right," says Nicole, holding Cassie close and eyeing the bloodstained bandage she'd wrapped around Cassie's wrist last night. Cassie had insisted that she must have been cut during the attack, but Nicole wasn't convinced. "We'll get through this together, but you have to tell the police."

"I'm not going through it all over again," says Cassie, her body shaking. "And it won't just be the police, will it? I'll have to tell Dad, a jury . . . then it will be all over the papers. Even if he's found guilty, my life will be over."

Nicole can't bring herself to tell her that her life has already changed forever. Her body may heal, but her mind will always be broken, her innocence shattered by a man the world looks up to. How is that right?

"We've at least got to tell Dad," says Nicole. "You can't hide up here. He's going to know something's wrong."

Cassie pulls at the nightie that Nicole had gently helped her into after giving her a bath last night. But the bruises that pepper her skin, darkening with every passing second, can't be disguised. "I'll be fine," she says, more to convince herself than Nicole. "I don't want him having to deal with this along with everything else he's got going on."

"Well, if you're not going to tell the police, do you at least want to tell *me* what happened? It might help to talk about it . . ."

"I-I should never have—" stutters Cassie. "I should never have left Ben's room . . . if I'd stayed with him, this would never have happened, but I was so angry and I wasn't thinking straight . . ."

Nicole's heart feels like it's stopped beating. "You were with *Ben* last night?"

Cassie nods tearfully. "Please don't be upset. I know what the papers said, but he swore it was all lies. He's just got back from America and I wanted to see him face to face to make sure he was telling the truth."

Nicole desperately wants to believe that this is another of Cassie's fantasies, which she has lived out so vividly in her head that she can't distinguish it from real life. But she can't accuse her of lying; not *now*, not when there is so much at stake. "And so what happened?" she asks, daring to play along. "What went wrong?"

"When I got there, he just didn't want to know," says Cassie. "It was as if he'd had a better offer in the meantime and needed to get rid of me as quickly as possible."

Nicole remembers feeling the very same and can't help but wonder if they've both been played.

"It was as if I meant nothing to him," Cassie goes on. "Like everything we'd shared had been forgotten."

Nicole balks.

"And when I started getting upset, he got angry and told me it was over, that he had another girl already waiting in a room down the corridor for him."

Nausea threatens to overwhelm Nicole as she listens to the parallels in Cassie's version of events and her own.

"We can't let him get away with this," she hisses, not knowing if she's referring to Michael or Ben.

"I got into Michael's car willingly," cries Cassie. "I even stupidly thought that if I slept with him, it would teach Ben a lesson."

"But it wasn't a choice you made in the end?" questions Nicole.

"No. I thought it, but would never have gone through with it. I kept saying no. I told him to stop. I didn't want him to do it."

Nicole's jaw spasms as she attempts to bat away the image. "He doesn't get to do what he did and just carry on living his charmed life," she seethes.

"He's Michael Delaney," sobs Cassie. "He can get away with doing whatever he likes."

"*No*," says Nicole, as she looks at her little sister. "Not this time."

38

I'm still reeling, dumbstruck by Zoe's revelation, when the doorbell rings again. I can't take much more and instinctively recoil away from the front door, but I can see the outline of the person I know to be my husband through the frosted glass.

"I didn't want to use my key," he says, when I eventually let him in.

"This is *your* house," I say, my brow furrowing.

"But I don't live here," he says, dourly.

It has been only four nights, but I suppose he's right. He doesn't live here anymore, and a panicked sob catches in the back of my throat as I acknowledge that he may never live here again.

"How are you?" he asks, his eyes searching mine for the truth, rather than the empty retort he's expecting.

"I don't know," I say honestly.

"Look, I'm not here to fight," he says, opening his arms in surrender. "I want to understand what's going on and how we can get through this. *Together*." He looks at me like he used to. "But you're going to have to trust me and believe that I had nothing to do with any of it."

I want to. God, how I want to. And I could almost believe it, because how could he possibly have found the tape with Ben's and my song on it—and then used Zoe to bring it to my door?

"I'm here to help you, not work against you," he says, as if reading my mind.

"How can I be sure you're not behind all this?"

He shakes his head in frustration, but tempers his response. "Why would I be?" he says, softly. "You're the best thing that's ever happened to me. We have a good life and I'm happy. I'm not going to destroy what we have for a quick fling, and I'm certainly not going to take our daughter away from the best mother I know."

His words hit a nerve, and I can't help but believe him.

"I don't want to make matters worse," he goes on, as I close my eyes and wonder how much worse it can get, "but I did some digging on the internet, just to get an idea of what happened back then."

It's something I've always avoided, knowing that it will only open a can of worms.

"And I've found an article that I really think you should read," he goes on.

I look at him skeptically.

"I'm not claiming to know what's gone on or going on—only you know that, and I trust you'll tell me all in good time. But I think this might help you start to make sense of things."

He opens his laptop and passes it to me. "Just take a look," he says, encouragingly, sensing my reticence.

"*HELP ME FIND MY DAUGHTER BEFORE IT'S TOO LATE,*" screams the headline across the center of the screen. "One man's final wish to be reunited with the forgotten victim of the Secret Oktober tragedy."

A knife pierces my heart as a picture of my family, the only one

I used to know, commandeers the double page. Happily posing for the perfect portrait, back when we thought a thousand more would follow. My face is so innocent and full of hope for what the future had to bring; blissfully unaware that my mother would be dead within a year and that a few months after that, I'd never see my father or sister again.

I stifle a sob as I trace my mum's happy smile with a shaking finger. If she'd stayed with us—had defied the odds—there's no doubt in my mind that the catastrophic events that hollowed out our family would never have happened. She would have made us *all* see sense before it was too late, before any of us had a chance to play a regrettable part in history.

"Your dad's dying," says Brad, his eyes downcast. "And it seems he really wants to speak to you."

I turn away, unable to look at the pictures for a moment longer as the sting of tears burns at the back of my throat.

Brad takes the laptop back from me, his eyes scanning the screen. "He feels there's so much more left to say . . ." He snatches a look at me before going on. "He doesn't want to go to his grave without clearing the air."

I stifle a sob. "It's too late."

Brad's mouth drops open and he instinctively comes over to me. It's only been a week since he's held me in his arms, but with everything that's gone on since, his embrace doesn't feel as safe as it used to.

"How do you know?" he asks, his suspicions as close to the surface as mine.

"His lawyer has been on the phone. Apparently there's a letter on its way, written by him . . ."

Brad's arms tense. "What do you think it's going to say?"

I've asked myself that question a hundred times already, but I'm almost too scared to answer. "I would hope that he regrets what happened and that he wishes he'd tried harder to find me when he had the chance."

"But you didn't exactly make it easy for him," ventures Brad.

I toy with the idea of telling him why, but it's gone as quickly as it came. "It was better that way," I say instead. "I didn't want *any* part of what happened to follow me here."

"But you denied yourself a father *and* a sister . . ." says Brad.

He has no idea what I denied myself.

"You didn't need to do that," he goes on. "Because what happened wasn't your fault."

My jaw spasms involuntarily and I bite down on my lip. "I know that," I lie. "But I needed a new start, away from anyone who knew my connection to the case. It would have dictated the rest of my life if I'd stayed in England."

Brad studies me as if waiting for the cracks to appear in my perfectly curated backstory.

"I get that, but you could have brought your family with you—in spirit, if not physically."

An involuntary wail comes from deep within my chest, making my shoulders convulse and my face crumple.

"Hey, it's going to be OK," he says, wrapping his arms tighter around me, but his empty words ring hollow.

"Brad, I-I need to tell you something . . ." I sob, knowing it's now or never.

He looks at me as if he's been waiting for this our entire marriage, and I can't help but wonder if the past twenty years have all been a sham. How can we have had a normal relationship when he knows nothing about the events in my life that have made me . . . *me*?

"What is it?" he says, holding me away from him.

"I don't want it to change anything . . ." I start. "I need you to promise me that."

He scratches at his head, as if assessing the tall order.

"That woman Zoe, who came up to us at Tino's . . . I-I don't think she is who she says she is . . ." I half mumble.

"OK . . ." he says, waiting for the part that's going to surprise him.

"I think she's pretending to be a writer, pretending to be looking into Ben Edwards's case."

I pull myself up with a start, the sound of his name on my lips so alien to me after all this time.

"You think she's got an ulterior motive?" asks Brad, his voice cutting into my guilt-ridden memories.

I nod and open my mouth, but my lips form around unspoken words.

"Which is . . . ?" he presses, tempering his impatience.

Say it, Nicole.

"She . . ." I swallow to moisten my dry mouth. "She has a tape . . ."

"OK," he says hesitantly.

"It's me and Ben singing."

His jaw tenses. "So, you made music together as well as being lovers?"

I nod. "It was a song I wrote for my mother, and it had a very special meaning. It meant a lot to me."

His brow furrows as he no doubt wonders how this is relevant in the whole scheme of things. "So how did Zoe get hold of it?" he asks.

I can't bear to look at him, knowing that what I'm about to say will change everything he ever thought he knew about me.

"She . . ." My heart is pounding so hard that the drumming is reverberating in my ears. "She . . ."

Say it, Nicole.

"She got it from her mother."

"And who is she to you . . . ?" prompts Ben, his patience wearing thin.

"She . . . she was someone I once knew," I say, bitterly disappointed that I have passed on my chance to be honest. But it seems I'm no more ready to tell the truth now than I've ever been.

39

Nicole almost expected the streets of London to be lined with grief-stricken mourners as her mother's hearse carries her to her final resting place in Highgate Cemetery, all beside themselves with the devastating loss of a much-loved woman at such a young age. But it seems that while Nicole's life has seemingly come to a standstill, the rest of the population is carrying on with gut-wrenching abandonment. Deliveries are being made to shops, children are being collected from school gates, friends are dining alfresco, taking advantage of the unseasonal warmth of the autumn day. How is the world still turning, when hers has stopped?

She takes hold of Cassie's hand and gives it a reassuring squeeze, in an effort to emulate their mother's natural ability to throw a metaphorical security blanket around them whenever they were in need. But Cassie snatches her hand away, her rigid jaw set in deep insurmountable despair.

Since the horrific incident with Michael, Cassie has withdrawn into herself, gone to a place even Nicole can't reach. Every time she's tried to talk to her, in an attempt to coax her out of the darkness, Cassie has seemed like an empty vessel, devoid of empathy or feeling, apart from the odd occasion when Nicole has seen a flash of something else cross her features. Was it anger? Hatred?

Whenever their dad has shared his concerns, Nicole has brushed them away and told him it was all part of the grieving process. Because if she told him the real reason *why* Cassie has distanced herself from real life, he would hunt Michael down and kill him. And that would be too kind, because there are better ways of making those that hurt us pay.

The cortege comes to a stop under the canopy of the crematorium and as the somber congregation look on, Nicole feels her dad's hand on the small of her back, a silent offering of strength as she gets out of the car.

"Your mum's right here with you," he says, sucking in a breath, as if it will last him all the way through the service.

It was meant to placate her—to calm the grief that has become her new normal. But the thought of her mother not being able to reach out to tell Nicole she's there makes it all the more painful.

She watches the wreath-laden coffin being gently lifted out of the hearse, waiting for the whisper of something against her cheek, the tingle of a hand holding hers—*anything* that tells Nicole that her mother is here. It's all she needs, to know that she can do this, but tears fill her eyes when nothing comes.

People grimace at her with pained expressions that are supposed to epitomize their sympathy, yet all they actually convey is pity. Pity that she lost her mother so young, pity for all the things she's going to miss out on, pity for the lessons she'll never be taught. Do they think she doesn't know all of that?

Among the mournful faces is her ex, Aaron, who Nicole only notices because his expression is one of resentment rather than compassion. She'd specifically told him, when he turned up at the house the night before last, that she didn't want to see him again—like she'd told him a hundred times before; for him not to listen is frustrating enough, but to defy her wishes on today of all days is beyond the pale.

A flush of anger infiltrates her veins, which only intensifies when she hears the first strains of "In My Life." She'd known it was coming, thought she'd prepared herself for it, but hearing Paul McCartney's music instead of her own reaches deep into her soul, squeezing the life out of her organs. It should have been *her* song that played to her mother on her last journey; *her* song that said everything that needed to be said. But Ben had destroyed her sacred words, taking them without respect or care, shattering any semblance of their meaning by using them for his own gain.

The sob, when it comes, is loud and ugly, taking her by surprise with both its ferocity and her inability to control it. But once it's out, it's as if the bitter intruder who has been festering inside her, feeding off her blood and draining her of energy, has been released.

The strength that Nicole had inexplicably managed to find lasts her through much of the service, only faltering when her father delivers his eulogy. He speaks not only of his daughters and the special bond they shared with their mother, but of his and Gigi's time before they came along. Nicole had selfishly convinced herself that she bore the brunt of the pain of losing the best friend she'll ever have, but the realization that her parents shared a life before her makes her father's grief even more insurmountable.

"How are you holding up?" Nicole asks Cassie later, as she sidles up to her at the wake, back at the house.

Cassie's mouth tightens into a thin line. "Like you care," she says acerbically.

"I'm trying to," snaps Nicole impatiently. "But you're making it really difficult. We're in this together—I've got your back and you should have mine."

Cassie snorts derisorily.

"I'm on your side," says Nicole. "But you need to let me in."

"If you were on my side, you wouldn't have done what you've done," says Cassie cryptically, before turning her back and purposefully walking across the living room to talk to a second cousin she can't stand.

Nicole shakes her head as she picks up a platter of tuna and cucumber sandwiches and offers them to those nearest to her. Amid the forced small talk and an overwhelming desire to tell everyone to leave, Nicole senses a sudden, palpable change in atmosphere, as heads turn toward the door and ribs get nudged with pointy elbows. If Nicole didn't know better, she'd imagine that her mother's nemesis has just turned up. But Gigi didn't have enemies—of that she's certain—so she, too, turns, with all the confidence of someone who has no fight to pick, except she couldn't possibly have foreseen this opponent. Her mouth drops open, her blood running cold with anger and panic.

"What the . . . ?" She can barely speak.

"I'm sorry, I had no idea it was today," says Ben, looking mortified as he stands in the living room doorway like a spare part.

"Get out of here," hisses Nicole under her breath, painfully aware that a starstruck audience is looking on in bewilderment and awe.

"I shouldn't have come," he says, looking like a reprimanded schoolboy. "But you wouldn't take my calls . . ."

"How dare you?" demands Nicole, choking back tears. "You have no right to be here."

Ben looks around aimlessly, as if hoping he'll be teleported out of the painfully awkward situation he's found himself in.

"*You!*" roars John, coming in to see what all the commotion is about.

"Mr. Alderton, I'm truly sorry to have imposed on you," says Ben, "but I just wanted to see your daughter."

John's nostrils flare. "She's not for seeing," he spits.

"But . . ." Ben starts.

"Not today. Not *ever.*"

"Mr. Alderton, if you'd just . . ."

"Just *what?*" spits John, stepping up to Ben so that their noses are almost touching. "You think being a high and mighty pop star means you can waltz in here, on today of all days, and demand to see my daughter?"

"Dad!" shrieks Nicole, taking hold of his arm, for fear he might hit Ben. "Let me handle this."

John laughs sardonically. "You have no idea what's been going on," he says disparagingly. "This sorry excuse for a man got your sister arrested for drugs."

A little piece of Nicole's heart breaks as she looks at Ben's confused expression, devastated, though not altogether surprised, that Cassie had been telling the truth. The shock is mirrored among the sea of faces of those around her—people who were there to honor the memory of her mother but are now being forced to witness the epic fallout taking place between those who loved her the most.

"She's sixteen!" cries John as Ben looks on in bewilderment.

"Hey, what's everyone—" comes a voice, *Cassie's* voice, before stopping short.

Nicole's head spins around, desperately looking for a way to prevent her little sister from being subjected to what's going on. But it's too late.

"What the . . . ?" starts Cassie, open-mouthed and frozen in the corner of the room, seemingly unable to believe the apparition standing in front of her.

Ben looks at her, and then looks again, his expression changing beyond all recognition.

"*You!*" he chokes, his hand going to his head. "I-I don't understand." He looks around at the gawping faces around him as if they'll provide the answer. "What are *you* doing here?" He makes a move toward Cassie. "Oh my god—are you OK?"

Cassie lets out an involuntary gasp. Nicole is on high alert as she watches, hoping with all her might that what's playing out in front of her isn't what it looks like. Because, despite herself, there's still a tiny part of her that wants to pretend that the relationship Cassie imagines she had with Ben is based on nothing but wishful thinking.

"Don't you take one more step . . ." warns John.

"I don't understand," says Ben, his face crumpling with confusion as he looks at Nicole. "Is she . . . is she your *sister*?" It's as if he's desperate for her to say no.

When she says nothing, he clenches his jaw. "I tried to get her help," he says. "You have to believe me. I did everything I could, but when I got back to the room, she'd disappeared."

Nicole winces, hoping that he stops there, because neither Cassie nor their dad need the night in question to be relived.

"I think you should leave," says Nicole, stepping forward.

"And then what happens?" he asks.

"You don't ever come back!" yells John.

"But I'm afraid I can't do that," says Ben, defiantly.

"And why's that?" John roars, pulling his arm back, as if getting ready to hit him.

Ben looks at Nicole with imploring eyes and the room goes silent. Everyone apart from the two of them seems to freeze in their positions, like toy figures whose windup clockwork has momentarily stopped as they wait for his answer. There's a pounding in Nicole's ears and her pulse beats through her skin like a thundering drum counting down the seconds to an execution. In the deafening silence that envelops the world outside her body, Nicole wills him to say the right thing, *do* the right thing—whatever that is—to preserve the hearts that aren't already broken.

"Because I'm in love with Nicole," he says, with unabashed clarity.

There's a wail—a gut-wrenching, bloodcurdling howl that reverberates around the room. Nicole instinctively puts her arms up to protect herself as a figure comes barreling toward her, but Cassie charges past her—past all of them—and out through the front door.

40

"I don't know how you didn't punch her," says Amelia, as Cassie lies on the grass bank outside her caravan. Amelia's mum is entertaining inside.

"I didn't know who to hit first: him or her," says Cassie, still in bitter denial that Ben was there for Nicole instead of her. She'd known there was every chance he would have been, bearing in mind they'd been sneaking around behind her back for the past month or so, but when she saw him standing in her living room, she'd still dared to believe that she was the reason for his visit. After all, how could Ben and Nicole's relationship have survived everything she'd thrown at it?

She'd known it was him the moment she picked up the phone extension to listen in to Nicole's conversation. And she thought she was going to throw up.

How was it even possible, she asked herself again and again. Was someone playing a sick game? Had their father got Nicole to set it up in the hope that it would deter Cassie from pursuing a relationship that he quite clearly disapproved of?

Her confusion had turned to pain, and pain had metamorphosed into an anger unlike anything she'd ever known. How dare they deceive her? How could the two people she loved more than anything in the world do that to her?

She'd imagined Ben ingratiating himself into their lives: picking her up from school in his limo, sitting at the family table for Sunday lunch, exchanging presents under the Christmas tree. But in all those fantasies, he was with *her*. The idea that he might do all those things but go to *Nicole*'s bed every night tore Cassie in two and left her entrails trailing behind her whenever she tried to put one foot in front of the other. It *couldn't* happen that way—she wouldn't allow it.

She'd thought that inventing a kiss-'n'-tell story for *The Sun* would be enough to detonate a bomb under their burgeoning relationship. She'd reveled in making up all the sordid details, imagining herself in the place of the naked girl from whose breasts Ben had allegedly snorted cocaine. When Cassie saw it in print the next day, she'd almost convinced herself it had actually happened, and she'd enjoyed watching her sister's discomfort as she relayed Ben's supposed indiscretion, safe in the knowledge that Nicole's pride and dignity would never allow her to be treated that way.

But then he had turned up at their house in the middle of the night, begging for Nicole to give him another chance. Cassie had sat at the top of the stairs in the darkness, listening to their hushed conversation in disbelief as he told her sister, the one person Cassie thought she could depend on, that she was the best thing that had ever happened to him.

It had taken all her resolve not to tear down the stairs and launch herself at them, not only because her hatred was so fierce that she was afraid of what she might be capable of, but because she knew it would only drive them further underground, and she needed them out in the open, where she could see them, so she could destroy whatever it was they'd convinced themselves they had.

She'd had to wait a few more days, and when the call came, she couldn't help but be disappointed to hear Nicole cave into his never-ending attempts to justify himself—not only because her sister clearly wasn't the woman she thought she was, but because it meant Cassie would have to go one step further to drive a stake into their relationship, once and for all.

On the day Nicole had agreed to meet Ben at the Langham hotel, Amelia had called her, posing as his assistant. She'd managed to work her wily ways and get a room for an hour—Cassie didn't ask what she'd had to do—and had ensconced herself, posing as Ben's "girlfriend" while he was supposedly in the "shower," so that Cassie could go and reclaim the relationship Nicole was seemingly so intent on stealing. But she hadn't reckoned on Ben's resilience and his love for her sister.

"So, what are you going to do now?" asks Amelia, chewing on her nail.

Cassie fixes her with an intense stare, wondering how much she should share. "What would *you* do?"

Amelia puffs out her cheeks. "If I found out Michael had screwed my sister, I'd cut off his balls and force her to watch."

Cassie wonders if the same would apply if she knew he was also capable of raping her best friend.

"You can't let them get away with it," Amelia goes on.

"I'm not intending to," says Cassie, not knowing whether she's referring to Ben, Nicole, or Michael, though in her mind they're all equally deserving of the punishment that's about to be unleashed upon them.

"So, what's the plan?" asks Amelia, her eyes darkening as the man she knows only as "Uncle" rounds the corner of the caravan.

"What you gonna kill her with today?" she calls out, her tone loaded with abject hostility.

He offers a black-toothed grin as he climbs the steps. "Whatever she wants to make the pain go away," he says, making it sound as if he's there for the good of her mum's health. "You want some?"

The girls look at each other, the unspoken words banging a drum in Cassie's head, as she wonders why she hasn't thought of it before.

41

The brown envelope goads me from the doormat, its postmark clearly overseas. The thought that, after all this time, across all those miles, a part of my father is this close to me makes me feel simultaneously anxious and comforted.

I'm immediately taken back to the last time I saw him, twenty-five years ago, as he shuffled into that courtroom. Having not seen him for six months, I remember being haunted by his gaunt and unkempt appearance. He was always a man of pride—proud to wear his Sunday best on every day of the week—but his suit was creased and two sizes too big for him, hanging listlessly from his prominent bones because there wasn't any flesh to cling to.

He'd looked at me with pleading eyes, as if silently begging me for forgiveness, but I didn't have the capacity to forgive anyone, least of all myself.

Had I known then that I would never see him again? And if I had, would I have done anything differently? I often think about that moment—about *all* the moments—when I saw the people in my life for the last time without knowing it; those final words, that last look, that parting touch, which I wouldn't realize until years later was the ultimate goodbye. Would I have held on tighter to my father for a little while longer? Would I have found it easier to forgive my little sister? Even now, after all this time, and after everything that went on, I still struggle to comprehend how the loving family I'd grown up surrounded by could be torn apart in such a spectacular fashion. But I guess killing someone can do that.

Still unmoving, I stare at the letter, wishing I had X-ray vision so that my eyes could preview its contents before my brain has a chance to be crushed by its lamentable words. In the twenty-four hours I've had to ruminate on what my father might have to say, I've realized that, good or bad, it can only hurt. If he shares his deep sorrow and regret that life has passed without us having a chance to reconcile, it'll wrench my heart and soul out. And if he spews hate and resentment, blaming me for the breakdown of our once-perfect family, I won't be surprised, but it will still cut deep. Though, if he hated me that much, why would he have left me his estate?

I edge forward, leaning down heavily to pick it up. It feels like a grenade in my hand, and I throw it onto the console table as if it's about to explode. Perhaps it's all a test, an elaborate ruse to smoke me out. Perhaps my father isn't dead at all, and it's a sick game to extract something I'm not prepared to give.

The conspiracy theories abound as I take deep breaths in and out, questioning what's the worst that could happen if I didn't open it at all. I've lived without his thoughts and influence for twenty-five years, so why do I need either now? And it's not as if anything he says can possibly change the course of my life. But perhaps I already know that there's a chance it just might—and that's what I'm most terrified of.

My hands are trembling, and I still my breath as I gingerly open it, half expecting my father himself to jump out. There's another envelope inside, its contents protected by a wax seal, with my maiden name on the front. It's unmistakably my father's spidery writing, and an involuntary sob escapes from deep within my chest as my finger traces the ink that ran from the pen he once held.

There are only two pages, so whatever he has to say, it's not much. But as I start to read, I'm immediately aware that the weight of his words more than make up for the weight of the paper.

Dearest Nicole,

I couldn't leave this world without telling you how sorry I am for the decisions I made when I was here. The consequences of my actions have followed me for my entire life—losing you as a daughter has certainly been the most costly.

All I ever wanted to do was protect my girls— and if you're now a mother yourself, you'll understand that.

Being a parent is tough, and although I didn't always get it right, I want you to know that I never stopped loving you, and truly believed that we'd see each other one last time. But if you're reading this, I guess that didn't happen, so this is my final chance to say what needs to be said.

There isn't a day that's gone by when I haven't thought about Ben, and what I did to him. If I could turn back the clock, believe me, I would, but in a moment of madness, I made a terrible mistake for which I have never been able to forgive myself. And I don't expect you to forgive me now. But I need you to know why I did it, because to go to my grave without telling you would be even more indefensible than the act itself . . .

I read on, because I have to, but the words have all jumbled themselves up so that nothing he says is making any sense. I close my eyes, forcing deep breaths in and out in an effort to stay calm, but my heart is racing and I feel so instantaneously sick that I have to rush to open the back door. I can't breathe, my lungs only half filling before collapsing again as I remember Ben—his smoldering eyes staring out at me from behind his guitar, that stomach-churning excitement that set my skin alight when he held me in his arms, the smell of him, even the thrill of the secret we were hiding in those sweet short weeks when we dared to believe it was going to be forever.

Bitter injustice rips through me and, as I fall to my knees, I vow to do what I should have done twenty-five years ago: tell the truth.

42

The press conference for Secret Oktober's surprise announcement is being held in the ballroom of the Savoy hotel, and Cassie sneaks in the back door behind Amelia, after her friend works her usual magic on their security guard.

There are only a few seats left, and they sidle up behind a journalist with a mass of curly hair, hoping that she'll disguise their presence.

"You sure you want to do this?" Amelia whispers.

Cassie nods as the microphone gets tapped with a dull thud.

"I'd like to thank you all for coming," comes a voice through the speaker, hushing the crowded room. "May I please ask you to put your hands together and give a warm welcome to Secret Oktober— Luke, Michael, and Ben . . ."

There's a smattering of applause and Cassie is grateful for the dimming of the audience lights. It means she can hide for a little while longer, though in any case the spotlight is quickly cast upon the boys as they make their way across the stage.

Cassie knew that seeing Ben would twist a knife deep within her soul, the depth of his and Nicole's deceit hitting her full in the chest. But it's the visceral reaction she has upon seeing Michael that takes her unaware. Her mouth dries up and her hands begin to tremble as he looks out across the sea of heads with a smile of self-satisfaction.

"Welcome to the hottest ticket in town," he says sarcastically as he takes his seat next to Ben behind the table on the stage. The pair of them don't even look at each other.

"Good to see you all," says Luke. "We're excited to be here."

The questions from the press come thick and fast, mostly about Ben's supposed indiscretion in America. Watching his face flicker between panic and resignation pulls at the back of Cassie's throat.

"We won't be making any comment on what's gone before," says Luke.

Ben's face glazes over, as if he's a thousand miles away.

"Yeah, this is about new beginnings," says Michael, smiling like a cat who's got the cream as he looks along the line at his bandmates without a shred of conscience. "We're going on tour—the biggest tour the world has ever seen . . ."

Cassie can't bear to look at him; even his voice makes her shudder.

"But what about Ben's drug problem?" calls a journalist. "Shouldn't he be going to rehab instead of embarking on a world tour?"

"Look, Ben's addressed his issues and he's got the help he needed," says Michael, patting Ben's back in a manner so condescending that even Luke, normally placid and unbiased, looks on nervously.

"So, the rumors that this press conference was to announce the band's breakup are unfounded?" asks another journalist.

"Absolutely," says Michael, before Ben can even open his mouth. "I don't know where you get these stories from."

"I heard there was trouble in paradise," says the journalist. "That you two weren't getting on so well these days."

Michael kisses his teeth. "We're brothers, man. There ain't nothing that can tear us apart."

"Not even the fact that Ben is making sweet music with someone else?" pipes up Cassie, earlier than she'd intended. "I can't imagine you being happy with that."

The crowd titter at the double entendre, but a hushed silence quickly descends as Michael makes a show of turning to look at Ben, forcing him to respond.

"I can't say I'm surprised that a tabloid hack is misinformed and barking up the wrong tree," says Ben dourly. "But once again, you've not checked your facts."

"Oh *really?*" says Cassie. "Because I have it on good authority that you've recorded tracks with an unknown artist called Nicole Alderton."

Ben's jaw twitches as he looks out across the packed ballroom, his silence speaking volumes.

"Is that something you'd care to tell *all* of us about?" asks Michael, sounding as if he was waiting for a reason to put Ben on the spot.

Cassie smiles to herself, grateful for the helping hand, even if it's being offered by someone who doesn't yet know that he stands to lose more than anyone.

"If I choose to collaborate with anyone else, it's not to the detriment of the band," says Ben, through gritted teeth. "None of us are contractually obliged. We're all free to pursue our own individual paths . . ."

Michael laughs inanely. "If *that* were the case, I'd be in Guns N' Roses." His caustic tone bites through the darkening atmosphere.

Ben throws him a derisory glance, the tension between them palpable.

"What?" Michael snaps, his nostrils flaring. "Do you honestly think I'd be in this shitty band if it weren't for my loyalty to you and Luke? Though I'm beginning to think that might be misplaced."

Ben shakes his head. "You are *so* deluded."

"What's *that* supposed to mean?"

"I'm not going to do this here," says Ben, looking away.

"OK, guys," says Luke, laughing nervously as Michael agitatedly clenches and unclenches his fists. "Who's got a question for us about the tour?"

"No, come on!" barks Michael, ignoring his bandmate's attempt to defuse the situation. "If you've got something to say, say it." He looks at Ben as if daring him to take him up on his challenge.

Ben's lips pull tight, as if it's taking all his restraint not to retaliate. "Do you know what?" he says, going to stand up. "I'm done here."

"You're *done* here?" mimics Michael, as he raises himself up to full height. "What the fuck is *that* supposed to mean?"

"It means, I'm done with this—I'm done with *you*."

The watching journalists move to the edge of their seats, with poised pens and trigger-happy fingers on cameras, as if waiting for the fight bell to ring.

"You gonna walk out on Secret Oktober, bro?" says Michael, looking to the audience and pulling a face. "*Here*, in front of the nation's press?"

"I'm done with you, and I'm done with the band," says Ben, turning his back to him.

"What do you think you're playing at?" yells Michael, as if suddenly sensing that he's serious. "You don't quit the band *I* started, the band that's made you a global fucking superstar, even with your limited talents."

"The band *we* started," says Ben, correcting him. "See, that's the problem: Your ego has become so oversized that you don't even know what's real anymore. You think this is the Michael fucking Delaney show—that we're all here to whistle to your tune. Well, guess what? I'm not doing it. You can't pull that shit with me anymore."

"If you walk away now, you're going to regret it," says Michael, taking hold of Ben's arm.

"Oh yeah?" Ben laughs acerbically. "What you gonna do?"

"I'm gonna fucking kill you."

As Michael's furled fist makes contact with Ben's jaw, the crack reverberates through the speaker system and the audience gasp, first in shock, then in a panicked rush to gather evidence of what must surely be the biggest band fallout in history; it's certainly the most public.

But Cassie stays where she is, unable to keep the smile from her face as she watches the fuse she lit explode. That was far easier than she thought it was going to be.

43

Horns blast and oncoming drivers gesticulate as I run a red light, so desperate to get there before it's too late that I can't see straight. When my phone rings, I fumble for it in the center console, but my hands are shaking so much that I drop it into the footwell. I lose my grip on the steering wheel as I make a grab for it, swerving into the middle of the road.

My breathing is louder than the music on the radio, yet the only thing I can hear are my father's words jumping off the page and sounding a death knell in my head.

"Please, god," I beg, willing someone I don't believe in to give me one good reason why he might be lying. But the resounding silence is deafening.

By the time I pull into the hotel parking lot, I'm convinced that Zoe's already gone, having given up on chasing a dead end. Or perhaps she'd known more than I had given her credit for? Did she know who I really was? What I'd done . . . ?

With my hand on the car door, I take a few seconds to force myself to breathe in and out long and slow, to stop myself from hyperventilating. I've only got one chance at this and I can't afford to screw it up.

My heart is still pounding out of my chest as I sprint into the hotel lobby and across to the front desk, demanding attention from the first person who looks in my direction.

"I need to speak to Zoe Mortimer. She's staying here and it's urgent." It comes out in a rush.

The receptionist taps a keyboard while I tap my nails, impatiently waiting for him to tell me that redemption is nigh.

"She's checked out," he says, as if it means nothing.

My legs buckle. *No, no, no, no, no . . .*

"Where was she going? Did she leave a forwarding address? Do you have a phone number?"

He looks at me as if I'm crazy, or at least thinks *he* might be losing it. "I'm sorry, madam, we can't—"

"She was going to the airport," interrupts a colleague without looking up from her screen. "About fifteen minutes ago."

My shoulders slump. I can't possibly catch up with her now. The thought that my only hope of making things right has left on the red-eye to London makes my throat close up.

"Are you looking for me?" comes a voice.

I swing around and a guttural cry catches in my chest. "Oh, thank god!"

Zoe's standing there with her coat over her arm and a suitcase at her feet.

"You can't go. I *have* to speak to you."

Her eyes widen. "I thought you didn't want to . . ."

"Something's changed."

She looks at me with tears in her eyes. "What can possibly have changed since yesterday? Everything you know now, you knew then."

"No," I say, shaking my head, vehemently. "I didn't know why all this was happening or why you were here, but it's all falling into place."

"I didn't come here to make things difficult for you," says Zoe.

"I know," I say, daring to believe that she might mean it. "And I'm sorry for shutting down on you."

"I don't want anything more from you than you're prepared to give," she says. "I just wanted to give you the chance . . ."

I shudder. Give me the chance to do what? To confess? To tell her how sorry I am?

She goes to step forward, but seems to think better of it and stays put.

"Where do we go from here?" she says in a small voice.

My jaw spasms as I look at her, knowing this is my last chance for my life to resemble anything close to normal. But what choice do I have?

"Do you know where he is?" I dare to ask.

She nods.

"Then I need you to take me to him," I say.

44

Nicole can't get to the Savoy quickly enough once Ben called to tell her that Cassie had been at the press conference, but that she'd disappeared before he could speak to her. "Who else would know that stuff?" he'd said, when she'd asked if he was sure.

After being up all night looking for her, trying anywhere Cassie may have gone to escape the pain of Nicole's deceit, she can't help but wonder why her sister would punish herself even more by going to the press conference.

"Excuse me, madam," says a uniformed guard standing by the lift. "Can I see your room key, please?"

Nicole huffs. She hasn't got time for this. "I'm going to room 239," she says, going to push past his outstretched arm.

"If you wouldn't mind reporting to the front desk first," he says, putting his hand in the small of her back to guide her toward reception.

"Look, I'm just . . ."

"I have a young lady here looking for room 239," says the man to the woman behind the desk. A brief conspiratorial nod of mutual understanding passes between them, making Nicole feel like a groupie trying her luck.

"Are you a guest of the hotel?" asks the woman, with her nose in the air.

"I'm visiting," says Nicole impatiently.

"And *who* might you be visiting?" she asks, getting ready, with smug superiority, to signal to the guard to remove Nicole.

Nicole almost doesn't want to give her the satisfaction of saying it out loud, but she *has* to find Cassie. "Peter Pan," she says.

The woman's assured expression becomes pinched as she gives the guard a reluctant nod.

As soon as his grip on her is released, Nicole races to the lift and pushes at the buttons indiscriminately, wondering if she'll find Cassie quicker if she takes the stairs. But the reassuring ping is almost immediate and, as she steps inside the mirrored box, she can't help but wonder what will await her when the doors open onto the parallel universe two floors up. Will Ben have found Cassie and be talking her round? Or will she have done something so unimaginable that none of their consciences will ever recover?

Of all the unthinkable scenarios Nicole's disturbed mind offers her, the one she hasn't allowed for was to find Michael prowling the second-floor corridor, pacing back and forth outside Ben's room.

"You'd better open this fucking door right now!" he roars, smashing his fist into what looks like an already splintered door.

Nicole momentarily freezes, knowing what this brute is capable of. But when she pictures Cassie's tear-stained face as he forces himself onto her, she's overcome with a rage so all-consuming that she can't hold back, painfully aware that if anything's happened to her, he's as guilty as she is.

"Where is she?" Nicole screams, running at him and beating her fists into his chest. "Where's my sister?"

"What the . . . ?" he yells as he grabs hold of her flailing hands and slams her back against the wall.

"I *know* what you did," she spits, writhing to free herself from his tightening grip. "And if anything's happened to her, I'll spend the rest of my life making sure you pay for it."

Michael's nostrils flare and he raises his hand. Nicole flinches, bracing for impact.

"Don't you fucking dare!" comes a voice.

Michael's arm freezes in midair and his grin makes him look psychotic as he turns to see Ben racing toward them.

"Are you fucking kidding me?" he sneers, as Ben takes hold of Nicole and pushes her behind him. "Is this *her*? Is this the reason you're not thinking straight?"

Michael's wide-eyed stare and dilated pupils set Nicole's teeth on edge and, despite jutting her jaw defiantly and willing herself to stand tall, the fearless fight she was happy to pick a few seconds ago has suddenly deserted her. Without even realizing it, she's backed herself up against the wall; as if sensing her discomfort, Michael smiles, making her feel as if she's a toy mouse on a piece of string.

"So, you're making music *and* fucking . . . ?" he sneers, whistling through his teeth. "Man, you never cease to surprise me. You could have any girl you wanted . . ."

Ben's jaw spasms at Michael's attempt to make Nicole feel worthless, but she pulls on his hand, holding him back from doing anything he might live to regret.

"So, you're just going to let Miss Yoko Ono here destroy everything we've worked our arses off for?"

"You've done that all by yourself," snaps Ben.

Michael turns to Nicole. "You must be really something if you've got the power to stop our boy in his tracks . . ."

"Nicole, go inside," says Ben, his eyes never leaving Michael.

She'd love nothing more than to do what he's telling her, but her feet are cemented to the ground, seemingly immovable, though whether it's from shock or fear she doesn't know.

"I can't see it myself," Michael goes on. "But then I've never had a redhead—and by all accounts they go like the clappers, so maybe I should give you a go." He pushes past Ben and thrusts himself at Nicole, making a grab for her breast.

Suddenly there's a flash of movement as Ben's fist hits Michael's jaw square on. His head snaps back and he momentarily lurches sideways as he attempts to find his footing.

"I'm gonna fucking kill you!" Ben yells, as he hits him again, sending blood splatters onto his T-shirt.

"Ben, no!" screams Nicole, attempting to pull him off as Michael staggers, trying to right himself.

"Stay out of this," yells Ben, wrenching himself free to lunge at Michael again. But he's had a split-second reprieve—enough time to retaliate.

The punch sends Ben backward, his feet momentarily leaving the ground and his body buckling under the force of Michael's knuckles. "You think you're so high and mighty," roars Michael, his eyes bulging out of their sockets. "But you're *nothing* without me." His spittle sprays the air, his words landing even harder than the punch.

Ben sways on unsteady feet and Michael can't disguise a smug grin as he wipes blood from his lip with the back of his hand.

As much as Nicole can't bear to see Ben hurt, Cassie is far more important than the bruised egos of two men who should know better.

She races into the room that Ben came out of, hoping to find Cassie there, out of harm's way. She no longer cares what may or may not have gone on between them—it's all become irrelevant since the funeral. All she needs to know is that she's safe. But the room is woefully empty, and Nicole races down the opposite end of the corridor from where Michael and Ben are still trying to defend their pride with warring words and physical exchanges.

"You need to get someone up to the second floor," she says to the guard as she emerges from the lift into the lobby. "They're about to kill each other."

If she'd known how prophetic her words were, and that they'd later be relied upon in a court of law, she would have chosen them more carefully.

45

Neither of us says a word for the first twenty minutes, but with another hundred miles to go, one of us has to break the deadlock.

"So, is your *mother* . . ." The word gets stuck in my throat. "Is she still alive?"

There's a deafening silence and I don't know what I want the answer to be.

"No," says Zoe, quietly. "She died about six months ago."

"I'm sorry," I offer.

"She was too young, but cancer doesn't discriminate." I can feel her turn to look at me. "But then, you'd know that."

The image of my own mother, smiling in happier times, makes my throat tighten.

"So, that's why you're doing this now?"

"I guess," she says. "The tape became sort of folklore in our house. She always imparted its importance to me, telling me that I should follow wherever it takes me, whenever I was ready."

"And it brought you here?" I ask, the pair of us daring to look at each other for a fleeting second.

"It felt like the right time," she says. "Everything seemed to conspire toward us coming together."

"Why weren't you honest about who you were when you first came to see me?" I ask.

She shrugs. "I suppose I was scared of how you might react. I didn't want to dredge up all the bad memories of a time I assumed you'd rather forget."

I can't help but be touched by how considerate she is, even though her undeserved empathy feels like shards of glass in my throat whenever I swallow.

I reach across the center console, taking her hand and giving it a squeeze. "Your father would be proud," I choke, unnerved by the feeling of her skin against mine. *His* skin against mine.

"When did you know?" she asks in a small voice.

I wipe away the errant tear that I can't stop from falling onto my cheek. "If I'm honest with myself, I think I probably knew the very first moment I saw you. Something about your eyes, the shape of your jaw, burrowed its way into my subconscious, although I was too scared to give it air to breathe."

"What are you frightened of?"

I snatch back my trembling hand. If only she knew.

"I'm not here to cause trouble," she says.

I refrain from asking why it seems that trouble has followed me around ever since she arrived.

"So, what *do* you want?"

There's a lengthy pause. "Answers, I guess. I want to know what really happened to my father. What happened to you. Why you ran away."

"I *didn't* run away," I say, far too sharply.

"It seems like you did, from where I'm sitting."

Is that honestly what she thinks of me? But then I pull myself up short. Why would she think any differently? All she's undoubtedly been told was that I left the very first moment I could, taking my version of events with me. Is it any wonder then that she wants to know more, *needs* to know more, about the event that has shaped her life and so many others' since?

"After the trial, I just . . ." My voice wavers as I remember taking the stand, knowing what I knew and waiting for it to be revealed. "I just needed to get away. I was still getting over what had happened, trying to hide myself away, but the trial meant that my entire world erupted all over again. It was day upon day, week after week, of questioning and speculating, both in court and in the media. They were desperate to tarnish your father's character, needing to prove that he deserved what happened to him, but I refused to give them what they wanted." I look to her. "Do you know why?"

She shakes her head.

"Because he wasn't entirely the man they made him out to be. Your father was a lot of things, but know this: had he lived to see you, to know you, he would have loved you unreservedly. He didn't deserve to die, and all of us who were there that day were accountable in some way or another. Every one of us played a part in what happened: me, Michael, Ben, my father, my sister . . . We were all to blame in some way or another, and it haunts me every day to know that it would have taken only one tiny variable to stop it."

"That's what I've always been told, too," says Zoe sadly. "That but for a particular sequence of events, none of it would ever have happened . . ."

I nod regretfully, ruing the sacrifices we've all had to make since that day, not least Zoe, who has missed out on so much since being born among the ruins of a shattered dream.

"I'm so very sorry," I manage. "If I could go back and change it, please know that I'd do so in a heartbeat."

"Funny—my mother used to say the same . . ." says Zoe, half smiling at the memory. "She always wished that things had been different. That she could have given me the real family she thought I deserved."

"So, she was honest from the outset?" I ask.

"As soon as I was old enough," says Zoe, nodding. "It was little things at first, like your tape in the attic. I don't think she was expecting me to find it—it was pretty well hidden—so when I started asking questions about it, I think she was taken aback. I was still young, and I don't think she was ready. But bit by bit, year after year, she opened up a little more, slowly revealing my history and telling me who I really was."

"She sounds like an incredible woman," I offer, though I can't help but admit that it pains me. "And to be so generous as to help you find me . . ."

"Oh, *she* didn't help me find you," says Zoe. "Aunt Cassie did."

46

"Are you looking for Cassie?" asks a voice, as Nicole hurriedly makes her way through the teenage throng that has congregated on the concourse outside the Savoy hotel. Hearing her sister's name, here, out of context, jolts her like an electric shock.

"Where is she?" demands Nicole, turning toward a girl who looks vaguely familiar—but with her scrambled brain, Nicole can't even begin to work out where she recognizes her from.

The girl chews on the inside of her cheek, as if contemplating whether to tell her or not, and it takes all of Nicole's self-control not to *shake* it out of her.

"Cassie told me what you did," she says, eventually.

"*What?*" says Nicole, her frustration mired with the alarm bell that's been set off in her head.

"She told me what you did," says the girl, almost cryptically. "You know, with Ben and stuff . . ."

The thought of a lynch mob suddenly descending on her only adds to Nicole's mounting problems. "Who even *are* you?"

"I'm Amelia, Cassie's best friend."

Since when? Nicole stops herself from asking. She's never heard of her, and in that moment she feels a pang of guilt for being so wrapped up in her own world that she doesn't know such a simple fact about her sister. "Do you know where she is?" she asks again.

"She's really upset," says Amelia.

"Why, what happened?" Nicole asks.

"Who does that to her own sister?" says Amelia. "Why would you even think of getting between Ben and Cassie?"

Nicole bites her tongue, seeing no point in putting her straight, because despite her sister's insistence that they were in a relation- ship, she is yet to find proof of anything more than an unrequited crush on her favorite pop star. Though she can't help but ask herself who's more deluded: Cassie or herself?

"Everything was going along fine until you showed up," Amelia goes on. "They were really into each other."

"She *told* you that?" asks Nicole, unable to help herself.

"I *saw* it," says Amelia brusquely. "Who do you think he was with the other night at the Langham, when you had the nerve to show up? They knew you were coming. That's why they had to change rooms, so they could get away from you."

A ticking time bomb goes off in Nicole's head. "*What?*"

"She told me she knew you'd overheard them making arrange- ments on the phone, and she knew you'd pitch up and try to ruin things, so she had to swap rooms . . ."

It's as if Nicole is being dragged through a vortex, back to when, despite her reservations, she'd succumbed to Ben's unrelenting pleas to see him. Back to when she'd arrived at his hotel room with a glimmer of hope that perhaps they could turn things around—only for any promise of utopia to be cruelly snatched away when a girl claiming to be his girlfriend opened the door.

"*You!*" she gasps, suddenly seeing the girl standing in front of her for who she really is. "It was *you* in that room!"

Amelia shrugs her shoulders.

"Fuck!" Nicole puts her hands on her head and walks around in a circle. "Ben wasn't even *in* the shower, *was* he?"

"Well, you weren't taking the hint," says Amelia, without an iota of irony. "You should have backed off when the story about the model came out, but that didn't seem enough to deter you either."

"Oh my god," shrieks Nicole, unable to help herself. "What kind of fucked-up game is that?"

Amelia's eyes shift, as if sensing for the first time that she may have been played by Cassie as much as Nicole has.

"Do you have *any* idea of the damage you've caused?" yells Nicole. "Of the delusion you've indulged? You helped Cassie create a fantasy in her head—one that was *never* going to happen."

"She loves him, and all she wanted was for him to love her back," says Amelia quietly.

"You can't force someone to love you," barks Nicole.

"Well, then she's going to die trying," says Amelia, turning to walk away.

Fear reaches its talons into Nicole's chest, making it feel as if her heart is being ripped out. "Where *is* she?" she roars, taking hold of Amelia's arm and spinning her around. "Where's my sister?"

Amelia fixes her with an unmoving glare. "She's gone to be with her mum," she says.

47

CALIFORNIA, 2011

"*Cassie?*" I gasp, my sister's name feeling like sandpaper on my lips, so used to banishing her existence to the depths of my consciousness. "So, she knows you're here?"

Zoe nods enthusiastically. "It was actually her idea to find you."

"But how . . . ? Why now . . . ?" I stutter.

"After Mum died and I found the tape again, I couldn't stop listening to your song:

> "*There are things I could never teach you, no matter how hard I try,*
> *Because only you can decide how high you fly,*
> *I can set you on your way and catch you if you fall,*
> *But only you will know . . . I would die for you.*"

I struggle to keep the steering wheel under control as Zoe's angelic voice fills the car.

"But the more I listened to it," she says, breaking off, "the more I needed answers. So, I lost myself in a bottomless pit of conspiracy theories, wishing I'd asked Mum more when I had the chance. But Cassie helped separate fact from fiction, though she said if I really wanted the truth, I'd have to find *you*. Because only then would I be able to put the final pieces of the jigsaw together."

"Is she here?" I find myself asking, fearing I already know the answer.

She nods, and an inexplicable anger floods my veins as I remember the way I steadfastly rejected Hannah's protestations that her "aunt" had picked her up from school, so sure that it was an impossibility. And the accusations I threw at Brad when he said my sister had been on the phone come back to haunt me, my conscience shamed by the memory of how I would rather believe him to be having an affair than for his claim to be true.

Was it Cassie at the convention center? Had she mounted the despicable attack against the seals just to call my reputation into question? Ripping it to shreds . . .

"I understand why *you're* here," I say. "But what does *she* want?"

Zoe shrugs her shoulders. "I think she's been feeling much like I have since you both lost your dad. She feels angry and aggrieved that they didn't resolve their differences before he died . . ."

I shake my head, shocked by my naivety. All this time, I've assumed they'd maintained their relationship long after mine ended. I tortured myself with picture-perfect imaginings of how they must have supported each other through the aftermath. How he walked her down the aisle. How he played grandfather to her children. But how could he have?

The letter he'd so painstakingly written comes back to haunt me, his every word etched with profound regret as he played out the consequences of his actions over and over in his mind with each letter he scrawled. What must it have taken for him to tell the truth after all this time?

". . . And she doesn't want to make the same mistake with you," Zoe goes on, snapping me out of my maudlin reverie.

"I think it's a little late for that," I say.

"Well, I think she's prepared to do whatever it takes to prove you wrong," says Zoe, looking at me. "She's determined to make sure that nothing remains unsaid between you."

An intense heat consumes my entire being, crushing me with panic and claustrophobia.

"I guess she's ultimately looking for a happy ending," says Zoe, seemingly oblivious to my distress. "And she thinks you're it."

48

I take a final look back at Zoe in the car as I pull my jacket around me, tucking my shaking hands under my crossed arms. The thought of what I'm about to do is so far removed from the romanticized version I'd so often fantasized about.

All this time, I've laughingly convinced myself that I would finally be at peace if I could just be honest. But standing here, knowing that the person in the house that I'm now standing outside of deserves to know the truth more than anyone else, makes my heart thump through my chest.

I take a breath, suddenly aware of how deathly silent it is. The hum of the freeway can no longer be heard and even the birds seem to have stopped tweeting—or maybe they know the enormity of what's about to happen and have flown farther afield, not brave enough to stay and watch the fallout. As I look up at the drawn curtains, imagining the person behind them, I can't say I blame them.

I close my eyes before lifting the metal door knocker, knowing this is the last chance I have to back out. But I can't. This *has* to be done, and if I'm not prepared to face the consequences now, I never will be.

As the door slowly opens and a head peers around it, I almost apologize and start to turn away, knowing that this man can't possibly be the boy I loved so deeply, so profoundly, all those years ago. His skin is lined and sallow, his hair gray and thinning, and his once razor-sharp cheekbones have been lost in plump jowls.

I can't help but be taken aback, because in all the millions of times I'd pictured this moment, he has always appeared exactly as I left him. Forever young, having never grown up and aged like everybody else. But it seems that time catches up with all of us in the end, because he can't see who I am either, no matter how hard he tries, his brow furrowed.

"Can I help you?" he asks nervously, clearly unused to visitors coming all this way into the Hollywood Hills without good reason. I daren't tell him that I've driven two and a half hours just to see him.

"Ben?"

He cocks his head, as if it will help, but his eyes—in which I can see no semblance of his old self—are still unable to recognize me.

"I'm sorry, I think you've got the wrong address," he says, going to close the door.

"Ben, it—it's me," I say, putting a hand out to stop him. "Nicole." He freezes. "*Nicole?*"

I nod and tears immediately spring to his eyes.

"Can I come in?"

For a moment, he looks as if he might say no, but then the door opens a little wider and he silently beckons me in, his voice shocked into silence.

"I'm sorry to show up like this . . . I didn't know how else to—"

"It—it's OK," he manages. "I guess there's a part of me, deep down, that's always been expecting you."

"You know why I'm here?" I ask, his revelation only adding to my sense of foreboding.

"I've got a good idea," he says, turning away. "Although you're five years late."

I choke at the reference, unable to believe that he'd remember our pact to meet in Los Angeles twenty years on.

"I guess neither of our lives panned out quite how we expected," I say.

"So, what took you so long?" he asks, as he leads me down the hall.

The living room is in total disarray: paperwork is piled in towering mountains; the mail lies unopened on the sofa, on the table, behind the clock on the fireplace; and vinyl record sleeves form abstract patterns on the floor.

"I was never brave enough," I offer quietly.

"So, why now?" he asks, going to the sideboard and pouring himself a double measure of whiskey into a tumbler. He knocks it back in one, scowling as the heat of the liquid hits the back of his throat.

"Because I need to tell you something," I say, before I have a chance to change my mind.

He waits with raised eyebrows, refusing to make this easy for me. I don't blame him.

"I can't even begin to tell you how sorry I am."

He fixes me with a look so intense that I suddenly see the man I used to know so well. I'm back in that recording studio, our faces so close that our noses are touching as we share the mic, naively daring to believe that the sense of utopia that we've inexplicably found, in the music we're making, could last forever.

"So, finally there's an apology . . ." he murmurs, with an air of detachment, as if he's talking about somebody else's life. I presume it's a skill he's had to employ in order to survive the grave miscarriage of justice that was bestowed upon him.

"It's been a long time coming," I say.

"Do you know how many journalists and armchair detectives have come knocking over the years, every one of them looking to unlock the *real* reason I did what I did?" He laughs falsely. "And yet not one—*not one*—suggested that perhaps I didn't do anything at all."

A viselike grip squeezes my airways, crushing my ribs. "I can't imagine what it must feel like to have spent all these years being punished for something you had no part in."

His lips pull thin. "Why are you here, Nicole?"

A single tear escapes and I hastily wipe it away. "Because everything has changed."

He studies me with suspicion before pouring whiskey into two tumblers and holding one out in my direction. I accept it readily with a shaking hand, needing something, *anything*, to dull my nerve endings.

"My father passed away . . ." I start.

His eyes narrow. "I wish I could say I'm sorry," he says bitterly as he swirls the amber-colored liquid around his glass.

I reach into my handbag. "I didn't have any contact with him after the trial. I hadn't spoken to him for twenty-five years before receiving this letter from him this morning."

There's a noise outside the room and I look up expectantly, first to the door and then to Ben, but if he hears it, he doesn't react. It suddenly occurs to me that we may not be alone in the house; he could have a wife at home, children . . .

"Are you OK to have this conversation here?" I ask, hating myself for not having checked before now. How hard has he had to work to build a new world for himself? He'd traveled thousands of miles to leave the past behind, hopefully met a loving wife, surrounded himself with a family of his own . . . Do *they* know who he is? What he's supposed to have done? I go to stand up, in case they don't. I had a huge hand in destroying his life once; I won't be responsible for doing it all over again.

"It's fine" is all he says. "Tell me what's in the letter."

I cough awkwardly to clear my throat, as if biding my time, but then I wonder why. He must already know what's coming.

"He asks for forgiveness," I start.

"Yours or mine?"

"Both," I say. "But it's only yours to grant."

"Only a coward waits until they're dead to tell the truth," he says bitterly.

"I think you'd be surprised at the strength and resilience it would have taken to lie for all these years."

"*Strength and resilience?*" he cries, his nostrils flaring as he displays his hurt and anger for the first time. "Do you have *any* idea how much strength and resilience I needed when they stripped me of my belongings, my clothes? When they threw me in a six-by-ten windowless cell for five years? When I remembered the life I had before . . . *That*'s resilience—not some lame confession, twenty-five years too late!"

He paces the room like a caged lion, his resentment palpable.

"And now I'm supposed to be grateful that your father has finally admitted that he lied."

I bite down on my lip as I picture my dad giving evidence in court: his hollowed cheeks, his empty eyes, his mumbled words as he tried to explain what happened that day . . .

"I-I went to the hotel looking for my daughter—Cassie . . ." he'd said. "She was . . . She'd gone missing . . . and Nicole . . . she'd already gone to the hotel . . . and I thought I should . . . you know . . ."

"Mr. Alderton, I appreciate how difficult this trial is for you and your family," said the prosecution lawyer as she approached the witness stand. "It must have taken its toll."

My father had nodded his assent.

"So, just take your time," she said. "Keep your answers clear and concise."

"O-K . . ." he said, forcing himself to take a deep breath in and out.

"So, after your younger daughter, Cassandra, had gone missing the day before, following a disagreement—which we'll come to later—your elder daughter, Nicole, received a telephone call from Ben Edwards to say that Cassandra was at the Savoy hotel."

"Y-yes, that's correct."

"But once Nicole left to find her, you felt that you should go too . . ."

"Yes, about an hour or so later, when I hadn't heard anything, I thought I'd feel more useful if . . . if I were there too . . ."

"So, when you got to the hotel, what did you find?"

"Well, there were girls everywhere and I didn't know where to start, so I looked in all the common areas—you know, like the restaurants and the ballroom, where somebody said the press conference had been . . . I even looked in the toilets, but I couldn't find her or Nicole and I was getting worried. Cassie was in a fragile state, and I didn't know what she might be capable of."

"So, after searching the common areas of the hotel to no avail, what did you do next?"

My father had looked down at the fidgeting hands in his lap. "I took the lift up and walked along the corridors. I don't know what I was expecting to find . . ."

"And what *did* you find, Mr. Alderton?" asked the lawyer.

"Erm, well . . . when I got to the second floor, I heard shouting . . ." He brought a shaking handkerchief up to his brow. "And then . . . then . . . I saw *him*."

The lawyer had snapped her head toward where my father was looking. "By *him*, do you mean Mr. Edwards?"

"Y-yes."

"Liar!" Ben had called out from the dock. "He's lying!"

My father had frozen, like a deer in headlights, his eyes the only thing moving as he peered around the courtroom, gauging whether people were believing him or Ben.

"And where was he, Mr. Alderton?"

Ben had stared at him, silently begging him to change his story.

"Mr. Alderton?" the lawyer pushed, when there was no response.

"He was going into room 245," my father had said, clearing his throat. "Michael Delaney's room."

Now, I look to Ben, whose eyes burrow into my soul, as if he can see the very same flashback. No doubt the scene has been on repeat in his head for years.

"I'm not expecting you to forgive my father for what he did," I say. "But I can only ask that you try and understand."

"How do you expect me to do that?" Ben says brusquely.

I think of Zoe sitting in the car outside, me promising I'd bring her in if it felt like the right thing to do.

"Do you have children?" I ask, remembering the dreamscape we'd naively created back when we were together. We were going to have three: two boys and a girl—Stevie, Eric, and Joni, named after our musical inspirations—who we were going to homeschool as we traveled the world on tour. A whimsical fantasy from another lifetime.

Ben shakes his head ruefully—yet another punishment he's had to endure.

I swallow my regret—not only for what he's missed out on, but for what we all, in one way or another, lost on that fateful day.

"I have someone I want you to meet," I say.

49

Amid all the furore of the press conference, it's easy for Cassie to snatch Ben's jacket—with its distinctive spray-painted logo—from the back of his chair and walk unnoticed to the lift. She lets herself into room 245 with the key Amelia had managed to extract from the bellboy in exchange for sexual favors.

There's a moment's hesitation as she turns the key in the lock, but as soon as Michael's musky scent permeates her nostrils, Cassie's suddenly underneath him again and all thoughts of backing out transform into a rabid ball of anger.

She helps herself to the minibar as she waits, drinking anything that will help numb her nerves and steady her resolve, all the while psyching herself up for when he eventually arrives.

She doesn't have to wait more than fifteen minutes for him to burst through the door and, as expected, he's blinded by rage and fury, so much so that he doesn't even see her sitting in the chair by the fireplace; as she watches him rip the ringing phone from the wall and listens to his embittered bellowing, a breath catches in her throat. She hasn't thought this through. She's thrown herself into the lion's den. She's enraged him before and look how that turned out. Why the *hell* has she done it again?

As he disappears into the bathroom, yelling expletives, she edges herself out of the chair and tiptoes toward the door. She's almost there—*just a few steps more*—but it's too late. He's spotted her.

"What the fuck are you doing in my room?" he roars, as blood runs down the side of his face.

All thought of doing what she came here to do vanishes. She *has* to get out of here.

She lunges for the door, but he gets there first, slamming himself against it, his body filling the entire frame.

"Please," says Cassie, making a feeble attempt to reach around him for the handle.

He pushes her and she falls backward, stumbling over the coffee table and onto the floor. Her face crumples as he comes toward her, but she refuses to cry.

"I asked you a question and I expect a fucking answer," he yells as he looms over her.

Cassie shuts her eyes tight, as if already giving in to what is surely about to happen. How had she ever thought that this wasn't how it was going to play out? It was a foregone conclusion, and she freezes, ready to accept her fate.

But the weight of his presence moves away and the hot breath that had hung over her in an ominous cloud quickly dissipates. When she dares to open her eyes again, he's pacing the floor in heated agitation.

"I swear to god, if I ever see him again I'm gonna fucking kill him," he spits, as if he's forgotten she was ever there. "He doesn't get to call the shots . . ."

Cassie lets out the breath she's been holding in and eases herself up onto a chair, grateful for the reprieve, but knowing that she's not in the clear just yet.

"Who the *fuck* does he think he is?" Michael rants.

This is her moment. The one chance she's got of turning this around. To do what she came here to do. If only she were brave enough.

"Ben Edwards?" she says, her mouth moving faster than her brain.

His head swivels and his dilated pupils drink her in, as if seeing her for the first time.

"I saw what happened down there," she says, willing her voice to stay on an even keel.

"He's gonna get it . . ." says Michael. "I swear to god, he's not going to get away with it . . ."

"I don't blame you," says Cassie. "He walks around as if he's untouchable, but he's nothing without you."

Michael's eyes soften, as if suddenly grateful for the sympathetic ear. "Exactly!"

"Why don't you come and sit down," she says, her trembling hands patting the sofa cushion beside her. "I've got something that might make you feel a bit better."

He raises his eyebrows questioningly and Cassie's chest feels like a boa constrictor is wrapping itself around it. She's aware of the dangerous game she's playing, but her hatred for him, and what he's done, is far greater than the risk. So, she pushes on through the fear and pulls out a foil parcel from her bag. It feels tiny in her hand, and she wonders if it's enough.

"What's this?" asks Michael, as she carefully unwraps the white powder.

"I'm reliably informed it will give you the best high you've ever had," says Cassie, her hand shaking as she offers it to him.

He grins as he takes it from her. "Well, then who am I to argue?"

She watches as he reaches into his back pocket and takes a bank card out of a battered wallet, then kneels on the floor to cut the powder into a line on the coffee table. "D'you wanna go first?" he asks, as he rolls up a ten-pound note.

Cassie shakes her head. "Be my guest," she says.

He roars as he snorts the first line, the animalistic cry coming from deep within as he throws his head back. "*Fuck*, yeah!" he calls out when he's able to form the words.

"I told you," says Cassie.

"That is some crazy shit," he says, his anger having immediately evaporated. "What the fuck!"

Cassie forces a smile.

"Where did you get this from?" he asks, going in for another line.

"I can get more," says Cassie, sensing a way out. "I can get as much as you want." She goes to get up, but he makes a grab for her, forcing her to stay put with a strong hold on her arm. His skin on hers makes her flesh crawl.

"Oh, man . . ." he says, as he collapses back on the sofa. His eyes roll into the back of his head, but his hold on her remains firm. She needs to get out. She's got more than she needs to make the phone call. The reporters will have a field day with this.

"Oh no you don't . . ." he mumbles as she tries to pull her arm from his grip. "You're not leaving me."

Cassie's heart pounds in her ears, drowning out his ramblings. She wonders how long it will be until he lets her go. She needs him to fall asleep, but what if that's not what this drug makes him do? What if he gets a second wind and wants to go all over again?

As she watches his flickering eyelids, she carefully reaches into her bag and takes out the Instamatic camera. If this is the only chance she's going to get, she needs to take the picture now, while he's semiconscious and surrounded by drug paraphernalia. He won't be able to charm his way out of this one, not if she's got photographic evidence.

"Stay with me," he slurs, as she gently pulls her arm from his loosening grip. "Promise me you won't leave. Because what will become of me . . . if you're not here to . . . to . . ."

His breathing slows and, once she's certain that he's passed out, Cassie takes the opportunity to rearrange the scene, making sure the foil and rolled-up bank note take center stage. It's only after she's taken a couple of shots that she remembers Ben's jacket, which she drapes casually over the back of the sofa so that any voyeur will all too easily be able to picture him just out of frame.

If Michael's going down, she's going to make sure Ben goes with him. It's the least they deserve.

50

Ben gives Zoe a cursory glance as she walks into the living room, and I wait for him to see something in her that he recognizes. Like I did, even though I didn't know it at the time—or maybe I was in denial.

Yet there's nothing but a muddled expression, as he no doubt asks himself why I need a stranger to help me say what needs to be said.

"Ben, this is Zoe," I say, my voice wavering as nervousness takes hold. "Zoe, Ben . . ."

Her eyes darken and her lips pull thin as she looks at him with nothing but disdain and contempt.

"I don't even have the words," she starts. "I've imagined this moment all my life, but now that you're here . . ."

"What's going on?" asks Ben, looking between us with a look of bewilderment.

"Twenty-five years ago, I did something that I"—my voice

cracks—"that I have never been able to forgive myself for. And I don't expect you to ever be able to forgive me either, but I have to tell you the truth, because I can't live the rest of my life with the guilt that I carry around with me every day . . ."

There's a daunting silence, but I will myself to go on, despite my heart almost beating out of my chest.

"I am *so* sorry that I wasn't brave enough to tell you, Ben . . ." I dare to look at him. "But I was young—we *all* were—and I was terrified that if I told you, told *anyone* . . ."

His jaw spasms as he looks between me and Zoe, trying to second-guess what I'm about to say. But he can't possibly imagine.

"Only one person knew . . ." I go on, before being cut off by the ringing of Zoe's phone.

We all look at each other, questioning whether there is anyone important enough to interrupt what's going on.

"It's Cassie," says Zoe, pressing the button to answer it.

My blood runs cold. I've had all these years to speak my truth, and when I finally find the courage, she comes in with a wrecking ball, as always. But I won't let her do it this time.

"She wants to speak to you," says Zoe, holding the phone out.

It feels like a hot coal in my hand as I take it, the thought of my sister being so close making my insides burn with a ferocious heat.

"So, you've finally found the balls to admit to what you did," she sneers, as soon as she hears my breath.

All the words I've saved for her are snatched away. "I have nothing to say to you."

"Have you told him yet?"

I open and close my fist, wishing I could reach through the phone and smash it into her face. "Which part?"

She laughs. "The part where he realizes that, if it weren't for you, his life would have turned out very differently."

Ben's eyeing me with increasing suspicion, no doubt wondering what I've brought to his door.

"It's over," I choke. "Dad wrote me a letter. He told me everything."

There's a drawn-out silence and I wonder if she's still there or already on her way to the nearest airport to avoid arrest.

"You were as much to blame as I was," she hisses. "Yet you think you're going to waltz off into the sunset with what's rightfully mine . . . *again*."

I laugh, unable to believe that she's still trapped in the imaginary relationship she thought she was having twenty-five years ago. But then it dawns on me: It's not about Ben at all.

"Is this about Dad's estate?" I ask, disbelievingly.

"You're not entitled to a penny," she seethes. "I'm the one who stayed here to face the music. I'm the one who had to deal with the fallout. That money is mine."

The breath I'd been holding comes out in a rush. She'd thrown a bomb into my life, not leaving a corner untouched, all because our father had called time on her deceit.

"You should have told the truth when you had the chance," I say.

"So should you!" she hollers.

"That's *exactly* what I'm *going* to do."

"It's too late for that," she says. "Justice was served a long time ago."

"*Justice?*" I croak, looking to Ben and Zoe, who stand paralyzed by unease and apprehension. "An innocent man was convicted of manslaughter and sent to prison for five years. How is that justice?"

"You're not taking me down with you," says Cassie, her voice laced with venom. "I won't let you."

"You can't hold me to ransom anymore. There's nothing more you can do."

"Are you sure about that?"

A cold shiver runs down my spine as I momentarily allow myself to believe that she still has a hold over me, but the shackles she's held me by for all these years are finally off. It's time we both paid penance.

"Goodbye, Cassie."

"Is admitting to something that happened twenty-five years ago really worth losing your precious family over?" says Cassie in a panicked rush.

"We're stronger than you think," I say. "You can't break us, and neither can the truth."

"I wouldn't bet on that," she says, before putting the phone down.

A second later, a text message pings through, and when I open it up my whole world crashes down around me.

51

If the phone hadn't been ripped from the wall, Cassie tries to convince herself, she would have used it to summon help—but who would she ring? Her father? No. Nicole? Absolutely not. If it weren't for her sister, none of this would have happened.

As Michael's lips turn blue, Cassie hurriedly looks around for anything that might shock him into breathing. Taking the flowers out of the vase on the coffee table, she throws the water into his face, hoping that it will wake him from his slumber, but he doesn't even flinch.

Nothing about this feels right, and panic swirls around Cassie's chest, constricting her airways as she dares to imagine the ramifications if anything should happen to one of the biggest pop stars in the country.

A tidal wave of images floods her mind: Michael being zipped into a body bag, tomorrow's headlines, the wig-wearing judge seeking justice for his untimely death. The torrent of premonitions almost stops her from breathing, but then she pulls herself together.

She hasn't done anything wrong. She only gave him the drug, which he would no doubt have taken from his own stash if she hadn't supplied the goods. She didn't force it on him; she didn't administer it. It was entirely of his own doing, and no court in the land would be able to argue otherwise.

"Michael, wake up!" she says, hoping it's loud enough for him to hear, but not for anyone passing outside.

His mouth begins to foam, and Cassie knows she needs to get help, but something stops her. Whether it's the fear of being embroiled in something she doesn't deserve or that she'd rather see him dead than alive, she isn't sure. But his life is ebbing away, right in front of her eyes, and she watches with morbid fascination, counting down the seconds until his pulse slows to a stop.

And as it does, a strange sense of calmness floods Cassie's extremities, an anesthetic of peace and equilibrium, making her feel that all is suddenly right in the world.

Making sure to put the camera in her bag, she surveys the room, imagining the scene in an hour or so's time, when the police will be scouring every fiber and surface for evidence of what led to the demise of one of Britain's biggest pop stars. Confident that she's removed all trace of herself, leaving only clues that will lead them to Ben, she's bizarrely satisfied that, by a sublime twist of fate, she's managed to kill two birds with one stone. It wasn't intentional, but the sense of gratification is intoxicating.

She places the DO NOT DISTURB sign on the door as she closes it behind her and turns the key in the lock.

"Cassie!"

She freezes, her blood running cold. She needs to take a breath to stop herself from passing out with fear, but her lungs are being squeezed by an invisible force.

"Oh, thank god," says the voice, getting ever closer.

"*Dad?*" she croaks, her brain trying to assess whether he is the lesser of the evils.

"Where the hell have you been? I've been going out of my mind!"

"I'm fine," she says, taking two steps toward him in a panicked rush to get him away from there. To get them *both* away from there.

"Is *he* in there?" asks John, his relief immediately replaced with anger toward the man he holds responsible for all his family's woes.

"Leave it, Dad," says Cassie, putting her hands on his chest as he forges toward the closed door of room 245.

"I swear to god, if I get my hands on him . . ."

"Dad, please!" says Cassie, feeling as if a steam train is thundering through her head.

"Edwards!" he bellows, slamming an open palm onto the door. "You piece of scum. Get out here!"

Cassie pulls at her dad's arm. She *has* to get him away from there.

"I'm not leaving here until he looks me in the eye," he roars.

Terrified that the commotion is going to draw attention, Cassie throws a glance down the corridor. "He's off his head," she says. "He's not making any sense."

"Well, he'd better make sense of *this*," says John, banging on the door again. "Because I swear, if you *ever* go near either of my daughters again, I'll fucking kill you!"

The silver key jumps from the lock and Cassie holds her breath as her father watches it fall, as if in slow motion, to the floor.

52

Nicole's despondency at not finding Cassie at their mother's grave turns to a sense of alarming panic when she gets back to the Savoy to see lights turning the air blue. There's no sound of sirens—as if it's already too late—just a crowd of hysterical teenagers tearfully screaming, "We want Ben!" and "Secret Oktober forever!" Girls lean on one another for support, fearing that if they let go, their grief will see them fall to the floor.

Nicole catches sight of a young girl sitting on the curb with her head on her knees, her shoulders convulsing as she laments the end of the world as she knows it. She looks up, her face stained with tears, as the crowd start up an impromptu rendition of "Souls," one of the band's few ballads. It makes her cry even more, the words of lovers passing in the night, evoking the trauma of two people who were once soulmates and now can't bear to be in the same room together.

"What's going on?" Nicole asks her, looking at the line of police barricading the front entrance. There's no way she's going to be able to get back in there now.

"They're saying there's been an accident," sobs the girl.

Nicole's brain scrambles as she remembers leaving Ben and Michael at each other's throats. She's probably jumping to ridiculous conclusions, letting her overactive imagination get the better of her.

"What's happened?" she asks, forcing herself to stay calm.

"It sounds really serious—someone said they heard Ben screaming and shouting. There was a girl . . ."

Cassie.

A burning heat envelopes Nicole's ears, shutting out the noise and commotion. She knows it's hearsay at its worst, but she has to know what's going on. Her whole world might be inside that hotel.

"I need to get in there," she says, going up to a policeman standing guard.

He smirks, as if she's a teenage fan chancing her arm. "That won't be happening," he says.

"I'm with Ben Edwards," she says, not only because it's the truth, but because she wants to test his reaction. A flicker of something crosses his features, as if he momentarily wonders whether she should be apprehended, but it's gone in a flash.

"So is every other girl here, apparently," he says with an air of smug superiority.

A siren sounds in the distance, the piercing wail getting closer with every passing second. There's a collective intake of breath as an ambulance appears at the end of Savoy Place, slowing as it contemplates turning in, but suddenly the accelerator goes down and it continues straight on.

Nicole looks at the four police cars parked at jaunty angles across the front of the hotel and can't help but feel buoyed by the fact that if there *had* been an accident, of *any* kind, then there would most definitely be an ambulance already in attendance—though her optimism is all too quickly extinguished when she realizes that there's no way they can bring anyone out of this entrance.

With burning lungs, she sprints around the block to the back of the hotel and is horrified to find two ambulances parked up with their blue lights flashing and sirens silenced.

"No!" she gasps, racing toward them.

A policeman sees her coming and holds his hands out in an attempt to stop her from crossing the invisible barrier he's trying to maintain.

"I need to see," she shrieks as she pushes past him.

"Now, now, young lady . . ." he says patronizingly, trying to get hold of the sleeve of her top. "You'll not be going any farther."

"Get off me!" she yells, breaking away from him and making a run toward the ambulance that a stretcher is being loaded into.

She stops dead as a robust man with graying temples is huddled out of the back door of the hotel. His face is ashen white and he's trembling so violently that he can't keep the blanket on his shoulders. The shock of seeing someone she knows so well in this unfamiliar context takes her brain a second to process.

"Oh my god—*Dad!*" gasps Nicole, struggling for breath. "What's happened?"

She stumbles in a state of confusion, unable to comprehend what he could possibly have done to warrant the handcuffs around his wrists.

It's only when she rights herself and looks at the stretcher again that she gets her answer. It's not a casualty being taken to hospital. It's a body bag being taken to the morgue.

53

My fingers prod at the digits on Zoe's cell phone in a frantic attempt to call Cassie back.

"I swear, if you do anything to hurt them . . ." I cry when it goes to voicemail.

"What the hell's going on?" asks Ben, perplexed.

I turn the phone to show him the photo Cassie has sent and he looks at it blankly, none the wiser.

"She's in my house," I say, as a searing heat wraps itself around me, making me feel as if I'm about to pass out. I look at my watch blindly, unable to see the time as my brain tries to work out where Brad and Hannah might be right now. But I don't even know what day it is anymore, my mind a jumbled mess.

A red mist descends as I dare to contemplate the hundred miles or more that stand between me and my family. How will I ever make it in time? How will I ever forgive myself if I don't? I head to the door, knowing that I can't stay here, the reason I came no longer important.

"Wait, what about the letter?" Ben calls out after me. "What did it say?"

"Where are you going?" asks Zoe, seemingly oblivious to the threat Cassie poses.

"I'm sorry," I say. "This was a mistake."

The rush of blood in my ears is deafening as I get in the car and slam it into drive. "Please pick up," I wail as the call to Brad's phone goes unanswered again and again.

I recall the image on Zoe's phone, of Cassie sitting on Hannah's bed, waiting for my sweet girl to get home from school. What will she say when she sees her "auntie" there? Will she call out in innocent surprise? Or will Cassie do something to silence her before she has the chance? I swallow the hot bile that rushes to the back of my throat every time I'm forced to imagine the worst-case scenario, and try Hank instead.

"Hank, she's at the house," I cry into the phone as soon as he picks up. "She's got Brad and Hannah . . ."

"Who has?" he says in a rush.

"My sister—the woman behind it all . . . She's at the house. Brad's not answering his phone and I'm going as fast as I can but . . ."

"OK, I'm heading there now," he says, and I can't help but feel pathetically grateful that he's not going to ask any more questions.

"Please hurry," I sob, pressing the gas pedal down to the floor.

Miles pass, but I have no recollection of them as my macabre thoughts take over my entire being. I imagine Brad being forced to watch as Cassie carries out her threat. How far will she go to protect herself? Does she really believe that holding my family for ransom will keep her secret safe? Does she not realize that I stand to lose them anyway once the truth comes out?

When I finally admit that *I* killed Michael Delaney.

If it weren't for the heroin I got from Larry outside Dallinger's that night. If I'd not stupidly left it in my rucksack. If I'd not told Cassie of my plan for revenge . . .

Who knows whether I would have been brave enough to plant

it on Michael myself, safe in the knowledge that a phone call to the police was all that would have been needed to bring about his downfall. But that's all that it was ever supposed to be. A wake-up call, to let him know that he couldn't carry on walking around as if he was untouchable. I wanted him to know what it felt like to have your dignity stripped, your innocence snatched away . . .

I was going to do it for Cassie—to show her that people don't get to do what Michael did to her and get away with it. But my bravery had deserted me just as her impatience had seemingly kicked in.

I realized the heroin was missing just before Ben called to say that Cassie had been at the press conference. I daren't imagine what she might do with it, but in that moment all I could think was that she would use it to do herself harm, such was her desolation.

But it seemed that that was never her intention.

"What the fuck happened?" I'd screamed at her as we were released from police custody after being held until the early hours after Michael's death. They'd wanted to know who I was, why I was there, my relationship to Cassie and the troubling connection between me and the man who had been found hunched over Michael's body, covered in his blood.

"They said Dad was trying to resuscitate him," I'd cried, as panic threatened to block my airways. "What was he doing there? Does he know that you gave Michael the heroin?"

Cassie had looked at me, wide-eyed.

"You need to tell me what happened," I'd yelled. "If they find out you took the drugs from me and gave them to Michael, we could both go to prison for a very long time."

Her brow had creased. "I didn't give the drugs to Michael," she said, matter-of-factly.

"Oh, thank god." I sagged with relief. "So, it wasn't my drugs that killed him?"

She'd bitten down on her lip, knowing that even one wrong answer could get her in deep water.

"Well, I don't know about that," she said, after what felt like an eternity. "Because I gave them to Ben."

"Fuck!" I yelled, my brain about to explode with the myriad of ensuing consequences. "What did you do *that* for?"

"He wanted to get high, and I thought it might make him love me again," she said.

I'd held on to the railings outside Charing Cross station to stop my knees from buckling as a tsunami of responsibility washed over me.

"But he went straight to Michael's room with it," Cassie went on.

I'd headbutted the unforgiving metal railings, drowning in a sea of guilt and deceit.

"It was Ben who killed him," she said, making it sound as if he'd done it with his own bare hands.

And I'd believed her. *Until now.*

I bang my hands on the steering wheel, swerving dangerously close to the central reservation as I dare to imagine how my father must have tortured himself over the past twenty-five years.

It's not difficult to envisage his heart-stopping panic when he realized his daughter was guilty of so much more than she cared to admit. And when the evidence against Ben began to mount, he must surely have wondered what harm it would do to add a little context to keep the police focus on the undeniable facts: his highly publicized drug habit, the fight in front of the world's press, the threats to kill, Michael's blood on his T-shirt, his jacket that lay casually draped behind Michael's corpse.

Maybe my father had convinced himself that he didn't see what he knew he saw. Maybe he was so intent on keeping Cassie out of the picture that his guilty conscience was easy to ignore. I can almost sympathize with the cross he'd had to bear, because now that my own family are at risk, there is *nothing* I wouldn't do to protect them.

54

Dusk is falling by the time I get home, and the darkening skies create an ominous aura. But there's nothing to suggest that my family are under siege or that my house is under surveillance. The windows are devoid of movement and light, and Hank's unmarked car sits idly across the street.

"Has anything changed?" I ask as I slip into the back seat.

He shakes his head without taking his eyes off the porch.

"Not since I went inside and checked," he says. "Which was about an hour ago."

"And you're sure that nothing was amiss?" I ask, my words strangled by the panic in my chest. "There was no sign of anything untoward in Hannah's bedroom? No sign of anything being out of place?"

"Not as far as I could see. Everything looked as it always does."

But Cassie had been there. I'd seen it with my own two eyes.

"Still no luck in getting hold of Brad on the cell phone?" Hank asks, looking at me in the rearview mirror. I shake my head.

"Listen, I'm sure there's a perfectly reasonable explanation," he says, attempting to assuage my agitation. "They may have taken the boat out and lost track of time."

I nod, grateful for the reassurance.

Perhaps Cassie wasn't in my house after all. Maybe that's what I chose to see as the photo flashed up on Zoe's phone, my levels of suspicion knowing no bounds. It looked like Hannah's room; I was sure it was her bed that Cassie had been grinning sadistically from, but maybe I was wrong.

"I'm sorry to have called you out," I say, hating that my paranoia has wasted his time.

"Do you want me to come in with you?" asks Hank.

I force a smile. "No, I'm fine. I'll keep trying Brad, and if they're not home by nightfall I'll give you a call."

The place that I've called home for the past twenty years doesn't feel quite the same, knowing that Cassie may have infiltrated it. I walk from room to room, turning the lights on, but the warm glow leaves me cold.

"Where are you?" I say out loud to the photo of the three of us that hangs in the hall.

I'm suddenly blindsided by the memory of Brad's threat to take Hannah to his parents' and force myself to acknowledge that, if he has, it would only be because her safety is paramount. And despite myself, I can't help but reason that it might be the best place for her right now. I take my phone from my pocket and call my in-laws.

"Betty, it's Nicole," I say, trying to sound as much like myself as I can. I wonder if Brad's told her what's been going on—I guess he would have had to, if he's taken Hannah there.

"Oh, hey there," she says, in her Southern drawl. "How y'all doing?"

Nothing about her suggests that she knows anything more about me than she did the last time we spoke, when she'd politely passed up my offer to make cornbread for the holidays. And nothing about her suggests that Brad and Hannah are there.

"We're good. I just wanted to double-check whether you needed me to bring anything next week." Now that I know she's blissfully unaware, I don't want to alarm her.

"Just your good selves," she says, cheerily.

"OK, great," I say, needing to move on to my next line of inquiry. "Actually, can I call you back? Hannah's just got home."

Tapping the side of my phone, I will myself to think rationally about where else they might be. They *may* have gone out on the water, but it's unlike Brad not to get back before sunset, especially given that one of the lights is out on the boat—but he bought a new one last weekend. Maybe they've gone to fit it and put it to the test.

I let myself into the garage, knowing that's where he'd put it, hopeful that if it's missing, there's every chance that Hank might be right. I reach for the light switch and, as the fluorescent bulb flickers to attention, it takes me a moment longer than it should to realize that Brad's truck is there.

He'd never go anywhere without it. He wouldn't know how to.

I shudder as my eyes travel to the ceiling, wishing I could see into our bedroom above so that I don't have to go up there.

I back out into the hall and look up the stairs, the gloom of the landing suddenly menacing. Brad *can't* be up there; Hank would have found him. Yet his pickup can't be here without him.

Despite several attempts, the landing light stays woefully idle, and my throat dries up as I contemplate the darkness that awaits. Every tread I take feels as if it's lifting me toward somewhere I don't want to go, even though it's a journey I've happily made a million times before.

I let out the breath I'd been holding when our bedroom light turns on the first time. I scan the empty room, but the oppressive feeling of not being alone sits like a weight on my chest.

I want to call out, desperate to hear Brad answer back, but fear chokes me into staying silent.

As I gingerly make my way along the landing toward Hannah's room, I trail my hand along the wall for support. Her curtains are open, and the moon's muted glow radiates across her bed. It must be a trick of the light, but it looks like she's actually in it, the shimmer rising and falling with the shadows.

"*Hannah?*" I half whisper, an irrational part of me not wanting to wake her if she's asleep.

I take a step closer, my eyes adjusting to the familiar outlines in the room. My hand reaches out to touch what still looks like a Hannah-shaped mound in the bed, but just as my fingers meet the fabric of her duvet cover, there's a dull thud from above me.

My pulse hammers in my ears, drowning out any remote possibility that I might have imagined the noise coming from the attic. As if on autopilot, I numbly put one foot in front of the other as I move toward the ceiling hatch on the landing. The window pole that we use to un-hook it and pull the ladder down isn't where it should be, so I revert to Plan B and drag a chair across the rug, snagging it on the corner. I pretend to inspect the hatch, but I'm just playing for time; delaying the inevitability of having to go up into a dark, confined space, knowing it would have been the one place Hank wouldn't have looked.

I know I have to go up there, for no reason other than to free my tortured mind of the thought that Hannah is being held against her will—and that I'm close enough to save her.

The metal ladder grinds against itself as I pull it down and lock it into place. I force a deep breath in and out of my lungs but feel momentarily suffocated as they struggle to inflate.

"Hello?" I offer pathetically, my voice not sounding like my own, as I stare up into the void.

My legs feel like jelly as they attempt to lift themselves up onto each rung, and I grip with whitened knuckles to keep myself balanced.

I stop, the top of my head level with the opening, knowing that the next step will either expose or assuage my darkest fears.

My eyes blink as they adjust to the cavernous space, delving into the pitch-black corners, searching for life. I sense it before I see it; the heat of an uninvited presence—the sickening realization that I'm not alone.

"Do you remember when we used to make a camp in the loft?" asks a voice, its sinister tone at odds with the childlike question. My chest tightens, restricting the rise and fall of my breath. "We'd smuggle all the treats up there and pretend we'd left home."

There's a flicker of light as a match is struck, and the wick of an oil lantern ignites. The burning flame sets Cassie's face aglow with an amber hue.

"What do you want?" I croak, desperately willing my voice not to reveal my terror. "Where's Hannah?"

My eyes follow the light as Cassie wordlessly moves to the far corner of the attic, where it settles upon a makeshift tent made out of bedsheets and broomsticks.

"I thought I'd show her what me and Mummy used to do for fun," she says.

My legs buckle beneath me as my feet blindly move across the uneven floorboards toward Hannah. I picture her in there, surrounded by the soft toys she calls friends, offering them imaginary tea and cakes from the play set Brad's mother bought her.

I want to claw at the linen, tear down this wolf in sheep's clothing, expose the malevolence that's being sickeningly disguised as an innocent adventure. But I stop myself, not wanting to impart my abject terror to a little girl who will wonder why I ruined her game.

"Hannah?" I choke, peering in. The muted light casts long shadows, but I can immediately tell she's not in there.

"Where is she?" I demand. "What have you done with her?"

Cassie lets out a hollow laugh. "What makes you think I would? *A guilty conscience?*"

"She's just a child," I say, appealing for mercy.

"Weren't we all?" comes the bitter reply. "Once upon a time."

"Whatever this is, whatever you want, keep her out of it. No good can come from involving her."

A barbed sneer of contempt rattles at the back of Cassie's throat. "How did you think you were any more deserving of Dad's estate than me?"

"I didn't," I say. "I always believed I was as much at fault as anyone—that *I* was responsible for what happened to Michael, to Ben . . . to *you*. For years, I've thought that if I hadn't got the drugs, you wouldn't have found them, Ben wouldn't have given them to Michael and he wouldn't be dead. That cycle of events has been on repeat in my head every second of every day since—as much as I've tried to forget it."

I fight to stop my jaw from spasming, my pent-up fury at what she had led me to believe at odds with needing to keep Hannah safe at all costs.

"But to find out that Ben had nothing to do with it . . ."

"You'll never be able to prove that he didn't give Michael the drugs," says Cassie, her tone brimming with gauche joviality.

I grit my teeth as I remember Ben's desperate pleas to the jury, willing them to believe that he hadn't been in Michael's room, that he didn't know how his jacket had got there, that he would never have given him drugs, that he hadn't touched them himself in over a year . . .

"I may not be able to prove that you gave Michael the drugs," I say. "But Dad's letter proves that *you* were there, that you watched Michael die, that both of you allowed Ben to take the blame."

"I think you've forgotten what you stand to lose," hisses Cassie. "Not just here and now, but in a court of law. Whichever way you try to spin it, it was *your* drugs that killed a man."

I chastise myself for my weakness, for not doing the right thing back when I had the chance to change the course of events. When

I should have owned up to what I'd done, instead of seeing the man that I loved go to prison for something I suspected, deep down, he was innocent of. Ben didn't take drugs. He would never have fed Michael's addiction. So how had I allowed myself to believe he would? Because otherwise I would have been forced to acknowledge that Cassie had lied—and that she was capable of so much more than I was prepared to accept.

"I'm not afraid to tell the truth anymore," I say to her. "I'm tired of running away from it. And if I have to pay my dues for Ben to be vindicated, then so be it. But know that I'll be taking you down with me."

55

"What the hell happened?" cries Amelia as she opens the door of her mother's caravan and ushers Cassie in. She looks like she hasn't slept or eaten in days. "I've been going out of my mind."

"I'm *so* sorry," says Cassie, pulling her friend in for a hug, unable to imagine what it must have been like to watch the news unfold on TV without knowing what's really going on. "Every time I tried to get here, the press would be on my tail. They've been camped outside our house all week and I didn't want to bring them to your door."

"I can't believe it," says Amelia, shaking as she lights a cigarette. "How can Michael be dead?"

"I don't . . . I don't know," says Cassie with tears in her eyes, though they're driven by fear rather than grief. "It doesn't feel real."

"B-but what went wrong? I thought you only wanted to expose Ben's drug habit—payback for how he'd treated you?"

"That was the plan," says Cassie, the lie rolling off her tongue.

"I just wanted him to get caught with it, but he took it straight to Michael's room and I can only assume . . ." Her words trail off.

"This is bad," says Amelia, rocking back and forth as she looks at Cassie wide-eyed. "This is really bad."

"Now, listen," says Cassie, desperately trying to keep her wavering voice steady. She needs to be in control—to stop Amelia from losing her shit. "We haven't done anything wrong. My sister gave me the drugs, and I gave them to Ben. That's it—end of story."

"But I *knew* you were doing it," shrills Amelia. "*I* helped set it up. *I* was complicit."

Cassie takes hold of Amelia's trembling hands, never thinking for a moment that *she*'d be the one to restore order. "You need to pull yourself together," she says. "None of this is our fault. The only person who has blood on his hands is Ben."

"Do you think he did it on purpose?" asks Amelia, the sudden realization catching in her throat.

"I'd be lying if I said no," says Cassie, the irony of her words not lost on her. "He was in such a state—saying how much he hated Michael and that he was going to kill him if he got his hands on him."

"Oh my god," croaks Amelia. "We set them on each other."

Cassie shakes her head. "We may have lit the fuse, but if it hadn't kicked off then, it would only have happened the next day or the day after that."

Amelia gives a conciliatory nod.

"It was a bomb waiting to go off," says Cassie, still desperate to instill the narrative that it had nothing to do with them. "We're the innocent pawns in this. We couldn't have known that this would be the outcome."

"Do you think there was something wrong with the drugs?" asks Amelia, wide-eyed.

Cassie has to admit that she's wondered the same herself. She's heard of dodgy batches and can't help but wonder if they got unlucky.

"I don't think there's any use in torturing ourselves with endless questions," she says.

"But maybe it was too strong, maybe it was too much . . ." shrieks Amelia.

"*We* didn't give it to him," says Cassie, not liking where this is going. She knew Amelia was going to be upset, but her hysteria is dangerous.

A bang on the open window makes them both jump. "Is Maeve around?" asks a man with a mullet and dirty jeans hanging down below his underpants.

Amelia gives him a derisory glance up and down, resigned to but not liking the constant coming and going of her mother's male visitors. "Who's asking?" she says.

"You can call me Uncle," says the man with a wry smile.

"What's happened to the other 'uncle'?" asks Amelia.

"He had a bad trip," he says, cryptically. "He didn't make it home."

Cassie's stomach turns over as she remembers the dead man's promise that his gear would give her the best trip she'd ever have. "You'll never go back," he'd boasted, as he handed her a foil package behind the shower block of Amelia's caravan park.

If Nicole hadn't failed her by allowing her cowardice to win out over retribution, then Cassie wouldn't have had to take matters into her own hands. But now it seems that perhaps her sister wasn't as weak as Cassie had her down for. Nicole had obviously got hold of some drugs herself and is now of the mind that it was those that led to Michael's demise. And for Cassie's part, it's not a bad thing. It won't hurt for Nicole to take some responsibility for what's happened; it's the least she can do after everything she's put Cassie through.

But as much as Nicole deserves to share the guilt, a sickening sensation creeps along Cassie veins. What if there *was* something wrong with the drugs she'd bought from "Uncle"? What if it *was* the same bad batch that *he'd* died from? And what if Michael's overdose could be traced back to her?

"I can't go to prison," cries Amelia, as the man walks away with his unsold stash still buried deep in his trouser pockets.

"Keep your voice down," hisses Cassie.

"You're gonna have to tell them where you got it from," sobs Amelia. "If it comes to it, you're gonna have to drop your sister in it."

"It won't come to that," says Cassie, adamantly.

"Maybe she knew it was bad—maybe she was hoping *Ben* would take it—in revenge for stringing her along at the same time as you. She might have known *exactly* what she was doing and frame you in the process."

"My sister is a *lot* of things," says Cassie. "But she's not going to set me up for murder."

"*Murder?*" whispers Amelia, almost to herself. "How am I supposed to explain that Michael was murdered?"

"Who to?" asks Cassie.

Amelia fixes her with a penetrating stare. "His child," she says, with a hand on her tummy.

56

"If I didn't know better, I'd say you were still rather smitten with him," says Cassie, sounding as if she's yet to reveal the ace up her sleeve. "Does Brad know about the candle you still hold for Ben?" My jaw clenches, but she can't see it. "Maybe I'll mention it to him next time I bump into him." A sadistic grin stretches her mouth wide, made all the more sinister by the muted light that dances across her face. "Though I'm not sure our paths will ever cross again."

An ice-cold hand reaches into my chest. "Where is he?" I ask, my voice hoarse.

She lets out a heavy sigh. "Let's just say he's taking a long walk on a very short pier."

It was an expression our mother used whenever she wanted someone to disappear—albeit metaphorically rather than literally. I suck in a breath, hoping that the sentiment remains the same when coming from her youngest daughter.

"If you've done something—to either of them—I swear . . ."

An empty laugh echoes around the vaulted space. "If you could have seen their faces when they headed out of the marina. So full of hope and expectation of the adventure that lay ahead."

"So, they've gone out on the boat?" I question, daring to allow relief to flood my veins.

"Yes!" says Cassie, overenthusiastically. "But without enough fuel to get back if they go too far, and without a radio to call if they're in distress."

I snort derisively, knowing that Brad would surely have checked both before they set off.

"And by all accounts, there was a whale incident a couple of miles out, and your caring husband didn't hesitate to head out there to help."

"You're a *fucking* psychopath," I yell.

"I may well be," she sneers. "But not enough to leave Zoe alone with Ben. I mean, in what kind of fucked-up world would you think that was the sensible thing to do?"

My brain scrambles to make sense of all the noise that crowds my mind, but it's a deafening cacophony that I can't quell.

"I guess he still doesn't know who Zoe is?" Cassie goes on, as I try to keep up with her dogged destruction of my life. "Would you not have thought to tell him, before leaving them together?"

I swallow, but my throat feels as if it's lined with knives, the enormity of what's going on slowly dawning on me. Had I been lured to Ben's, a hundred miles away, leaving my family at Cassie's mercy? Had Zoe left a trail to Ben's door so that, when something happened to him, I'd be the prime suspect?

"She wouldn't . . . ?" I croak, barely audible, as I picture Ben and Zoe alone in his house.

"You couldn't blame her if she did," says Cassie. "After all, she *is* the daughter of the man he was convicted of killing."

57

"What is it going to take to make this stop?" I ask, as images of Ben, Zoe, Brad, and Hannah flood my beleaguered brain.

"I want what's mine," says Cassie. "Dad had no right to leave it all to you."

"Shouldn't you be thankful for what he did for you when he was alive, rather than resent what he didn't do in death?"

"Not when you're just as guilty as me," she spits.

"*I* didn't ask him to lie for me," I yell, unable to hold my vitriol back any longer. "He was a good man, but you put him in an impossible position. He lied under oath that he'd seen Ben go into Michael's room, to save your skin. How do you think that made him feel? Having knowingly sent an innocent man to jail?"

"What about how I saved *your* skin? What thanks do *I* get for not telling the police that *you* were the one who supplied the heroin that killed him?"

"Did Dad know that?" I can't help but cry. "Did he know that you got the drugs from me?"

Cassie scoffs, her tone telling. "He knew *everything*. He found out what Michael had done to me by reading my diary. He developed the photos on my camera and saw what I'd done to him." I gasp at the memory. "He told me that he would protect me, but I had to be completely honest and tell him exactly what had happened."

"So, you told him you'd taken the drugs from my bag without permission?"

I hold my breath as I remember my father's cryptic final words in his letter. "*You can't take something that was never there. No matter how many lies you have to tell yourself to pretend that you did.*"

"He held you just as responsible as me," she says, sounding as if she's almost enjoying my distress. "Even more so because you were the adult—the big sister who was supposed to have my back."

"*Did you tell him that you took the drugs from my bag without permission?*" I ask again through gritted teeth, desperate to be told in words of one syllable whether my father meant what I think he meant.

"Yes," she says.

A rush of air escapes from my chest and my knees threaten to buckle beneath me. "It wasn't mine," I say, almost to myself. "It was *never* mine—and you *knew* it."

"Wh-what?" Cassie falters, as if the reality of what happened twenty-five years ago is as alien to her as it is to me.

"You couldn't have taken the heroin from me," I mutter numbly.

"What are you talking about?" snaps Cassie. "Of course I did. How else do you think I got it?"

"Fuck," I gasp, as the enormity of what she's done—*of how evil she is*—bears down on me. I grab hold of a wooden joist to stop my body from falling, as every nerve and muscle folds in on itself, paralyzed from the deceit. "Dad must have found it. He found it in my bag and took it."

Cassie laughs sardonically. "Are you so deranged that you're going to blame our dead father now?"

"How could you let me believe that it was *my* fault?" I rasp. "How could you have allowed me to spend the best part of my life blaming myself for something I played no part in?"

Cassie tsks derisorily.

I shake my head, as all the pieces fall into place. "Oh my god, I handed it to you on a plate, didn't I?" I rake a clawed hand through my hair as I remember the conversation we had in the hours after Michael's death. I'd spoon-fed her the narrative that they were my drugs—that she'd taken them without permission—and she'd run with it. Never once faltering. Never once stopping to consider the consequences. Never once showing compassion by putting me out of my misery.

"This was all you," I choke. "It was only ever you."

There's a sudden rush as she launches herself at me, grappling for any part that she can sink her nails into. I crash to the floor and feel a tightening around my neck as her weight pins me down. I kick with all my strength while my hands flail, attempting to wrench her fingers away from my air supply.

We thrash around and I push my foot against an attic beam, using the traction to twist myself away from her. But she's too quick and counteracts the bid by slamming my shoulder down into the floor, her hands around my neck as she squeezes the life out of me once more.

I manage to suck in a desperate mouthful of air, and it pulls me back from the edge of consciousness, fueling my need to fight back. But she's straddled over me, her features contorted as her thumbs slowly shut down my lifeline. I look at her, breathless, eyes bulging and, as I feel myself slipping away, all I can see is Hannah's innocent face, questioning whether I deserved it.

58

I gasp what I'm sure is my last breath just as the weight of Cassie is lifted off me. I can hear what sounds like Brad's dulcet tones faintly in the distance, but don't dare to allow myself to believe it.

"No!" screams Cassie, wailing like a banshee.

A beam from a flashlight floods the attic and I instinctively sob with relief. "Where's Hannah?" I croak, to nobody in particular, as I scramble to my feet.

"It's OK," says a familiar voice. "She's safe. We both are."

Brad's strong arms wrap themselves around me, my chest convulsing as it desperately chases the air it has lost. I collapse into him, trembling, my body spent from running from the past.

"Cassie said you went out on the boat . . . and that she—"

"I know," says Brad. "But we're OK—thanks to Hannah sending an SOS signal on her Rapunzel walkie-talkie."

A choked laugh catches in the back of my throat.

"Which made the rescue boat's job a lot easier," says Hank, placing a reassuring hand on my back. "I'm sorry, I should never have left you here on your own. Are you OK?"

I manage a nod.

"I'll make sure she never darkens your door again," he says, as he secures Cassie's wrists behind her back with handcuffs.

Her eyes search mine as she's dragged away and, despite everything, I can't help but feel sorry for her. For what she never had. For what she always wanted. And for what she's lost.

"It's over," says Brad, as if reading my mind. "You can stop looking over your shoulder now."

I fall into him, daring to believe he's right, when an incoming alert on Hank's radio pulls me up short. "An officer from LAPD has called in a potential homicide," says the caller, her terse voice reverberating around the enclosed space too many bodies are packed into.

Hank pulls a face, as if questioning how that's got anything to do with him. "It's out of my jurisdiction," he says absently into the walkie-talkie clipped onto his shirt pocket.

"Yeah, but there appears to be some crossover on this one," comes the response. "Because a suspect's name has been put forward . . ."

"Who?" barks Hank impatiently.

Cassie turns to look at me as a warped grin spreads across her face.

My pulse pounds so loudly in my ears that it drowns out the answer—but, as Hank's eyes widen and Brad's arms fall away from me, I realize that I'd been a fool to think she wouldn't try to take me down with her.

ACKNOWLEDGMENTS

First and foremost, I would like to pay homage to those who inspired this novel: a pop group called Duran Duran. Simon Le Bon, John Taylor, Nick Rhodes, Roger Taylor, and Andy Taylor were not only instrumental in forming the seedlings of the idea, but they were also hugely influential during my teenage years, when I could think of little else—much to my parents' and teachers' chagrin! Because, while I should have been focusing on homework and exams, I was instead tearing up and down the country, chasing after my idols in real time; waiting for them outside TV and recording studios, walking through airports with them, camping outside their houses—and just about anywhere else they'd dare to go!

It makes me cringe when I think of it now but, before you judge me too harshly, I should emphasize that I was always respectful and enjoyed what I thought was a mutually beneficial relationship with the band. We talked, we laughed, they knew my name, and they were, in the main, happy to see us. And by *us,* I mean the staunchly loyal fan community of twenty or so girls—some of whom I still count as good friends today.

Between us, we knew where the band were staying, what flights they were on, their personal appearances a month in advance . . . all without the aid of mobile phones or the internet! Like Amelia, we were certainly industrious, but Simon would sometimes help us along by dropping the name of a hotel into conversation, and John would whisper where they were going next as he jumped into a limo surrounded by screaming girls. And yes, my toes *were* run over more times than I care to remember! And yes, I *was* left dangling from the BBC railings after snagging my white leather trousers on a spike. And yes, I *was* on the ten o'clock news as I saw the band off at Heathrow airport! But although this book is more autobiographical than any others I've written, the similarities stop there! I'm no Cassie . . . but I acknowledge that I might sometimes have crossed the line and, to Duran Duran, I'm sorry!

There have been a lot of changes to my stalwart dream team while I've been writing this book—some of whom I regrettably won't be working with on the next one. Vicki Mellor, my fabulous editor at Pan Macmillan—thank you for your patience and guidance these past six years. You've made every structural, copy, and line edit so much easier than it might otherwise have been. Tanera Simons, my brilliant agent at Darley Anderson—thank you for seeing something in *The Other Woman* and putting your faith and belief in me. I will always be indebted to you. And to my editor Catherine Richards at Minotaur, who moonlights as Wonder Woman—I can't wait to do it all again!

Finally, to my wonderful readers—thank you for choosing my books. I look forward to hearing your thoughts on *I Would Die for You*. Get in touch on IG @sandiejones_author and do please leave a review on Amazon—it makes a world of difference to authors.

Love,
Sandie x

ABOUT THE AUTHOR

Harriet Buckingham

Sandie Jones has worked as a freelance journalist for more than twenty years and has written for publications including *The Sunday Times, Woman's Weekly,* and *Hello!* magazine. She lives in London with her husband and three children. *The Other Woman* was her debut novel and a Reese Witherspoon Book Club pick.